# THIRTY DAYS LATER
## Steaming Forward: 30 Adventures in Time

Support public libraries and explore a world of steampunk fiction!

- Revenge and greed threaten to tear apart lovers and families!
- Dragons wreak havoc!
- Sasquatches dabble in politics!
- Revolution is in the air, and in the streets!
- A cursed *netsuke* threatens the life of a young girl.

*Thirty Days Later* will have you on the edge of your seat and ripping through pages, racing to find out what happens.

# TWELVE HOURS LATER
## 24 Tales of Myth and Mystery

Myth! Intrigue! Dirigibles! Literacy!

- Thrill to round-the-world and round-the-clock action!
- Go on adventures in ancient Egypt, Greece, Japan, and more!
- Get swept away in a whirlwind of steam, legends, spy-craft, and the occasional forest demon!

So, put the kettle on, pour a strong cuppa, and curl up on the couch for a rollicking good read with *Twelve Hours Later*!

## Other Fiction

*Debris Dreams* by David Colby

*Beyond the Fence* by Marilyn Horn

*Sibling Rivalry* by Anthony Francis

# SOME TIME LATER

## Fantastic Voyages
## Through
## Alternate Worlds

*Edited by*
*AJ Sikes*
*BJ Sikes*
*&*
*Dover Whitecliff*

Thinking Ink Press
Campbell, California

Published by Thinking Ink Press, P.O. Box 1411, Campbell, California, 95009

First printing, 2017

Ebook edition ISBN 978-1-942480-21-1

Print edition ISBN 978-1-942480-20-4

Printed in the United States of America.

## Project Credits

Cover design: Robin Ludwig Design Inc. www.gobookcoverdesign.com

Clock deisgn: Anthony Francis

Layout: Betsy Miller

Proofing: Anthony Francis, Keiko O'Leary, Liza Olmsted

A moment, a minute, all we are
And there is so much black 'tween the stars

—From "Who Mourns Eos?" by Alyssa Rosenbloom and
Nathaniel Johnstone

# CONTENTS

Notes from the Editors................................................................ix

**The Story Begins**.................................................... **11**

Three Men and a Vampire
By Harry Turtledove.................................................... 13

Ely and the Medium
By Kirsten Weiss ........................................................25

Weekend Near the Asylum
By Katherine L. Morse & David L. Drake........................... 37

The Wheel of Misfortune, Part I
By Lillian Csernica...................................................... 47

Cheque for a Pulse First, A Miranda Gray Mystery
By T.E. MacArthur...................................................... 61

Two Weeks of Hell
By Anthony Francis..................................................... 71

Solarpunk Gauguin, Part I
By Janice Thompson .....................................................81

Here Abide Monsters, A Boston Metaphysical Society Story
By Madeleine Holly-Rosing........................................... 83

Cock of the Walk
By Dover Whitecliff..................................................... 101

The Descent
By BJ Sikes............................................................... 111

The Cannoneer's Tale
By AJ Sikes............................................................... 123

Flowers of London
By Sharon E. Cathcart ................................................. 137

Seeking Atlantis
By Michael Tierney...................................................... 145

When Johnny Chimes Came to Town
By Richard Lau .......................................................... 159

**Some Time Later** ............................................... **165**

Three Men and a Werewolf
By Harry Turtledove ................................................ 167

Death Stalks Closer
By Kirsten Weiss ..................................................... 179

All Warfare Is Based upon Deception
By By David L. Drake & Katherine L. Morse ...................... 187

The Wheel of Misfortune, Part II
By Lillian Csernica .................................................. 197

Tiger, Tiger, A Miranda Gray Mystery
By T.E. MacArthur .................................................. 217

The Day of Reckoning
By Anthony Francis .................................................. 229

Solarpunk Gauguin, Part II
By Janice Thompson .................................................. 243

Home, A Boston Metaphysical Society Story
By Madeleine Holly-Rosing .......................................... 245

Playing Chicken
By Dover Whitecliff .................................................. 247

Into the Order of Glaucos
By BJ Sikes ........................................................... 257

The Confectioner's Tale
By AJ Sikes ........................................................... 267

Flowers of Paris
By Sharon E. Cathcart .............................................. 271

Reaching Atlantis
By Michael Tierney .................................................. 279

The Last Stand of Johnny Chimes
By Richard Lau ...................................................... 289

About the Authors .................................................. 299

# NOTES FROM THE EDITORS

Adventure, espionage, horror, love, death, and the lunatic fringe. Come and get it, and get it here.

Seeking the supernatural? We have it. Vampires and werewolves join three men and a dog in Harry Turtledove's laugh-a-minute adventures in old London. And don't forget the things that go bump in the night, or the things that should not be, here with an alt-history twist. Make that a double-twist in Anthony Francis's stories of Liberation Academy cadet Jeremiah Willstone.

We have war on offer, if you're into that sort of thing, but don't expect the usual suspects—no brass bands, lost squads, or upright decorum here, thank you very much. AJ Sikes presents two views on the ages-old feud between the haves and have-nots. Drake and McTrowell return to do battle with time itself, and run into some truly colorful (and costumed) characters along the way.

How about stories of seduction? We have them, from the romantic to the demonic. Temptations abound in no fewer than nearly all of the tales in this collection. A straying heart and a hearty dose of psilocybin befuddle a scientist's mission in BJ Sikes's Bahamian adventures. Elsewhere, a rakish engineer nearly progresses to his end in Sharon Cathcart's stories of Thaddeus Flowers and his plans for air travel. Dreams of riches tempt airship pirate captain James MacNee to scour the seas for signs of the fabled island of Atlantis in Michael Tierney's tales. Janice Thompson weaves a skein of somber omen in her poems about Paul Gauguin's flight to warmer climes.

Here are more of the characters you've grown to love from our previous anthologies, *Twelve Hours Later* and *Thirty Days Later*. The Madam Archaeologist returns to London to rescue a friend from a scoundrel's avaricious grasp in the latest of T.E. MacArthur's Miranda Gray Mysteries. Kirsten Weiss's secret agent Ely Crane stumbles upon state secrets while trying to disprove a medium's act in New York City. Lillian Csernica's British ex-pat physician, William Harrington, must open his mind and heart to the reality of poverty in Meiji-era Tokyo to escape a vengeful spirit. Kenna Wolfsdaughter wants to join the fight, but is more liability than leader until she's shown the path to the real arena in Dover Whitecliff's off-world adventure tales.

And we've added some new faces to the mix, too.

Be sure to spend some time with Madeleine Holly-Rosing's tales of the dark supernatural along the Underground Railroad set in the world of her Boston Metaphysical Society graphic novels. And—fanfare—this year, for the first time, we are including stories by a Clockwork Alchemy participant! Join us in welcoming Richard Lau, whose Weird West stories about the metallic lawman, Johnny Chimes, won a place in this anthology. The competition was fierce, and we look forward to (possibly) running a similar contest for our next collection, The Next Stop.

By diving into these stories of adventure, mayhem, romance, and madness, you'll also be helping someone else learn to read; a portion of all sales of this anthology will go to local literacy charities, so you can feel even better voyaging to alternate empires. Now turn the page, turn back time, and find out what happens Some Time Later.

—AJ Sikes, BJ Sikes, and Dover Whitecliff.
Davis, California, January 2017

# THE STORY BEGINS

# THREE MEN AND A VAMPIRE

*By Harry Turtledove*

It's the most extraordinary thing, it really is. None of this would have happened if I hadn't made a silly mistake.

But life is like that all the time, isn't it? A chap I know married the girl who fell into his lap—yes, literally—when, as was his habit, he stuck out his long legs and big feet in a crowded train compartment and dozed off. Such stories haven't always happy endings. Some years later, I had to trade places with him at a fancy dinner party; they'd seated him next to her, and she was, by then, his former wife.

A happy ending to this particular tale I'm about to tell you? Let us not, as the shilling shockers say, anticipate.

George and Harris and I were coming out of the Oaken Barrel (not the real name of the place, and don't ask it of me, for I shan't tell you) not long before closing time one Friday night: which made it Saturday morning, if you're a stickler for such things. Three or four pints apiece left George and me uncommonly contented with the world. Rather more than three or four

13

pints left Harris wanting to sing a comic song. Take no alarm, dear reader; we did not let him.

But it was the nearest run thing you ever saw in your life, as Wellington, with so much less at risk, said of Waterloo. Thinking of our narrow escape called to mind other times when we were not so lucky. I also recollected another man's "comic" song I once heard, and that is what led me to my mistake.

For, after we'd managed to quieten Harris, looking up I saw walking along the pavement not ten yards ahead of us a man who was, at least from behind, the very spit and image of Herr Slossen Boschen. The fellow was tall and lean, as was the German musician. He dressed in an old-fashioned, almost excessively formal style, as did Herr Slossen Boschen. And the gas lamps clearly showed an upstanding pouf of white hair like that affected by the man of my acquaintance.

When I sped up and left my companions behind, George called after me, "Here, J., what in tarnation do you think you're about?"

"Making up to an old friend," I answered over my shoulder. Friend doubtless stretched the point, but heaven knows I did want to make up to Herr Slossen Boschen. Along with a roomful of other people, I've owed him an apology for lo these many years.

And I owe it to him yet. When I tapped the man on the elbow, he of course turned around to see who it might be. "Yes?" he said.

Like Herr Slossen Boschen's, his accent was indeed Teutonic. I realized at once, though, that I'd never once before set eyes on him. "I beg your pardon, sir," I stammered. "I took you for someone I knew."

"Till now, I agree we have not had the pleasure of each other's acquaintance. Let me remedy that. Abraham van Helsing, at your service." He bowed stiffly, from the waist, and held out his right hand.

As I shook him by it, I murmured something in what I hoped was German. They made me take the language in my schoolboy days, but I gladly gave it back soon afterwards. George and Harris caught me up then. Reveling in my fragmentary grasp of German, I also used it to present them to Herr van Helsing.

He smiled thinly. His narrow features had no room for any wider kind of smile. "You are kind, to look to bespeak a foreigner in his own tongue," quoth he, "but, though I know the speech of the Kaiser's Empire, I come from Holland, and it is not mine from birth. English will do more than well enough, I assure you."

Didn't I feel a right fool then! Not only had I thought he was someone he wasn't, I'd thought he hailed from a country he didn't. The disadvantage to paved streets, I find, is that you can't sink down through them no matter how embarrassed you are. My friends weren't about to let me forget it, either. What are friends for but reminding you how big a chucklehead you were while they chanced to be there to see it?

I started to give the Professor—that, I soon learned, was his proper title—the best apology I could (in English), but he held up a hand to show he did not want it. "Perhaps we are after all fortunately met," he said. "Providence works in mysterious ways its wonders to perform, and I confess to you all that the services of three bold young men would be of great value to me now."

I nearly wrote that I don't know why he reckoned us bold. I do, however: he must have been looking at George's blazer. You would never dream George works in a bank, not by that blazer. It would make you guess him to be the intimate acquaintance, perhaps even the taskmaster, of young women in the custom of earning the wages of sin.

But I digress. It is a bad habit of mine, digression. I may try to tell a story in the most simple and straightforward fashion, but somehow Uncle Podger and Montmorency will find themselves in the narrative whether they belong there or not. Perhaps it has something to do with the ink with which I prime my pen. Or it may ...

Your pardon, pray. I quite forgot. That shall not happen again.

Resplendent in his gaudy blazer, George asked, "What do you think we can do for you?"

"Have you gentlemen"—Professor van Helsing spread his hands to take in the three of us—"any acquaintance with the supernatural?"

"Ghosts are splendid in tales told after supper, especially on Christmas Eve, when it's almost hallowed to tell them," Harris said.

"That's an acquaintance with stories about ghosts. It isn't an acquaintance with ghosts." George, despite his villainous taste in haberdashery, keeps both feet firmly on the ground. If ever you should see George with his head in the clouds, you may be sure they've risen from his pipe.

"I've told some of those Christmas Eve ghost stories," I said slowly, "and some of the ones I've told are true, or as true as I could make them."

"Fishermen peddle the same nonsense," said George with a snort.

"Never mind, my friends," broke in the professor. "I only wished to assure myself that you would not dismiss the notion out of hand. I see that is true for two of you, at least. Sir"—this to George—"if you do not wish to continue with us, I promise I shall not think the less of you."

"You won't get rid of me so easily, not when you've scratched my bump of curiosity." George struck a phrenological pose. "If there's nothing to it, I'll have a laugh. If there is something to it, you'll need someone who has too much sense to get all hot and bothered. Here, that means me."

"I could get Montmorency," I said. "We're only three streets from my room."

"He'd give the doubters a bit in the way of brains, anyhow," said Harris. George glowered and growled. He's a large, solid man, George, but his bark is worse than his bite. When Montmorency sinks his teeth into something, he means it.

"This Montmorency is—?" enquired van Helsing.

"He certainly is," I agreed. "He's my dog."

I looked for him to say we needed a rascally fox terrier even less than did the cat who owned the young lady upstairs from me. I don't suppose he'd met the young lady upstairs—or the cat—but he would have known similar cases. What he did say, however, was, "Excellent! Against the *vrolok*, the *vrkoslak*, all aid is welcome."

I had no idea what he was talking about, which proved just as well. Neither did George. Harris looked thoughtful, as if the strange, barbarous words meant something to him even if he wished they didn't. Or it may be that the bitter he'd downed was having more of its way with him than I imagined.

We went upstairs on tiptoe so my landlady would not feel put upon. You would understand why had you ever heard her wax eloquent upon that feeling. You would also wish never to provoke it in her again, in which wish, she being what she is, you would find yourself disappointed.

I opened my door, scraped a lucifer on the sole of my shoe, and lit the gas. Montmorency lay asleep not in his basket but on my favorite chair, where the hair he sheds is more visible and more readily transfers itself to my trousers. He opened his eyes. George and Harris he is used to; he takes them for other pets of mine, which is not so far wrong. He didn't try to bite Professor van Helsing's ankles, showing himself either impressed by the man or too sleepy to bother.

Before he fully woke, I snapped a leash to his collar. That would, I hoped, keep him from pursuing cats and other distractions. If only people could so easily be kept from haring off in all directions.

"Now," I said brightly, "where are we going?" Montmorency wagged his tail. He was ready to go anywhere.

"Why, to Abney Park Cemetery." Van Helsing clucked. "Excuse me. I thought I already told you, or that you could have plucked the answer from my brain like fruit from a low-hanging tree. It is not far—no more than two or three kilometers."

He used those funny Continental measures, foreigner that he was. Well, I have crossed the Channel often enough to understand that he meant a mile or two. Half an hour's brisk walk, say.

It had been clear when we went in to get the dog. By the time we came out, only ten minutes later, fog was rolling in from the river. The lamps that lit the streets seemed to shrink in upon themselves. They cast little wan puddles of light at the feet of the poles they topped. Between the poles, darkness and mist held sway over all.

"Is the, the *vrkoslak* at the cemetery … in the cemetery?" asked Harris as we walked along. His voice sounded oddly muffled, as if the fog attenuated it like the streetlamps. Or he may have known more than George and I did, and liked what he knew less. By the way he pronounced the odd word van Helsing had used, he had indeed run across it before.

"Yes, I believe so." The Dutchman sounded grim. "I aim to run it off—to destroy it, if I am able—and to rout as many of its confederates as God may grant me the power to do."

"What are we talking about here?" I asked. "In plain English, I mean."

"You will have read *Varney the Vampire*, J., I'm sure," said Harris.

"Mm, parts of it," I allowed. *Varney the Vampire* is not a shilling shocker. It's a penny dreadful, from the days before I was born. Few have gone all the way through it, for it's two or three times as thick as the Bible, Old and New Testaments together. The pair of hacks who perpetrated it also wrote *The String of Pearls*, which loosed Sweeney Todd upon an unready world. They have much to answer for, in other words. I turned to Professor van Helsing. "You don't mean to say—?"

"Never mind what I mean to say," he told me. "Believe what you see, what you hear, what you feel. Forget all else, and act on that."

"Good advice," said George. His thinking so was not the worst argument to the contrary, but I let it pass.

I had trouble believing van Helsing could find Kingsland Road, but he did. Kingsland Road became Kingsland High Street, which became Stoke Newington High Street, all without a kink. He, and we, turned off Stoke Newington High Street at Stoke Newington Church Road. Soon we came to the gate of Abney Park Cemetery.

Anyone who knows me knows I am not wild for graves and tombs, except those of my kin. Still, of its kind, Abney Park Cemetery is quite fine. It is one of London's Magnificent Seven. (Curious—as I write that, I feel I ought to hear dramatic music playing, though I can't imagine why.)

"Better to use this entrance than the main one," murmured Professor van Helsing. "Coming off a road named for a church can only be a good omen." What about forgetting everything save what one saw, heard, and felt? Yes, what about that? Since van Helsing was already walking into the cemetery, I let it pass, too.

Abney Park is an arboretum as well as a burial ground. It houses all manner of rare and foreign trees and shrubs and flowers, but the flowers were closed for the evening, you might say, and with the fog the shrubs and trees might as well have been. Professor van Helsing nevertheless bestrode the paths like a colossus who knew where he was going. The rest of us followed as best we could. Montmorency, in fact, tried to follow the professor in front of him a couple of times, till I shortened the lead so he couldn't.

A tawny owl hooted from ... well, from somewhere. I believed I could hear it, but I didn't believe I could see it, or much of anything else. The fog seemed thick as meringue, though it tasted of coal-smoke rather than sugar. A properties manager putting on the Scottish play would have set a man who could do bird calls in the rafters to produce that eerie effect.

Little skittering noises came in amongst the rare and foreign foliage. My frightened imagination wanted to believe wolves and bears were making them, and never mind that England has been centuries free of such savage beasts (but for those that walk on two legs, not four). Reason insisted they came from creatures more on the order of cats and rats, mice and hedgehogs. In the dripping fog, though, reason was an *ignis fatuus*, one that shed little light.

One of us—I don't believe it was me, but I may be wrong— muttered what sounded like a prayer. It was likelier to have been in Latin than English. Even to the sturdiest nonconformist or C. of E. man, Latin feels more powerful than his native tongue. Latin is old. So is God. Therefore ... Almost a syllogism, don't you see?

I hadn't worked out whether it was or not when Montmorency yipped, snarled, jerked the leash out of my hand, and charged away. I could just about see him when he was at the end of the lead. He didn't take more than two bounds before disappearing altogether.

Fresh snarls came from off to our left, and then a thin screech that did not burst from a dog's throat. Like any terrier worth his table scraps and tasty bones, Montmorency is a ratter born. The only thing to delight him more than killing a rat is killing one rat after another. That thin screech didn't sound as if it burst from a rat's throat, either, but nothing seemed likelier.

We all hurried over towards where we thought we heard it. How we didn't get separated from one another and lost in the swirling mist I cannot tell you. I merely report the fact.

Then a flame sprang up in our midst. Van Helsing had, not an ordinary paraffin lamp, but something smaller and neater. "What the devil—?" said George. I couldn't have put it better myself.

"It is a Döbereiner's lamp. I light my pipe with it," said the professor. "An ingenious device. A valve releases *waterstof*—ah, hydrogen—over a platinum sponge, which causes it to ignite in the presence of air."

The faintly bluish flame faintly showed Montmorency. Even more faintly, it showed something that made my stomach turn over: the corpse of a naked young man, his throat torn out. I stared at my dog, who was licking from his muzzle I know not what, nor ever want to learn.

"Ah, poor Stivvings. Pity it had to end like this," said van Helsing sadly. He turned the valve on his lamp so darkness swooped in again. Then he continued, "He was in rat form when Montmorency took him. It is a stage on the road to vampirism; I cannot explain better than that. Only in death did the poor devil return to his birthshape. Christ have mercy on his soul!" He drew a cross in the moist air in front of him. For a moment, it glowed blue like the flame from the Döbereiner's lamp.

I saw that. Did I believe it? I didn't see a rat turn into a man upon death, but I saw the dead man. Did I believe Montmorency could have slain him had he been in human form all that time? Did I believe a naked man would skulk through the undergrowth in Abney Park Cemetery on such a dank and foggy night?

I can tell you what I believed. I believed I'd fallen in deeper than I ever dreamt I might.

"Come, all of you." Professor van Helsing's voice grew urgent. "If his amanuensis is so near, the fiend will rise at any moment. God bless your dog, sir. He may well have saved us from an attack from behind."

God bless my dog? God bless Montmorency? God bless my soul!

How van Helsing found the path again is one more thing I cannot tell you. I can only relate that he did. We pattered on, staying together more by the scrape of our feet on the paving stones than by sight. Montmorency, trotting along beside me, seemed content now to stay on the leash. Perhaps one miracle of an evening sufficed even for him.

On we hurried, now left, now right, now straight—it was worse than the maze at Hampton Court, for there was no one to rescue us if we went astray. With the fog and the black night, I have no idea whereabouts in the cemetery we wound up. Van Helsing seemed sure of where he was going. Sure, of course, need not mean right; let anyone who doubts this hang about with George for a bit.

A sudden boom followed by the noise of dirt rolling off something large came to our ears. Many caskets are designed with signaling devices to prevent the horror of premature burial, but I had trouble imagining someone prematurely buried possessing the preternatural strength to throw off the coffin lid and the earth atop it.

Yet I heard what I heard. Did I believe it? I blame the blistering pace of nineteenth-century life in general for how I reply; things were happening too fast for me not to believe it.

Professor van Helsing made the sign of the cross once more. This time, it did not merely shine blue; it blazed like lightning, piercing the fog as if it were a lighthouse lamp warning steamships away from jagged rocks. And what it showed …

When you hear the phrase a *fiend in human shape*, what crosses your mind? Shame on you if it's your least favorite relative. Shame, too, if it's your least favorite politico, though, given the run of politicos these days, your sin there may be more venial.

As for me, I saw the genuine article that night. Mad eyes glowing like an animal's, fangs longer and sharper than Montmorency's, a pallor as of the grave from which the horrid thing had just emerged … My hair stood on end. It truly did; I could feel it lifting my hat.

"Begone!" cried Professor van Helsing. "This tomb, this city, this land are not for you!" He sketched the cross yet again. The mystic, purifying sign glowed brighter than ever. That glow hurt the vampire, which flinched away as if from a hot poker.

Yet the foul creature was made of stern stuff. "Damn you!" it cried, its mouth sounding stuffed with dirt. It rushed at its tormentor, and at my friends and me.

Van Helsing coolly pulled a pistol from his pocket. He did not fire it at the fiend, however, for it spat water rather than bullets. The good professor did not seem the sort to annoy his friends with a squirt-gun, but there you are. He did more than annoy the vampire—when the drops touched its skin, it shrieked as if they were vitriol.

"Holy water," said van Helsing. "Quick—fall on it whilst it is weakened!"

We did. Even Montmorency grabbed a trouser leg in his jaws and did his best to impede the monster. Heaven preserve me if ever I meet a vampire at full strength. Weakened as it was, the creature seemed a match for George and Harris and me, to say nothing of the dog.

Along with his squirt-gun, the professor proved to carry a stiletto. He stabbed the vampire again and again. No blood flowed from the wounds. Then the long, thin blade must have pierced its heart. The vampire collapsed in a puff of ashes and dust. In an eyeblink, the opera suit it had worn was empty. Only a faint foul odor lingered in the air.

The cross signs faded away, leaving us again in darkness. "I say," drawled George. "Not the way I planned to spend the small hours, but not the least interesting little while I've passed, either."

"That must be what they call English equanimity," said van Helsing. "Against such, the *vrolok* might well have struggled in vain even without my trifling intervention. But better, I think, to take no chances."

Montmorency barked agreement. I also thought the professor was right. As a proper Englishman, though, I was of course too modest to say so.

# ELY AND THE MEDIUM

*By Kirsten Weiss*

REPORT FROM ELY CRANE
SEPTEMBER 3, 1849
NEW YORK CITY

Let's get something straight off the reel. There's no such thing as ghosts. But there are spies, and there's not much worse than having one cavorting in your backyard. And that's the *only* reason I volunteered to attend a table rapping run by Miss Persephone LaPorte.

Getting a ticket was dashed difficult. All of New York's high and mighty were yammering to push in on one of the lady's conversations with the dearly departed. Death is a strange business. There was worry that certain folks of a more desperate persuasion might be saying to Miss LaPorte things they shouldn't. State secrets—military documents, mostly—had found their way into the wrong hands. The trails led directly back to some of Miss LaPorte's table rappings.

So I dusted off my top hat, and there I sat in my best brown coat and cravat, holding the hands of a peppery industrialist and a high-society matron. The industrialist's muttonchops were gray, and his palms were sweaty. But since this was his house, I didn't see fit to complain. On the snowy tablecloth lay the tools of the medium's trade—a tambourine, a drum, a fife. Candlelight gleamed off the rose-patterned wallpaper.

"Let us now close our eyes," Miss LaPorte intoned, "and think on our dearly departed."

I studied the medium through my slitted eyelids. I reckoned she was in her late twenties. Her clothes were elegant and fashionable, but not too showy. Her skin was the color of tobacco, and her accent hinted of warm Caribbean breezes.

It's my job to know things. And I knew for a fact she'd been born into bondage in Virginia and brought by her owner to live in Washington City. That was where she'd won her liberty and discovered an island dialect. The capital was desperate for labor, and Washington City had devised its own revolting version of the South's peculiar institution. Slave owners acted as employment agencies, hiring out the men and women they'd bought. The slaves lived on their own—saving the owner from the costs of roof and board—and remitted a portion of their earnings to their owner. Miss LaPorte had saved enough money as a medium to buy freedom for herself and her mother, and the two had promptly moved north, changed names, and tried to put the whole ghastly business behind them.

After what Miss LaPorte had suffered, I reckoned she could fleece as many rich fools as she wished. But selling military secrets to civilians was another matter.

War was coming.

If good people were to end the disgusting business of slavery, then the North would have to win. And we would, as long as the recent advances in mechanical technology stayed secret at the highest levels.

The red velvet curtains stirred, a whisper of cool air chilling my cheek. The candle flames blew sideways, and we were

—

plunged into darkness. The lady beside me gave a little jump and a gasp, squeezing my hand. Now our only illumination was the moonlight shifting through the blowing curtains.

The industrialist snored softly. Carefully, I slipped my hand from his grasp and withdrew my borrowed goggles from my waistcoat. I flipped the dark-seeing lens into place and pressed one side of the goggles to my right eye. Through the lens, the room turned a sickly green, but I could see everything as if we sat beneath full daylight. I scanned the room for Miss LaPorte's confederate.

I frowned, seeing no one aside from our group of hapless table rappers. That meant the medium's assistant was hidden by more than darkness—perhaps lurking behind the curtains or inside the wooden chest near the door.

The table shifted, and the industrialist awoke with a snort.

"What? What?" he asked.

"The spirits are with us," Miss LaPorte intoned.

And though I knew she was a fraud, I came all-overish. A shiver like crawling ants raced up the back of my neck. I feared that the industrialist would remember to take my hand, but at that moment the instruments rose into the air.

I nearly dropped the goggles.

There were no strings.

Now, I'd tested these goggles under all sorts of conditions. If those instruments dangled from strings or wires, I should have been able to see the cords. I'd swear to it there were none.

The table jumped again and scraped across the floor, ramming into my midsection. I did drop the goggles then. Turning my mistake to an advantage, I stooped to retrieve them, taking my chance to lift the tablecloth and scan for contraptions.

Nothing! No wires, no confederate, no odd bolts or devices. It was enough to puzzle a Philadelphia lawyer.

And then Miss LaPorte started talking, her voice an eerie, masculine crackle. "My darling Belle."

I jolted upright, banging my shoulder on the table and making my neighbor screech.

The society matron leaned forward and sobbed. "Harold?"

"I love you, my dearest," the medium rasped. "That key you're looking for is in the laundry room."

"But I've looked there," the matron said. "I've looked everywhere!"

"Try the third flagstone from the left."

"You mean ... beneath it?"

But the medium's voice switched again, turning childlike, and she called out for her mama.

A dignified lady on my left fainted and slid in a heap to the Oriental rug.

Her neighbors at the table leapt to their feet to attend her, and I figured that was that. But the evening wasn't over.

"Death," the medium said, her voice a razor whisper.

The hair rose on the back of my neck.

"Death stalks closer, Ely."

My jaw clenched, and I muttered a thousand and one silent curses. I'd not only introduced myself as Mr. Horace Drake, but I'd worn a disguise complete with bushy eyebrows and a squashed nose. Somehow, Miss LaPorte had found me out.

Someone raised the lamp wick. Miss LaPorte blinked, sagged forward, and straightened.

Then the show really did sputter to an end. I lingered, covertly examining the room to figure out how Miss LaPorte had played her trick. If I'd had more time, I'm sure I could have winkled out the truth. But our hostess, the industrialist's wife, shuffled us all out.

Miss LaPorte was growing more and more intriguing. But I wasn't going to get beat by a lady. So the next day, and for the week thereafter, I watched Miss LaPorte in her humble abode in Dutchtown. She lived with her mother in a three-story framed tenement beside a rowdy beer hall below Houston Street. I guessed they'd settled on the place because it was cheap, but with her dusky skin, she stood out among the pasty Germans like a rose in a desert.

To my surprise, the ladies' neighbors treated them both with respect … to their faces. Behind their backs, the neighbors gossiped, eyes wide with anxiety. I guessed the LaPortes had threatened hoodoo to any who molested them. The German immigrants understood the power of a good hex.

I trailed after Miss LaPorte for days, changing my disguise, following the agent handbook on sneaking around and a few rules I'd codified on my own. She didn't know I was there, I'd swear to it. But her days were mundane—trips to the market, helping her mama with the laundry, a visit to the library.

And then one early morning I trailed her to a Manhattan park. She sat still as a statue on a dew-covered bench and stared at a highfalutin Queen Anne brownstone across the road.

Weaving like a drunk, I curled up beneath a buckeye tree, its leaves turned golden. I pretended to sleep, one eye fixed on the medium.

The sun made its slow perambulation across the sky. The air had a snap to it, and the cold from the ground seeped into my bones. A small boy kicked my shin, taking me for dead. I glared at him through one eye, and he ran squealing to his nanny.

And still the medium sat.

I had one bad moment, when a manservant from one of the neighborhood's grand houses came to run me off. But we discovered we'd been in the same army unit, and he took pity on my fallen state.

Miss LaPorte sat, unmoving.

Darkness fell, the temperature dropping, and I began to worry maybe she was in a trance. But finally, she rose, stretched, and returned to her tenement.

When I returned to my hotel room, I found an invitation from Miss LaPorte for another table rapping in five days—at the brownstone she'd been studying with such concentration. No doubt she saw me as a new mark, but I wondered if she'd somehow caught me watching her.

Through a series of telegrams, I determined the brownstone was the second home of a wealthy Southerner. He traveled frequently to New York to oversee the sale of cotton to the northern mills.

I sent an affirmative response to the invitation.

The next day, Miss LaPorte and I repeated the process. I found a different tree to curl under, and she sat on her bench.

A small carpetbag rested on the bench beside the medium. Her dainty hand lay lightly atop its bone handle, as if warning any thieves from trying to separate the two.

At nine in the morning, the master of the house exited. His lady followed soon thereafter. And then three maids departed, giggling.

Quick as a wink, Miss LaPorte was across the street. She vanished behind an arrowwood shrub.

I rose, ready to follow.

And then Miss LaPorte was scampering up the corner of the brownstone. Her skirt had been shed and replaced by loose men's trousers. The carpetbag was slung at her back. She wriggled through a high window beneath the roof.

I stood gawping like a great big gawper. Finally remembering myself, I settled down on the tree roots to watch. An hour later, she returned, clambering down the wall like a spider and dropping into the arrowwood bush. She emerged wearing her demure checked brown skirt and waltzed down the street.

When she'd vanished around the corner, I trotted across the road and examined the brownstone's wall. Tiny scuffs on the stone told me all I needed to know.

Now, a good agent should be prepared for anything. While I hadn't expected this, I had a set of metal climbing claws in my coat pocket. Shrugging from my ragged coat, I slipped the clamps onto my boots and hands and tightened their leather straps. Up I went—not quite as elegantly as Miss LaPorte—reaching the window without breaking my neck. I slipped inside an empty servant's room—a maid's, judging by the jam jar of flowers on the table.

Oh, Miss LaPorte was a clever one, there's no doubt about it. But she was no match for a trained agent. It took some doing, because the lady had been careful, but even she'd left a trail for me to follow. In the attic, I found her careful cuts in the floorboards. She'd covered the evidence with a steamer trunk. Judging by the thick dust she'd left footprints in, her perfidy wouldn't be discovered any time soon.

I pulled up the puzzle piece of floor and found myself looking *between* the home's walls.

For once it came in useful that I resemble the crane that is my family name. I reckoned that hole Miss LaPorte had created was just wide enough to accommodate my shoulders.

Climbing claws back on, I made my way through the gap, shimmying between the walls. It was a tight fit, and there were a few bad moments, but eventually I found it. A wide, flat, empty plane diverged to my right—a gap between the ceiling and floor of the first and second floors. Wedged inside the space was a device.

I crawled inside, wriggling flat on the ground. The ceiling pressed close against my spine, forcing me to take shallow breaths. As I slithered toward the device, dust and spiders dropped onto my head. Every movement threatened to get me stuck. The floor above bowed downward, compressing me as I got closer to the machine. When I was within good visual range, I gave a snort and inhaled a mountain of dust.

"What's that up there?" a woman cried out below me.

I pressed my hands to my nose and mouth and struggled to suppress the coming explosion.

"Peter?" the woman said. "Peter! We got rats! You here? The mistress won't like rats in them walls."

I managed not to give myself away further, and retreated, grinning.

◌◌◌

It was a glittering, cloudless night. Ladies in silk gowns and gentlemen in white gloves milled in front of the brownstone.

I skirted the crowd and slipped, unseen, behind the arrow-wood. Quick as a wink, I was up the wall. As I'd suspected, the window was again open. I clambered inside and made my way to the attic without encountering any maids.

The dark-seeing goggles were strapped to my head and the aether weapon I'd purloined to my thigh. The gun was silent and looked lethal. I expected Miss LaPorte's partner would come along with little trouble when confronted with the weapon.

Silently, I clambered down the inside of the walls, bits of plaster falling like snow. Approaching the crawlspace between the first and second floors, I slowed my descent. I wanted to catch the lady's partner by surprise, but I was also curious to see her machine in action.

Faintly, the murmurs and laughter of hopeful table rappers drifted through the walls. I could clearly make out Miss LaPorte's melodious tones. And was that the British ambassador? What the devil was he doing in New York?

I took a cautious glimpse inside the crawlspace. Then a longer one. The machine was there, its outlines visible with my dark-vision goggles. But I saw no confederate. I bit back a curse. Had I arrived before her partner? There was no dratted place to hide from him, jammed between the walls as I was.

A light flicked to life on the mysterious machine. A faint hum vibrated through the crawlspace, and more plaster drifted downward.

Distance control! Miss LaPorte had a machine with distance control! Good gad. This sort of technology was only now being explored by top military scientists. If a civilian had it—

"The spirits are with us," Miss LaPorte intoned below me.

I adjusted my goggles. Had the machine lifted slightly into the air? It was too far away for me to see clearly, but it seemed … It was! It hovered half an inch off the ceiling below.

Now, I knew a scientist who worked with aether technology, and this machine would be something she'd dearly like to examine. She was also the lady I'd "borrowed" the goggles from, and I figured I owed her a treat if I ever intended returning to her lab.

I needed to get closer to that machine.

Gritting my teeth, I slithered into the crawlspace. The floor and ceiling seemed closer tonight, and I regretted the hearty meal I'd eaten earlier. I crept forward, wriggling on my belly like a snake. The floor above pushed into my spine. It was definitely bowed—I hadn't imagined it. I reached for the device, and the machine zipped silently sideways, evading me.

A woman below shrieked. "They're floating!"

Her companions shushed her.

I could imagine what was happening at the séance below. The machine probably used magnets of some sort, no doubt enhanced by aether, and those magnets were moving the small metal objects on the medium's table. But how the devil was the machine itself flitting about? And why hadn't my brass pocket watch gone airborne at the first séance?

I made another lunge—so to speak—in the tight crawlspace. Again, the blasted contraption darted out of reach.

Footsteps sounded above me. I raised my head and banged it into the second floor. Grimacing, I bit back a yelp. But the pain made me reckless. I shifted forward, determined to catch the blamed device.

And my shoulders stuck.

Grunting, I tried to pull back, but I was stuck like a cork in a bottle.

"Brandy?" a man with a buttery Southern accent asked above me.

I wriggled experimentally. It wasn't just my shoulders that were trapped. The lowest point of the floor pressed into my upper back, pinning me like a butterfly.

I heaved forward and back, breathed out, compressed my ribs. Above, the men joked, and below, the spiritualists gasped, and I was well and truly stuck.

The devil with it. My mission was to expose Miss LaPorte, and I was quite willing to come crashing through the ceiling to do it. I drew the aether weapon from the holster at my thigh.

"And if war comes?" The Southerner asked above me. "What will Britain do?"

I froze, my head cocked.

"The people have no sympathy for slavery, sir," the British ambassador said. There was a long pause. "However, the government understands certain realities."

The Southerner gave a bark. "You mean your government is still smarting over the last war."

"We did burn your capital to the ground," the ambassador said dryly.

"Not my capital, sir!" There was a long pause, and I held my breath. "Then it is possible?" the Southerner asked.

"Certain quarters would need to be appeased, but yes, it is possible."

I groaned and banged my head on the floor. Ceiling. Whatever the devil it was.

The British working with the South? This was actionable intelligence and vitally important. Now I couldn't bust into the séance and reveal Miss LaPorte as a fraud. The traitor above would suspect I'd overheard. Worse, this hidey-hole would be the perfect spot for future eavesdropping.

I was well and truly fixed, and I settled in to await Miss LaPorte's rescue. After all, she'd have to return for her marvelous machine sometime, wouldn't she?

Wouldn't she?

# WEEKEND NEAR THE ASYLUM

*By Katherine L. Morse & David L. Drake*

Dr. Sparky McTrowell stared sullenly into the distance, piloting the Peregrine air yacht mechanically, almost as if she were an automaton herself. She'd flown the Peregrine in some truly trying circumstances, but today she felt like the atmosphere in the cabin between her and her fiancé, Chief Inspector Erasmus Drake, was so heavy that she marveled at the little craft's ability to stay aloft. Their confrontation at Cape Wrath with the man responsible for her father's death had sorely tried their relationship. Even though a day had passed, neither Sparky nor Erasmus could bring themselves to bend to the other's position.

"Darling, perhaps we should discuss what happened at Cape Wrath," Drake ventured.

"You promised we would never speak of that again," she replied stonily without taking her eyes off the darkening horizon. "I'm tired and hungry, and it's getting dark. I'm going to set down at Lincoln. They have a tiny port there, just two small towers, where we can tie up for the night. I don't see any reason to press on to London in the dark."

"Yes, dear."

CREO

"The White Hart? That sounds serviceable," Drake offered cheerfully, hoping to bring up Sparky's mood.

"It's pretty ordinary, as the name suggests, but it's the only thing open at this hour near the airship 'port.'"

They walked silently together for half a mile before the pub came into sight, the only business lit in town at that hour. The only other light was the faint glow from upper-story residences. Without conferring, they both came to a halt to observe a disturbance unfolding in the street outside the White Hart. It exhibited the characteristics of a schoolyard bullying with the ugly soupçon of drink. By reflex, Drake extracted his police whistle from his waistcoat pocket and blew three short blasts while running toward the melee. He could hear McTrowell close upon his heels.

"Chief Inspector Erasmus Drake of Scotland Yard," he shouted authoritatively as he dashed into the middle of the dustup, shoving back an antagonist and hauling another one away by his collar far enough to assist Sparky, who had bent down to help the victim up from the street.

"I'm a doctor," Sparky said. "Let's get you into the light of the pub so I can examine you." But the injured party was out cold. Sparky reached for the neck to check for a pulse and the initial touch caused the head to roll to the right. The light spilling from the lamp over the pub sign gave Sparky a clearer view of his face. His? The brow and jaw were strong, but the light was insufficient for the flight surgeon to tell whether there were whiskers or not. Was that a hint of an Adam's apple or just a shadow? Sparky remembered her Hippocratic duties and checked for a pulse; fortunately there was one.

Having rousted the assailants, Drake bent down to lend a hand, asking, "Is he alive?" Sparky nodded. He continued, "Shall we get him back inside so you can examine him more thoroughly?" She nodded again and moved around to pick up the victim's feet so Drake could get a grip under the shoulders.

The pub patrons all stopped their conversations and turned their attention to the door as Drake and McTrowell shuffled in with the inert patient. Sensing the hostile atmosphere, Drake peremptorily announced, "Chief Inspector Erasmus Drake of Scotland Yard. There will be no more physical confrontations this evening. Publican, is there a quiet place we might assist this man?" The pub owner shuffled unenthusiastically from his post behind the bar to lead the adventurers to a side room with a rough table and chairs. He left without uttering a single word. Drake and McTrowell settled their charge on the table. Erasmus pulled all the chairs back to the walls while Sparky turned up the gaslight to get a better look.

What the two of them saw when they turned around brought both of them up short for the second time that evening. The victim's ensemble was a peculiar mishmash of clothing articles from different time periods: a contemporary overcoat, rough medieval era boots, a style of shirt that Erasmus recognized as being at least a century old, and a pair of breeches that looked like they'd just arrived from the court of the Sun King. His headwear was even more remarkable. His tattered top hat was adorned with a pair of goggles bristling with lenses of different magnifications mounted on slender retractable arms. The hatband was stuck around with bits of mechanical detritus, half of which Sparky couldn't identify.

"Ah," the flight surgeon sighed slowly.

"Please tell me that utterance means you have an explanation for this," Drake probed.

"There's an asylum a few miles down the road. The delusion of being a famous personage out of history is not uncommon. They may have humored, um, him by allowing him to dress this way. Let's search all the pockets to see if we can find any other evidence of his identity."

"What do you mean by 'um, him?'"

McTrowell didn't bother to look up as she began a thorough ransack of pockets. "*He* is dressed as a man, albeit from a lot of time periods. But the casual indicators of sex aren't definitive in this context without removing at least some clothing or performing a manual examination through the clothing, not that it matters under the circumstances. Aha!" she declared, extracting a small, worn, leather-bound notebook from a pocket hidden inside the overcoat under the arm.

"What have you found?"

"How is your cryptography?" She held the notebook open to a random page to show Drake. "There are some peculiar mechanical drawings that would take some time to analyze, but there are also many pages like this one." The offered page was covered from top to bottom with a list of names, last name first, each followed by a string of nine digits in three groups of three.

Drake stroked his beard. "Clearly it is not a Caesar cypher since each one has only nine digits. There are too many for house numbers, and neither the format nor all the digits fit dates or times. Even the Bank of England cannot have this many safe deposit boxes, nor have I ever seen a combination lock with numbers this high. It could be some kind of identification code, but with nine digits, it could account for approximately eighty percent of the people on the planet!" Drake was unsettled by his last conjecture because it implied a global enterprise engaged in identifying and cataloging everyone on earth. The immensity of such an undertaking was too much to imagine. He shook his head. "That cannot be the answer."

"Perhaps we should just wait for our victim to wake up, and then we'll just ask … him. In the meantime, I'll get us some dinner and sit watch. You might see if you can cajole some useful information out of the locals."

"Yes, a Chief Inspector from Scotland Yard interviewing local ruffians in Lincolnshire; that is guaranteed to produce fruitful results," he quipped sardonically. Sparky wordlessly dropped a peck on his cheek before returning to the main room of the pub in search of comestibles.

❦

Having fortified himself with the passable shepherd's pie, the Chief Inspector sallied forth to investigate the assault. Almost immediately he spotted a pair of the assailants at a table in the far, dark corner of the bar. He was striding purposefully toward them when the publican stopped him with a firm grip on Erasmus's arm.

"I don't want no trouble in my establishment."

"I assure you I am not a man of *unnecessary* violence," Drake asserted, and he firmly pulled his arm away. He closed the distance to his target. "I am Chief Inspector Erasmus Drake of Scotland Yard. I have some questions about the altercation I witnessed outside just a few moments ago."

"You got no authority here," snarled one of the men.

"I am an agent of Her Royal Majesty. You will answer my questions or it shall go very badly for you, I promise." He let the threat sink in for a moment. "What was the nature of your conflict with the victim?"

"Victim? Hah! That one is dangerous. Mad as a hatter!"

"Only a few forms of insanity carry the threat of violence to others. What precisely was the nature of the alleged madness you observed?"

"How should I know? He was screaming in some strange language and pulling at my clothes?"

"What language?"

The previously silent co-conspirator spoke up. "It was kinda like Spanish?"

Sensing he had identified the more useful witness, Drake pressed the second man. "Are you sure? What do you mean 'like Spanish?'"

The witness offered, "I sailed some when I was younger and had some reasons to learn a few words of Spanish." Drake wondered if by 'sailing' the man meant 'pirating,' but he didn't interrupt. "It was like he was speaking Spanish, but some of the letters was wrong."

"Could you make out anything he was saying?"

"It sounded like he was asking what year it was, which didn't make no sense, and he asked where he was."

Having observed the man for a couple of minutes, Drake concluded that he wasn't drunk ... at least not yet. He also realized he wasn't going to get any more useful information out of either belligerent. He made a mental note to report the incident to the local constabulary in the morning. "In the future, I advise leaving strangers alone. One never knows when one of them might turn out to be dangerous in actuality," he smiled menacingly at the two assailants before returning to Sparky, who was tending the victim.

CR&SO

"Er, huh?" The victim stirred groggily. Sparky got up from her chair and approached slowly so as not to startle him. "*Em que ano estamos? Onde estou?*"

Sparky considered these utterances before commenting to Drake, "Not Spanish. Probably Portuguese, which I don't really speak." She addressed her patient, "*¿Hablas español?*"

"*No.*"

Sparky looked back at Drake. "Well, that's strange. He claims not to speak Spanish, but clearly understood me enough to say so." She tried again with the patient. "*Me llamo* Sparky McTrowell."

"Thomas Trent."

Drake responded first. "That sounds like an English name."

To which Thomas replied, "It is."

"You are English? Then why were you speaking Portuguese?"

"I was expecting to be in Brazil. What year is it?"

"1852. What year did you expect it to be?"

"Anything but that."

Drake and McTrowell exchanged a meaningful, could-matters-get-any-weirder look.

⋙⋘

"Hello, I'm Dr. Sparky McTrowell. This is Chief Inspector Erasmus Drake of Scotland Yard. Do you recognize this man?"

"Woman," the female desk clerk at The Lawn replied.

"He introduced himself to us as Thomas Trent."

"Thomasin," the clerk responded curtly.

Despite the unpleasant brevity of the encounter, it was fruitful because it confirmed Sparky's assessment that their victim was a resident of the asylum.

"Gender doesn't matter in the future," Thomas/Thomasin interjected.

"I can hardly wait!" Sparky retorted before re-engaging the woman behind the desk. "We are returning him or her to your custody. Several fantastic claims were made by your resident," Sparky continued, awkwardly resorting to passive voice to avoid further engagement on the gender question. "Might there be someone with whom we could discuss these assertions?"

"She's close with an old woman named Violet, but she's senile."

Sensing his fiancée's frustration, Drake asked politely, "Could you please take us to Violet?"

ᘓᘔ

"She was always building strange devices. She swore they were going to make her rich in the future. Like this here one," Violet offered, pointing at a makeshift siege engine at the edge of lawn.

"Um, isn't that a trebuchet?" Sparky asked.

"Quite correct, my dear," Drake affirmed.

"You know I'd never even seen one until I met you, and now they're everywhere we turn." Sparky turned back to Violet, "This one has an awfully long throwing arm for such a small sling. What was she planning to do with it?"

"She said it was for testing airship engines." Sparky did engineering gymnastics in her brain for a full minute before concluding this made absolutely no sense for any of the airships she had ever encountered. "Did she happen to say how?"

"You're supposed to put a frozen chicken in there"—the old lady pointed at the sling—"and fling it into the engine," she waved her arm vaguely in an arc over her head. The airship pilot's hopes of clarification evaporated; her brain just hurt. She concluded that the attendant had been completely accurate in her assessment of Thomasin's mental faculties.

ᘓᘔ

"I propose we review the evidence," the Chief Inspector suggested once they had returned to the privacy of the Peregrine.

"Yes, dear," Sparky replied while readying the air yacht for the last hop back to London.

The Chief Inspector extracted his notebook from the pocket of his cape coat. "We have an individual diagnosed as insane who claims to be a time traveler. Despite the diagnosis, there are some facts that are not explained by simple insanity."

"Insanity is never simple."

"As you say. A person who has never left England suddenly turns up speaking Portuguese. She has in her possession a list of names and associated numbers by which she claims one will be able to contact that person in the future, no matter where they are."

"That would be very handy. I need to give those mechanical drawings a more thorough review, but I'm almost certain that they require machining tolerances that are not feasible … at least not yet."

"Demonstrably, she has invented an apparatus for testing external airship engines of a configuration that even you cannot imagine."

"And I can imagine quite a lot. Please throw off the anchor line."

Drake reached outside the hatch and opened the toggle linking the Peregrine's anchor line to the tower's tether. "Finally, and most importantly, there is her worrisome claim that a war will consume the world sixty years from now, and both Brazil and the British Empire will be engaged, the latter to its immortal peril."

"As farfetched as that sounds, if it's true, the fate of your empire depends on our intervention. Oh, shouldn't we be referring to the Trent individual as 'he,' his chosen gender?"

"Ah, yes, and there is the matter of the claim that gender will be irrelevant in the future. I believe investigations farther afield are in order."

"Another of your transatlantic sailing adventures?" Sparky quipped, reminding Drake of their inordinately long rescue of Edwin Llewellyn that had taken them all the way to the Hawaiian Islands and back. She opened up the Peregrine's throttle and pulled back on the yoke. "Please tell me that this time I'll at least be given the time to pack a bag properly."

# The Wheel of Misfortune

## Part I

### By Lillian Csernica

Dr. William Harrington strolled the Hachinaga-dori, a broad avenue in the expatriate section of Kyoto. The cool evening air helped him savor his cigar. Cherry blossoms graced the city with their annual mantle of pale pink beauty. A scattering of petals clung to Harrington's black wool topcoat, burgundy waistcoat, and gray trousers. He'd just enjoyed a fine evening of billiards and conversation with some of the other members of the British expatriate community. Japan had welcomed him with more hospitality than he'd expected. Still, it was good to be in the company of his own countrymen, so much so that he'd stayed past midnight.

A shortcut through the alleys would help him arrive home more quickly. Harrington turned right down a side street that took him between houses built of wood, their sliding doors paneled with the thick paper that kept out wind, rain, and snow. A left turn brought him parallel with his own street, just a few blocks away. Somewhere behind him, wagon wheels rumbled over the hard-packed dirt. The hoarse growl of an angry Japanese man disturbed the night's peace. Something peculiar about the sound of the wagon wheels made Harrington glance back. A single wagon wheel as big as an entire carriage rolled toward him. Flames streaked back from the spokes. From the hub sprouted the huge head of an old man with wild white hair and blazing eyes.

"*Gizen-sha!*" the old man shouted. "*Gizen-sha!*"

Instinct overcame shock. Harrington ran. The wheel pursued him, the flames painting the houses around him with reddish light. Its horrible voice kept chanting that one phrase in tones that promised violence. Harrington spotted a gate that stood ajar. As he came abreast of it, he threw himself sideways into the garden beyond, landing hard on the gravel pathway. Ignoring the pain, he scrambled up onto his feet and shut the gate.

The flaming wheel rumbled past. The harsh voice faded.

Harrington leaned on the gate, trying to catch his breath. He looked back down the street. No flames, no embers, not even a spark. Why hadn't anything else caught fire?

Six weeks. Just six short weeks had passed since he'd captured the shapeshifting cat monster. Would it never end? He'd brought his family to Kyoto because one simply did not say no to Her Royal Majesty Queen Victoria nor to the Emperor of Japan. Harrington still wasn't entirely certain why they'd chosen him to be the personal physician for the abbot of Kiyomizudera Temple. One thing he did know with absolute clarity: No one had told him his new situation meant frequent battles with gods and monsters.

Now this wheel monster, huge and angry and bent on deliberate mayhem. Had it been waiting to ambush him? Harrington tidied his coat, brushed the dust from his trousers, and set his jaw. Whatever this creature was, whatever its purpose, he had no intention of involving Madelaine. This time he'd get to the bottom of the matter himself.

CR80

At the breakfast table in the morning Harrington drank his tea and spread bitter orange marmalade on his toast. His wife, Constance, and their nine-year-old daughter, Madelaine, had embraced the spirit of springtime. Constance wore a morning dress of green figured silk. Madelaine wore pale blue calico. Her dark hair had been plaited into two braids and tied off with matching blue ribbons. As lovely as both ladies were, they were also having a difference of opinion.

"Mama, don't you see? The flames must have been magical or simply an illusion. None of the monsters I've read about damage property."

"Lady Montague's housekeeper was quite definite. A rolling bonfire that spoke with a human voice. Lady Montague very nearly sent her footman to ring the fire bell."

"Better to be safe than sorry." Madelaine conceded the point in a tone of such mature consideration that Harrington had to hide his smile behind his teacup.

"It's refreshing to hear you say that, young lady, given your recent adventures." Constance poured more tea into her own cup. "There might be fairies in an English garden, but I daresay Japanese gardens might be home to something altogether more exotic."

"Yes, Mama. That's the point. I want to compare the two and see if there's a different species here."

Constance paused, her hand hovering above the scones. "You won't be sticking pins in them and putting them under glass, will you?"

"Mama!" Madelaine laughed. "These aren't insects. They're magical creatures."

"Really, Madelaine. You're getting a bit old to believe in magic."

Harrington chewed his toast. The bitterness of the marmalade echoed his mood. Part of him hoped the flaming wheel was nothing more than a hallucination brought on by an excess of tobacco and brandy. The Abbot had told him that, having become one of the Abbot's guardians, Harrington would attract the attention of supernatural entities. This flaming wheel with the face of an old man seemed even more dangerous than the cat monster.

"Maddy," he said. "May I borrow some of your books on folklore?"

Madelaine looked up, eyes bright. "Certainly, Papa!" She pushed back her chair.

"Just a moment, young lady." Constance's stern voice stopped Madelaine in midstride. "You will sit down, finish your juice, and ask to be excused."

Madelaine took her seat, drank the rest of her juice in four ladylike sips, then patted her lips with her napkin. "I say, Mother dear, might I be excused?"

"Very well."

Madelaine rushed off, feet pounding up the stairs.

Constance winced. "Honestly." She buttered her scone. "Doing research, are you?"

"A little cultural reconnaissance."

"Tonight we're expected at the home of the Malloys to play whist."

Harrington grimaced. "You accepted this invitation, Constance. I expect you to rescue me when Augustus Malloy begins to recite his medical history. Again."

Constance patted his hand. "Mr. Malloy is just a poor old hypochondriac. I'm sure it brings him considerable comfort to confide his medical worries to a British physician."

"There's nothing wrong with him that can't be cured by a good dose of salts."

"Now, now." Constance rose and dropped a kiss on Harrington's cheek. "Go and do your research."

⟨≈⟩

An hour later Harrington sat back in his armchair staring at one particular book lying open on his desk. Madelaine had everything from nursery fairy stories to more scholarly works. Attached to several pages in the more serious books were sheets of paper covered in Madelaine's painstaking cursive writing. She must have found someone to tell her the stories associated with the illustrations. Among them he found his new nemesis.

The *wanyudo*. A big wheel from an ox cart, aflame with fires that never died. At the hub, the head of an old man, bitter and angry and vengeful. The "Wheel Monk," also referred to as the "Soul Taker."

One book claimed the Wheel Monk was the spirit of a Japanese lord, a *daimyo*, so evil that, upon his death, he became a monster doomed to roam the midnight streets, hunting corrupt priests and other evil people. Another book said the Soul Taker guarded the gates of Hell. Both books agreed on the most frightening point: the flaming wheel crushed its victims, tore the souls from their dead bodies, and dragged those souls down to Hell.

It made no sense. Why would this vengeful demonic creature chase down a foreign physician appointed to attend the Abbot, a righteous and upstanding monk? Harrington must have been in the wrong place at the wrong time, stepping into the path of the monster when it was already pursuing its latest victim. That made more sense, although he'd seen no one else on that particular street last night.

Harrington shook his head, closed the books, and stacked them neatly on the corner of his desk. The *ofuda* still hung on the front gate. Granted, it was merely a strip of parchment on which was written a Sanskrit *sutra*, but Harrington's household had enjoyed six weeks without supernatural interference. He didn't want to say or do anything to make Madelaine or Constance worry. That being so, there was no truthful way to get out of leaving the house to play whist with the Malloys. Perhaps one of Mr. Malloy's imaginary ailments might make itself useful. As soon as he began complaining of tonight's symptoms, Harrington could call an early halt to the whist party by prescribing a stomach powder, perhaps a mild sedative. Few things were better for the body than a good night's rest.

CRSO

Harrington sat in the carriage, both hands resting on the head of his walking stick, watching the more Westernized buildings of the expatriate neighborhood pass by. It had been a tiresome evening. The problem of the Wheel Monk had left him far too preoccupied to pay proper attention to his cards. That had not endeared him to his hostess and whist partner, Mrs. Malloy. The additional vexation of Mr. Malloy's rather nasal voice, finding every excuse to bring up this or that largely imaginary medical malady, did not improve Harrington's concentration. Harrington wanted to be home, safe and sound behind his own walls.

"William?" Constance sat beside him, lovely as ever in plum taffeta with jade green accents, her dark hair in an elegant chignon. "You're in quite the blue funk."

"I find Malloy's company exceedingly tedious."

"The poor fellow just needs a sympathetic ear. Mrs. Malloy told me Mr. Malloy doesn't make friends easily."

"Somehow that does not surprise me."

"Really, William. Surely you could manage the appearance of cordial interest?"

"Connie, please. Such people are not to be encouraged."

"Civil attention is not the same as active encouragement."

"Mr. Malloy needs an agony aunt, not a Fellow of the Royal College of Physicians."

Constance turned to look at him with deep concern. "This isn't like you at all. I can understand a certain amount of impatience due to the lateness of the hour, but this? Such—such disdain?"

Harrington sighed and rubbed at his weary eyes. As much as he longed to confide in Connie, he could not let her know the extent to which the supernatural continued to invade their lives.

"You're right, my dear." He patted her hand. "Perhaps we might invite the Malloys over for tea sometime soon. I will give him my complete attention."

Constance smiled and squeezed his hand.

The carriage rolled on through the quiet streets. Harrington allowed the rhythmic clip-clop of the horses' hooves to lull him into a more tranquil state of mind. Constance leaned forward, looking out the window on her side.

"How strange. There must be a shrine festival this evening."

Harrington glanced past her. Dancing orange shadows filled the side street just ahead. The carriage drew abreast of it. Flames. Blazing eyes. A snarling mouth. Harrington grabbed Constance by her shoulders and yanked her down across his lap. He pushed them both off the seat and rolled over, shielding her with his body.

The Wheel Monk hit the side of the carriage, splintering that door and shoving the entire carriage sideways. The horses screamed and reared.

"*Gizen-sha! Gizen-sha!*"

Harrington got to his knees and flung open the door on his side of the carriage. The horses jerked at their traces, making the carriage rock back and forth.

"William!" Constance clutched at his coat. "What—Why—"

"Get out!"

Constance stared over Harrington's shoulder. The Wheel Monk's flames blazed in Constance's wide eyes. Harrington grabbed the doorframe and wrapped his free arm around Constance's waist, swinging her out through the doorway. She landed on her feet, staggering forward.

"Run, Constance! Run!"

Constance fled.

*"Gizen-sha!"*

"Shut up, damn you!"

Harrington snatched up his walking stick and shoved the handle through the Wheel Monk's spokes, then down between the spokes of the carriage wheel. He turned the stick so the handle lay perpendicular to the spokes, locking it into place. The Wheel Monk roared, pushing forward against the walking stick's heavy oaken strength. Jumping down from the carriage, Harrington backed away, calling out to the driver.

"Dobson! Run, man!"

The driver climbed down from his seat and ran for his life. Harrington's walking stick snapped. The carriage toppled over onto its side with a tremendous crash. Rolling through the wreckage, the Wheel Monk crushed the undercarriage, breaking the front axle. Free at last, the horses galloped away. Harrington took to his heels, racing after Constance.

CRSO

Harrington woke up angry. The Wheel Monk had dared to threaten the health and safety of his beloved wife. Harrington meant to put an end to the problem today. He bathed, shaved, dressed in charcoal grey trousers, a crisp white shirt, and a waistcoat of emerald green paisley. For his cravat, he chose silver gray silk. His black morning coat completed the picture of somber respectability.

On the days he visited Kiyomizudera, Harrington shared a carriage with Fujita, his translator.

"Fujita-*san*, can you tell me the meaning of the word or phrase that sounds like 'GHEE zen shah'?

"The closest approximation of '*gizen-sha*' in English would be 'a fox in lamb's clothing.'"

Harrington noted the similarity to 'a wolf in sheep's clothing.' He frowned. Why would the Wheel Monk accuse him of pretending to be harmless so he could sneak up on his prey? That made no sense, not according to Madelaine's folklore books.

"What does the term mean when shouted by one Japanese at another?"

"To be addressed as 'gizen-sha' is to be called a liar, a fraud, a charlatan."

"That sounds quite the serious insult."

"Indeed, Harrington-*sensei*." Fujita nodded. "In the days of the samurai, such an insult would demand immediate action."

"Drawing swords?"

"Precisely. No samurai would tolerate being accused of such dishonor."

Harrington mulled that over. Why would the Wheel Monk accuse him of claiming to be something or someone he was not?

Harrington's routine examination of the Abbot went well. At the venerable age of eighty-five, the Abbot still stood straight in his white *kimono*, the black *kimono* over that, and the golden sash wound around his torso. Through Fujita, the Abbot invited Harrington to join him for green tea and tiny, exquisite cakes. Harrington forced himself to bear with the usual pleasantries. In Japan, it did not do to rush straight to the point.

The Abbot studied Harrington, then spoke.

"Harrington-*sensei*," Fujita said. "The Abbot would like to know if there have been any recent … disturbances."

"Twice now a great flaming wheel has attacked me. Last night it smashed my carriage and very nearly killed my wife."

Fujita translated. The Abbot's brows rose. On his normally tranquil face, that indicated considerable surprise. He spoke again.

"Please, Harrington-*sensei*," Fujita said. "Tell us exactly what this wheel looked like, what noises it made."

"I can tell you its name. *Wanyudo*."

"*Wanyudo?*" The Abbot made several comments to Fujita, speaking in an urgent tone.

"Harrington-*sensei*, the Abbot is most distressed. The *wanyudo* is among the rarest of the *yokai*, very fierce, very dangerous." Fujita gave him a shrewd look. "Is this where you heard the phrase 'gizen-sha'?"

"Yes."

Fujita relayed that. The Abbot frowned, then spoke.

"Harrington-*sensei*," Fujita said, "the *kami* and *yokai* who have appeared to you came to punish you for some offense or rescue you from that punishment."

Harrington nodded. Amatsu Mikaboshi, God of Chaos, wanted vengeance. The gods with shrines at Kiyomizudera had protected Nurse Danforth against his schemes. Next came the shapeshifting cat monster who'd tried to kill Madelaine because Madelaine knew her for what she was.

"The *wanyudo* is cursed to punish those who have failed to fulfill their duties." Fujita looked distinctly uncomfortable. "Forgive me, Harrington-*sensei*, but there are questions that must be asked."

"Ask anything you like, Fujita-*san*. I want to be rid of this creature at once."

"That may not be possible, Harrington-*sensei*. Your answers to the Abbot's questions will determine the proper course of action."

"Very well."

The Abbot spoke, looking Harrington in the eye.

"The Abbot wishes to know if you have ever lost a patient, Harrington-*sensei*. He means that in the Western manner."

"Yes, I understand." The memory of that horrible night forced its way into Harrington's mind much like the Wheel Monk smashing into the side of his carriage. He'd been a young physician, newly made, and rather full of himself. One night Mrs. Carmody called for him, claiming chest pains. For months, he'd been treating her for a poor digestion. On that particular night, Harrington had tickets to the theater with Constance, the first evening of what he hoped would be a successful courtship. He was in love, and he was in a hurry. He gave Mrs. Carmody's servant a prescription for a stomach powder with orders to eat bland food and keep to her bed. While Harrington was out dining with Constance and amusing himself at the theater, Mrs. Carmody had suffered a heart attack and died.

"Ten years ago, at the very start of my career, one of my first patients was an older lady preoccupied with every little ache or sniffle." Harrington steadied himself. His mentors had assured him he need not feel guilty. "She died of a sudden heart attack."

"You were not treating her for an illness of the heart?"

"It appeared to be more a matter of her digestion. The symptoms certainly pointed that way." Harrington suddenly felt flushed, the smell of the incense too strong, his woolen garments too heavy in the confined space of the Abbot's private room. He hated calling to mind what had happened to Mrs. Carmody. "From that point on, if I had reason to believe a patient might have an illness pertaining to one particular organ, I referred that patient to the appropriate specialist."

Fujita translated. The Abbot spoke again.

"The Abbot wishes to know if you feel you did everything you could do to treat your patients before you sent them to another physician."

"I was only just out of medical school. I knew I didn't have the experience or the judgment. I thought it best to have such patients seen immediately by a specialist so they might receive the most accurate diagnosis."

When Fujita had translated Harrington's words, the Abbot bowed his head. Harrington didn't need a translator to sense the Abbot's sorrow, even pity. The Abbot spoke in a tone of gentle chiding.

"Harrington-*sensei*," Fujita said, "the Abbot now knows why the *wanyudo* has come. You abandoned your patients to the care of other physicians."

"I did not abandon them!" Harrington gulped more tea, giving himself time to regain his composure. "I saw to it they received the best care available."

"Please, Harrington-*sensei*, it is essential that you understand why the *wanyudo* is hunting you. If you had made the effort to treat your patients yourself, you would have grown stronger in your knowledge and your skills."

For ten years, Harrington had told himself he was doing the right thing. He had learned, and he had grown, but nowhere near as much as he might have? The *wanyudo* was right. Harrington's selfish neglect resulted in Mrs. Carmody's untimely death. The enormity of his crime left him gasping, sickened beyond words.

"What—what can I do?"

The Abbot spoke. His tone was firm, his expression stern.

"Harrington-*sensei*," Fujita said, "there is no single act that can mend the bad karma arising from the failure to fulfill your duty. Serious atonement is not without cost."

"Please, Fujita-*san*. Help me understand."

"Healing one single person will not be enough. To drive away the wanyudo, you must begin caring for those who have been neglected, abandoned, forgotten. You must go on caring for them. Can you do that?"

"Yes." As the word left his lips, Harrington knew he'd made a binding promise.

"Then go and find these people. Once you have found them, the Abbot will send a monk with you. The presence of that monk will show everyone you act with the Abbot's blessing and you are under the protection of Kannon herself."

"This sounds dangerous."

"Lives are at stake, Harrington-*sensei*. Do your duty."

# CHEQUE FOR A PULSE FIRST

## A Miranda Gray Mystery

### By T.E. MacArthur

September, 1892

The alley behind the office of Mercer and Van Ruthan—Importers of Fine Coffee—was square and small, brightly lit from one end and brutally dark at the other. Fog poured over the third story roof and swirled in the alleyway trap.

Lucy hurried as fast as her petticoats and dignity allowed. Leaving quickly from the side door of the office with those posted warnings that had stopped her before tonight, she tried her best not to look guilty. The premises were restricted and no one was to enter. Such a terrible risk to take. Yet her prize was clutched under her arm, hidden in folds of an unfashionable but very practical cloak for an evening's burglary. It is worth it, isn't it, she thought. Such a small thing—a treasure to her. If only she'd had time to find those damnable cheques.

Still, as childish as it felt, she had her prize, and a cabbie was waiting for her in the lit street ahead. She was going to get away with it.

"Rushing off somewhere, Miss Mercer?" The man's voice stopped her flight. She knew his voice. "You do know that your father's office"—the tone of his voice emphasized the fact that this was not yet her inheritance—"is locked and boarded by the police. You have no right to go in there."

Lie quickly. "Mr. Franklin, I—I'm aware of that. But I ..." Lie fast! "I wanted to see the place. My father and I spent so much time there, as you know."

"Just to be in the place?" The gentleman emerged into better light, with another fellow behind him—a fellow clearly not a gentleman. "Really? Perhaps I should have you searched, to see if you stole anything."

Lucy turned sharply on him. "How does one steal from one's self? Everything in that warehouse is mine."

"Not yet, my dear. The court will decide that. As you are so very fragile, I'm sure they won't burden you with the weight of running a business. Not for a delicate," he paused, "hysterical girl like you. Now, tell me what you stole and I won't inform the police."

"I *stole* nothing."

"Damien, please assist the young lady with her acquisition."

Damien pulled out a knife and made some fancy twirls with it, demonstrating to her that he was quite proficient with it.

A piece of broken brick landed at Franklin's feet. It had been thrown, neither tossed nor dislodged from the crumbling buildings on either side of him.

"I shouldn't like it if you were to assault my friend, Mr. ...? Did I hear her say Franklin?" Lucy knew that voice. "Franklin, of Franklin Importers? How very curious to find you here."

It had been so long—so terribly long—since she'd seen her friend Miranda Gray. Miranda would be as cool as an iceberg, she thought. "You found me," Lucy whispered.

"I rather assumed you'd be here." Miranda, who was some-what tall and angular for a woman, strolled up behind Lucy, took her by the arm as old friends are wont to do, and stared at Franklin and his man. "Lucy dear, I think you should call out for the police. There's usually a constable within the block. I'm certain they will be far more disturbed by a threat of assault upon a woman than by a lady in mourning seeking a moment's comfort in her time of distress." Miranda threw an angry glare at Franklin. "Would you not agree?"

"She's stolen something from the office. The Magistrate was clear: no one was to enter or to remove any items from this place until Mercer's will is final. All parties agreed …"

Lucy interjected, "I did not agree!"

"It was decided for you, my dear, being as you are of such a delicate mind."

Miranda straightened up to appear taller, as if that were possible, and coated her voice in clear resentment. "Are you calling my friend a liar? My—gentlemen are just not what they used to be. Rude and frequenting dark alleyways."

Damien, not being a gentleman, was impatient and started forward. "I'll handle these two girls. Easy picking …"

The sound of a rifle bolt was pronounced in the small alley. Lucy took extreme satisfaction from the sight of both Miranda producing a long-barreled pistol and the arrival of a tall, slender man with an Enfield rifle already at his shoulder. She saw Miranda glance slightly toward the rifleman.

"Colonel—you found my note," Miranda cooed, not taking her eyes off Damien. "I was not expecting you, but your timing has grown impeccable over the last year. You look surprisingly well—and pleasantly alive." When the Colonel only nodded and remained focused on Franklin's man, Miranda leaned over to Lucy. "Lucy, may I introduce you to my friend, the Colonel. Colonel," she continued, still pointing her weapon at Franklin and Damien, "this is Miss Lucy Mercer, *owner* of Mercer and Van Ruthan, Importers."

"A pleasure to meet you, sir," Lucy whispered. She didn't like the look of this *Colonel* fellow, with his slouch hat, older tweed suit, and a cigarillo held between his teeth. But, he was on her side. She'd need to see him in better light, but if Lucy wasn't mistaken, he appeared to have been beaten badly—and recently.

The Colonel began to smile around his cigarillo. "All right there, big man, move along. The lady told you she hasn't stolen from the place. I think you'd be wise to turn about and mind your own business."

"I was going to suggest the same to you, sir," Franklin growled. "Come along, Damien. We'll let Miss Lucy go about her day." He signaled his man to follow him. The man put away his knife. "Oh, and Colonel, you might want to be careful. Poor Miss Lucy is not right in her mind. That's why the court isn't turning over her father's assets to her. We all know she may need to be committed to—to—somewhere that will give her the treatment she needs."

"You miserable liar! You're just trying to buy my father's business for pennies ..."

Miranda's hand wrapped tighter around Lucy's arm, and Lucy knew that was her friend's way of warning her.

Once in the hansom cab Lucy had waiting, while her friend and her friend's acquaintance were still boarding, she couldn't help herself. "Miranda, I'm so sorry. When I asked you to come and help, things hadn't been so bad. And—well—I ..."

"You did lie a little, didn't you?" Miranda's voice had an amused lilt to it. "What did you take from your father's office?"

"A little painting. It wasn't what I went looking for, but it was something I couldn't leave there, especially if the court—oh Miranda, I'm in such a pickle."

Lucy slid over to allow Miranda to sit next to her. The Colonel sat opposite, sliding a leather rifle sock over the length of his odd-looking rifle.

"My dear Colonel," Miranda smiled. "Superb timing."

"Your note at my club said I should come looking for you here." He looked directly at Miranda. "Until then, I wasn't sure if you'd ..." His voice dropped off.

"That makes two of us." She smiled at him. "Thank you for coming."

Miranda turned to Lucy. "I'm sorry, Lucy dear, I didn't mean to leave you out, but the Colonel and I have had—well, let's call it an adventure."

Lucy perked up. "Oh, please tell me. I could use the distraction."

The Colonel and Miranda stared at each other, wide-eyed, as if thinking the same, horrible thing. The expression on both their faces made it clear that no story was coming.

A hand clamped down on the door before the cab could take off. People were just appearing out of nowhere, Lucy thought, catching her breath. There was a drunken sot attached to that peculiarly dirty hand. Oh, what had he been doing now?

"Miranda, you do remember my brother, Ernst?"

Ernst teetered for a moment before speaking. He was the same size and general coloring as Lucy, with the exception of bright cheeks and a reddish nose. "Miranda Gray. It's been a while. Come back to help little Lucy get all of Father's money and property?"

"I've come back to be with a friend of mine while she is in mourning. We all need—and seek out—our own forms of comfort."

"Well, don't believe everything little Sissy tells you—oh, hello there, sir, didn't see you—anyhow, you won't find things as they used to be. No, sir. Things are very—very different now." He tried wiping his hands on his trousers, leaving dark streaks.

"Oh, Ernst," Lucy said, wishing she could disappear into the shadow of the cab.

Miranda purred out her words. "When one loses a parent ..."

"Mourning, oh yes, I'm in mourning. In mourning for the dear departed father who cut me out of his will completely, giving it all to my sister. Anyone knows," he aimed his words at Lucy, "women are bad in business and shouldn't look outside the home for anything. Anything! I'm the man of the house now ..."

The Colonel called out, "Driver! We need to go now!"

"Off to write more cheques, Sissy, to spend money we don't have, and to leave me with nothing. Tell your friends how forgetful you are. How easily manipulated. The business is dead, and it's your fault."

The Colonel reached over, plucked Ernst's fingers from the door and banged his other hand on the roof of the cab.

CR&SO

An empty house, the Colonel noted. Lucy had told them on the way that nearly all the furniture was gone. All the paintings Mr. Mercer had collected. The Early Revival vases. All the usual things rich people had, he thought. One or two items remained, but it appeared that the creditors had come in and stripped the place nearly clean.

"Do come upstairs. I can't afford to heat the whole place, but I do keep Father's study warm. I don't think it will be long before I'll have to leave." She opened the door to reveal a room with some remaining books, an old sofa, and a nice fireplace. "I don't have any refreshments for either of you. I really, really must apologize." She seemed close to sobbing.

The Colonel walked over to the fireplace and started a small fire. Miranda sat next to her friend.

"I did tell one lie, but not entirely. You see, I took this from the office." She held up a small, remarkably ornate frame with a clumsy, dark painting in it. The frame was gold and far too good for the contents. The object was no larger than a book, but the frame took up most of the size.

"Sentimental value? It's not a very good painting." Miranda tried not to laugh.

"Oh, I know. I painted it. It's quite dreadful. Don't you think, Colonel?"

He nodded. "That frame, however, could keep you in this house for another week or so."

"Oh, but I couldn't. You see, I painted this when I was twelve. Father was so proud of me. Then his business partner, Mr. Van Ruthan, saw it and had that beautiful frame specifically made for it. I was so honored—Mr. Van Ruthan was such a collector of famous paintings. I simply couldn't part with it unless it was the very last thing I had."

Miranda nodded. The Colonel seated himself in an over-stuffed chair. "Time to unload all the baggage, my dear Lucy."

Lucy looked at the Colonel, a little startled.

"It's alright, Lucy dear. The Colonel and I—have developed a respect for one another."

He gave Miranda a relieved glance.

Miranda held Lucy's hand. "Tell me—us—what is happening?"

"Where to begin? Well, Father died about a month ago. He left everything to me in his will, bypassing Ernst, his only son. You know Ernst, Miranda. His drinking is getting worse, though he told the court—when he contested the will—that I was making all that up. That I just wanted him discredited. That I was the one who was disturbed. That if anything, he wants the court to have me committed to some sanatorium and to give him all the property—money, business, all of it."

"You seem sane to me, if a little overwhelmed," the Colonel noted.

Miranda looked at him, as if she'd never thought he'd say such a thing. He was a tad surprised too.

"My brother and the man he wants to sell the business to …"

"Franklin?" Miranda asked.

"Yes, Mr. Franklin. They both say they have proof: that I wrote about a dozen cheques in the last month that have completely ruined the business. While Father did have debts that had to be paid on his death, there was plenty of money for that. Or so I thought. I agreed to pay the debts, assuming that I would have access to the money, but suddenly, there isn't any. And I'm being blamed."

Miranda was silent, clearly contemplating it all. "If you didn't write the cheques, it should be provable. Ernst and Franklin have made the accusation, but if they can't …"

Lucy dropped her face into her hands and pushed away tears. "They can. Oh, Miranda, I don't remember writing them, but Ernst showed them to me. It looked like I'd signed them, but I can't remember doing so. Then of course the cheques were locked up in the office where no one can see them until the court makes a decision."

"And the court can't make a good decision without looking at the cheques." Miranda stiffened. "You have explained everything to the court?"

"Yes, but everything I tell them is countered with—with my being crazy or incompetent. That I'm hysterical and cannot be trusted. So my word is not equal to Ernst's."

"Or Franklin's, no doubt. It sounds as if he'll do anything to buy the business."

Lucy looked up. "No. Oh no, he told me he doesn't want to buy the business—not in a practical way. He's far more interested in the contents of the warehouse than the whole business itself.

And of course, the office. There's nothing in there except furniture, records, and some items from the late Mr. Van Ruthan."

The Colonel took out a cigarette, noted the two ladies present, and put it away. "Don't forget the cheques, too. If the business owns plenty of goods ..."

"We haven't received a shipment in several months. We aren't due to. You see, we work with a Dutch supplier, who used to be part of Father's business—hence the Van Ruthan side of things—but when Mr. Van Ruthan died a year ago, Father simply left the name in place—to honor the gentleman. The warehouse is almost empty—we sold the contents and were expecting another shipment from the Indies in a few more months." Lucy laughed a little. "I miss Mr. Van Ruthan; he was a lovely and very generous man. He even adored my painting as much as Father did. I never knew why. But then, he always treated our family as though it was his." She sat and stared into the fire. "Well, the debt collectors came because I said I'd pay, but with the bank accounts locked shut to me or empty, I had no way to pay them except to sell everything."

"Why did you call in Madame Archaeologist here?" He used her agency name, aware, she was sure, that her friend wouldn't know what the reference was for.

"I've been receiving strange visits in the night—men at the window who flee the moment I bring up the lights. Odd little notes. I feel as if someone is constantly watching me. I'm sure it's merely thieves looking for opportunity with a quickly emptying house, but—it's more."

Something crashed downstairs, and all three were on their feet, racing down the staircase. Collapsed at the door was Ernst—bloodied and clutching his side. Lucy screamed. The Colonel withdrew a small caliber pistol from his pocket, and Miranda rushed to Ernst's aid. The man had been stabbed. More than once.

Lucy knelt down next to him and cradled his head in her lap.

"This is all your doing," he spat out, blood bubbling on his lips. "You did this to me."

"Oh Ernst, I would never …"

"Took everything—all of it. You and those damn …" He was having difficulty breathing. Lucy looked up at Miranda, who shook her head. Lucy began weeping uncontrollably and whispering to her brother—drunkard or not—how much she loved him. She didn't seem to care that he blamed her for things outside of her control.

"Had to have been that Damien fellow. You saw how he handled a knife." The Colonel flung open the door and walked out into the night air. "No one's here now."

He returned to find Lucy completely hysterical, Miranda entirely fuming, and Ernst quite thoroughly dead.

# TWO WEEKS OF HELL

*By Anthony Francis*

Soul-sick, Liberation Academy Cadet Jeremiah Willstone watched that great airshark, the *Prince Edward*, slide past her perch on the ramparts of Edinburgh Castle. Perhaps the most celebrated airship of the Victoriana Defense League, the *Prince Edward* was cheered on by a thousand cadets, mostly Falconers, all desirous for a posting within its bronzed hide.

Jeremiah's lip quivered. Not ten meters away, but it might have been a thousand. The empty space around her told the tale: no cadet wanted the stink of *washout* on them. Neither did she, but her real quandary was: *what to do when a traitor's got your back?*

"Jeremiah! You're out of hospital!" Cadet Erskine Spencer cried. "When you stopped visiting me, it was two weeks of hell— and when I found out you'd ended up not one wing away from me, I went through it all over again—"

"Erskine!" Jeremiah cried, hopping up into his embrace, damn the proctors—and the damning evidence in her back pocket that he was a Foreign sympathizer. "The doctors said you came to the coma ward *every day*, leaving notes *most* imprudent from a first-year to a third—"

"I had to wake you somehow. Is it true? You crashed a pair of Falconer's wings—"

"And washed out," Jeremiah admitted, recounting how her inner ear had failed her mid-flight, down to the corkscrew trail of vomit—an image which, she noted with sadistic pride, turned the underclassman a bit green. "I was never meant to fly."

"Jeremiah," Erskine said, touching her shoulder. "I'm so sorry—"

"I'm still an Expeditionary, in training, at least—what's wrong?"

"Nothing," Erskine said—then shook his head, eyes far away. "No, I won't pass it off like last time; that landed me in hospital. Do you ever feel," and he uneasily looked over his shoulder, "like you're being watched?"

"Yes, by proctors," Jeremiah said lightly. She guessed why he'd gone on high alert; last time he'd shrugged off that feeling, they'd ended up cornered in a dark alley by a horde of clockwork rats. Still, she reached for his hand. "Care for a go at eluding them?"

CR&SO

From the darkness of a shuttered classroom behind them, the two glowing eyes of Senior Expeditionary Commander Jeremiah Willstone stared straight through a half meter of opaque wood, stone, and metal, tracking the antics of her younger, more carefree self.

The elder Jeremiah folded her arms as the younger took her lover by the hand and darted into a back stairwell, perhaps for a tryst—well, her memories were muddled by time, both by its passage and her own meddling, but if she was still herself, *no doubt* for a tryst.

But through three, no, now four walls, she saw, tucked away in the transparent mass of clothes and flesh surrounding the skipping skeleton that was her younger self, the *device*. Erskine's device—her younger self was using this tryst to gain his trust.

That meant the cadet was starting the path that would one day make her a matahari. Clearly, the younger already suspected Erskine; strange, then, how much the elder found she romanticized this early relationship. First man she fought alongside, and then—well.

Still, as skeletons intertwined, metal creaked in protest as the elder leaned against the wall, spreading her brass dragonfly wings a bit as she settled in—as wood would creak, she grumpily imagined, when young flesh met young flesh in the darkness of the hall.

Jeremiah was glad she couldn't quite visualize that from this distance, even with the eyes of the Burning Scarab—but still, she couldn't *not* see the skeletal bumping and grinding, unless she turned off her X-ray vision, which would defeat the purpose of the exercise.

She checked her springback bracer for temporal anomalies, then used her delicate brass antennae to review the briefing on her iPhone while she used her front-facing, human-looking eyes to keep a lookout for Foreign perils threatening her younger self.

This was going to be two weeks of hell.

CRSO

"So, Erskine," Jeremiah said, struggling, as she buckled her blue vestcoat—*her* vestcoat this time, forgoing the romantic tradition of cadets swapping blues—to finesse a question about the device Dean Navid Singhal had asked her to investigate. "Found this in my satchel. Yours? What is it?"

Jeremiah held up the device, a cross between a spyglass and the keys of a trombone. It had a neat little eyepiece, some well-worn punches, a slot filled with a half-sized wax cylinder—and a glittering circuit within, almost certainly Foreign to the Earth.

"My *astrolathe!*" Erskine said, seizing it happily before she could react. He appraised it with an expert, *loving* eye. "In your satchel? Impossible. Someone must have planted it—"

"How can you be sure it wasn't in my satchel? Did you search it? You *did*—"

"I—" Erskine spluttered. "Of *course!* We'd swapped our blues after our, ah, picnic. I lost track of my astrolathe after the attack and wagered it would be in your effects—and it's *engraved*, so it could have gotten you a citation."

"Oh!" Jeremiah said, reddening. Many military *marriages* started in Liberation Academy, but its proctors still frowned on fraternization. "Quite sensible. But whatever *is* it?"

"My astrolathe," Erskine repeated, chuckling. "As familiar to me as your calculers are to you, Cadet Specialist Engineer. *Every* cadet specializing in Foreign Affairs has their own astrolathe for recording wax cylinders from astronomical instruments."

"Oh!" Jeremiah repeated. "So how did it end up—"

"Who knows," Erskine said, smiling as he buttoned a pocket of his vestcoat, the device safely tucked inside. "But *you*, in particular, are skating thin. Let's not have a device with an underclassman's name engraved on it turn up in your effects, eh, Cadet?"

He kissed her impulsively and darted off, to his next class, as he'd said. Jeremiah touched her cheek, realizing that in-the-open romantic peck meant more to her than all that clandestine pounding in the stairwell ... and that she naturally thought of Erskine and marriage together.

*Then* she realized he'd walked off with the enigmatic device Navid had given her.

"Oh ... oh ... *bollocks!*" she cried.

CR8O

Watching the show from a service hallway, Senior Expeditionary Commander Jeremiah Willstone put her hand over her mouth and laughed silently, antennae twitching with each spasm. She'd *quite* enjoyed seeing the young matahari-in-training get outplayed at her own game.

"Any luck?" Dean Navid Singhal whispered from behind her. Jeremiah glanced back: even with her eyes, she hadn't noticed that side passage. Navid knew all the tricks, and must have been quite the hellion. "Have you, ah, has she, learned anything—"

"No, I was young and inexperienced and let him walk off with it."

"Oh, *bollocks!*" Navid whispered.

"Relax, sir, I'm on it," Jeremiah whispered—though she had to admit, looking at Erskine now was a painful act. Still, she scanned through the walls and soon found him: in his class, as he'd said, near the front, dutifully taking notes, sitting in proper military posture, the device still buttoned away. "I'd planted a Scarab microtracker on it … but it shorted out."

"The device has countermeasures," Navid whispered. "It's an active threat."

"And we're leaving it to the cadets." She shook her head. "I should intervene—"

"No!" Navid said, grasping her arm, his hand bearing a prosthetic finger gained on *his* time travel misadventure. "What if Erskine saw you, and told you about yourself? Even if taken into confidence, the information would be *in* him, a time bomb, as long as he lived—"

Jeremiah tried to control her expression, but Navid caught the look—and blanched.

"Lord." His hand went to his mouth. "What's going to happen to Cadet Spencer?"

"Reckless, prying in the future," she said. "The device. It's an astrolathe."

"Of course." Navid's raised hand shifted from shock to pensiveness. "An antique model—I think my uncle had one. But this one was modified with what looked like Foreign technology—certainly like, if it reacted to your tracker. What has it *become?*"

"Why not ask," Jeremiah said, eyes tracking Erskine. "He's bringing it to you."

CRR80

Tailing Erskine, Cadet Willstone slipped into the priest hole behind Navid's office, confident that the Dean would approve, or he wouldn't have showed it to her. But, still, she had an eerie sense of *déjà vu*, feeling like she'd be caught, as the secretary let the traitor in.

In the attic above, Commander Willstone watched discreetly as the young cadet tilted her head at the inverted *camera obscura* projection from the pinhole. The elder's eyes inverted the image easily, but it was more effort to remember what the cadet felt when first she saw it.

"Cadet Willstone claimed she found this in her satchel," Erskine said casually, raising the astrolathe. Jeremiah clenched her fists; clearly her lover, a first-year, had won more confidences from the Dean than she had in three! "I thought you might have an explanation … sir."

"Did she now," Navid said. "And you think I can explain, *Cadet?*"

"Sir," Erskine said, stiffening. "Sir, the cadet knows that you and—"

"And Cadet Willstone work closely—a reasonable surmise, but off point," Navid said sternly. "That device. It's an astrolathe. An antique, like my uncle used. But it's been modified, it was found in suspicious circumstances, and it has your name engraved on it. Explain … *Cadet.*"

"Sir," Erskine said, "it's my astrolathe, sir. It is an antique, my grandmother's. My mother had it engraved when she gave to me. And *I* modified it to work with modern couplings—the Academy's equipment is newer, but I—"

"Save it. That circuit looks Foreign. *Explain.*"

"Sir," Erskine said stiffly. "That, I'm not at liberty to say."

The Dean's jaw clenched. "That won't work on me, Cadet!"

"Sir," Erskine said, anguished. "Professor Dyson *insisted*—"

"Did he?" Navid asked, standing. "Horse's mouth, shall we?"

ᘒᘓ

Cursing her stupidity, Cadet Willstone raced from secret passage to service passage, leaving the covert warren of tunnels connecting the faculty offices behind in favor of the overt but little trafficked corridors servicing the classroom laboratories, counting doors as she went.

Jeremiah hadn't counted on Navid's authoritarian streak. She hadn't the experience to keep Erskine from walking off with the device, but even she could see that bringing the question to Dyson without a way to cross-check the story would leave them even *more* in the dark.

In moments, she was in Dyson's lab. The well-groomed elder professor, known for his neatly trimmed moustache and his dryly wry lectures on Foreign Affairs and the perils of other worlds, was carefully feeding a half-sized wax cylinder into a harmonic analyzer.

"Professor Dyson," she began.

"Ah, Commander," he said, turning. "Any progress—oh my."

"Commander, sir?" Jeremiah asked, puzzled. "Should I expect a promotion—"

"Clearly I mistook you, *Cadet*," Dyson snapped, and she came to attention. "What is it?"

"I—" she stammered, as Dyson absently spun up the harmonizer. *Was that wax cylinder from Erskine's device—and was that a glittering circuit?* Was *Dyson* in on this, whatever it was? She'd thought he was working with the Dean! Jeremiah thought quickly: what question could she ask that would provide the maximum information? *Aha! Assume trust!* "Any progress, sir?"

"What?" Dyson asked blankly.

"On the cylinder from the device the Dean asked me to investigate," she said, pointing at the harmonizer, calculating how to catch Dyson in a lie. *Confabulate a miscommunication?* "I gathered you were going to analyze it for Foreign influence, or did I mishear?"

Dyson clenched his jaw, then fussed with the harmonzier. "Eavesdropping again?"

"Sir, no, sir," she said, "but if the cadet did so, sir, it's at the Dean's orders, *sir*—"

"Save it," Dyson said, staring at the display. "The Dean's taken me fully into confidence, and I can say *with* confidence neither he nor I want you eavesdropping on us." Dyson engaged the harmonizer's reader. "And if you do, you're likely in for an unwelcome shock—"

Then the device exploded with clockwork tentacles.

Dyson flinched and screamed—but even as the articulated gearwork grasped for him like the bony hands of a metal witch, Jeremiah was already drawing her twin *Kathodenstrahl* blasters, nailing tentacle after tentacle with glowing blue-green beams of aetheric fire.

Firing two-handed was no mean trick, and Jeremiah found it hard to sustain the steady one-two, one-two rhythm that made the Austrian weapons effective. Then a *second* pair of beams lanced into the harmonizer, expertly blasting a newly formed metal claw. She caught a quick glimpse of a dark, running form, wrapped in a black cloak, firing, just like her—*but who?*

"Erskine?" she asked—just as the tentacles sprang on them again.

"I'm here!" he cried, leaping in from behind, slamming his astrolathe into the second slot of the harmonizer. Beating tentacles back with a bloody hand, he engaged his device. "There! Have a dose of your *own* medicine!"

The tentacles thrashed as the harmonizer erupted in a dissonant scream, and Jeremiah felt herself lifted bodily as Erskine grabbed her and Dyson by the collars and dragged them away. Then the tentacles shorted out, collapsing like a dying spider.

"Ha!" Erskine cried, helping Jeremiah to her feet with one strong hand, then releasing her so he could lower Dyson to the floor. "I inverted the phase, then fed the original cylinder back through the harmonizer, so that ought to—oh, oh, *bollocks!*"

He lunged forward, but it was too late: the cylinder in his astrolathe went up in smoke.

"Both copies ruined," Navid snapped, storming into the room with a fireaxe in one hand and a blaster in another. He hefted the axe, then saw that the tentacles were truly dead. "Blood of the Queen, we're fumbling about like first-years on a picnic in the park—"

"Oi!" Jeremiah said, then clapped her hand to her mouth. "Beg pardon, *sir*—"

"No offense taken, none meant," Navid said with a sly smile, his glance surveying the two cadets as they both turned beet red. "Who am I to call the proctors down on a little tomfoolery? I was conceived at Academy, after—"

"Hang the jokes, we lost valuable advantage keeping knowledge about this affair too compartmentalized," Dyson snapped. "Still, Cadet Spencer, you saved our lives—and you, Cadet Willstone, saved me from a nasty infestation. I'm lucky I didn't end up like Feldkirch—"

"Stiff upper lip, Dyson," Navid said. "I'll fetch aid. And, cadets—well done."

CRSO

Within half an hour, a team of Expeditionaries from the airship *Prince Edward*—a team of *Rangers*, not Falconers, Jeremiah noted with interest—had secured the site, and, after another hour of inspection, investigation, and interview, freed the cadets to return to their rounds.

The first moment they were alone, Jeremiah turned and hugged Erskine gratefully. They kissed, embraced, then darted to a side hall—both unaware that, behind wood, stone, and metal, were two glowing eyes that could see straight into Erskine's gear-infested skull.

The elder Jeremiah felt she'd learned three things. First, as she suspected, the real danger was in the Foreign signal the circuits received, not the circuits themselves. Second, her unseen foe was actively meddling in time; events had transpired differently from her memory.

And third, her foe's agent ... was Erskine.

Jeremiah glared at the machinery consuming her young lover's brain, a process she was intimately familiar with—and infinitely more expert at than the clumsy gearwork butchering his delicate tissues. Why, there'd be nothing left of him.

Soon, there must be a day of reckoning.

# Solarpunk Gauguin

## Part I

*By Janice Thompson*

For many years, Paul brokered stocks successfully,
Which well sustained his wife and growing family.
He purchased art and socialized with artists who
Preferred the Paris cafes for their rendezvous.
Paul painted, too, but only when he had the time,
And thus his life was happy, full, and quite sublime.
Then all at once, the market crashed; his savings ebbed,
For paintings could not pay the bills or keep them fed.
So Paul's wife, Mette, proposed to Denmark they should move
And live there with her parents till their state improved.
Though Paul at first resisted, he at length agreed.
Alas, this move would lead to his calamity.
Jobs failed because he could not speak the native tongue,
And enmity at home with Mette had soon begun
To undo any benefit he'd hoped to see

In moving there. Thus he would back to Paris flee.
But Paris in his absence had transmogrified,
And in that art world he no longer could reside.
He traveled to Tahiti for a better start,
Imploring Mette to join him there with all his heart.
His darling would not budge, no matter how he pled.
No, Mette would stay in Denmark with her kin instead.
Her gainful job and pressure from her family
Ensured that, though she loved him, she would never leave.
His frequent letters eulogized the island life,
But nothing could inveigle his adoring wife
Although the air seemed colder than it ought to be
For Copenhagen's summer months. Was it just she?
Then autumn's heavy snow confirmed a dire report
As Europe was invaded by the arctic North.
Soon glacial sheets advanced in unrelenting crawl
While oceans froze and threatened to entrap them all.
She bundled up the children, grabbed a few things and
Together with her household sought which trains still ran,
Then to the coast they travelled, hoping that a ship
Might still be in the harbor, thus complete their trip
To far away Tahiti, leaving all behind,
And fearful whether they would make it there in time.
For in their wake the sea was freezing over still,
And no one could but panic of their state, until
That ghastly white offensive slowly eased away
Allowing subtly warmer winds and seas to play.
Whole fleets of ships had left the most affected shores
For islands equatorial, and safety, sure.

# HERE ABIDE MONSTERS

## A Boston Metaphysical Society Story

### By Madeleine Holly-Rosing

Carrying nothing but a scraping knife and a flint pouch, Duncan and the escaped slave woman ran for their lives. A demon was tracking them.

Duncan tripped over a tree root and fell face first into the dirt.

"Get up! You saw what it did to Benjamin," the woman pleaded.

She was right. The demon had used one talon to rend the man named Benjamin from his crotch to his neck with a single stroke. Bile came up Duncan's throat at the mere thought of it. As part of the underground railroad, he had dealt with slave traders, unscrupulous militia, tax collectors, and the trackers known as "paddy rollers", but never such as this.

Sent to Richmond, Virginia to pick up a load of willow bark for his father's small tannery on the south side of Boston, Duncan knew there was always an element of risk. Not for the bark, but for what their cart transported in a secret compartment underneath the floor boards—escaped slaves.

Duncan, having just turned twenty, had taken the route many times with his older brother, Jonah. This time, however, Jonah's wife was bearing their first child and he refused to leave her side. Their mother had rolled her eyes at her love-struck son, but respected his wishes.

The family had decided that Duncan should take the trip without him as various tax collectors and militiamen were accustomed to seeing them on a regular basis and they feared their absence would be noticed. They were also worried that if no one went, any slaves that had escaped and managed to get to the way point would be caught and killed.

Duncan stood up and noticed the woman's shadow in the fading sun.

At almost six feet tall, the young woman's head reached his nose. She looked to be around his age. Sweat and humidity made her light brown cotton skirt and blouse stick to her skin while her obsidian hair peeked out of an indigo dyed scarf. The color set off her high cheek bones and bright eyes. They held intelligence and something else: a drive, a passion, a force of will.

She sucked in her breath. "There be a bog nearby?"

"A marsh—mile or so east," Duncan replied, in a light Irish brogue.

"We go there."

Duncan struggled to keep up as the woman took off in a sprint.

The MacGuire family was but one of several in Boston who aided those who longed for freedom. There were a few Middle District families who helped the cause by gifting the Mac-Guires with horses, carts, and items that were needed on the road. Though they had more wealth than Duncan's family, their social standing restricted their movements and subjected them to more scrutiny. The MacGuires were their link to a network that stretched from Georgia to the Queen's Canada. If Duncan were caught, one link would be shattered.

Low branches whipped across his face as he ran after her. His lungs seared in pain and his throat constricted. Every muscle cried out in agony, but he could not stop. He had seen the hatred behind the demon's molten iron eyes and knew it brought torment, then death. He prayed that whatever the woman planned was going to work.

The sun had buried itself into the orange-brown horizon by the time Duncan realized the bottom of his woolen pants were wet. He stopped and saw the woman shove her way through reeds and floating logs into a deeper portion of the marsh. A night heron flew away in protest at the intrusion, but otherwise it was quiet.

She gestured him to follow her.

Not knowing what else to do, he obeyed.

The odor of dead carrion wafted up behind them. Duncan turned to look, but caught only a glimpse of something shimmering and fading into the forest.

The woman grabbed the front of his shirt, dragging him under water.

At first he struggled, but soon understood her intent. The water, though cool and dark, stung the cuts on his face. Duncan let out small bubbles of air and tried to remain as still as possible. She took his hand and they half-swam, half-pulled their way through the murky marsh. Just when he thought his lungs would burst, she shoved him upward.

Duncan found himself hiding within a large clump of rushes and reeds. It was shallow enough for him to sit on rotting vegetation and keep his chest above the water. The woman sat arm's length from him.

She bobbed her head. "We be safe here. For a little while."

"From that?" Duncan snorted. "You bought us time. That's all."

"What would you have me do? Give up?"

"No. I'm sorry, Miss. It's just that I've …"

Her lips grew thin and tight. "Never been hunted like an animal before? Never been helpless? Always had … freedom?"

"Aye. But that's why I came. To help free you," Duncan retorted. "Slavery is an abomination. Like that thing out there."

The hum of propellers silenced them.

Duncan peered into the sky to see an airship hovering about five hundred feet above them. Beams of light swept the marsh in slow defined patterns. He knew from seeing them up close that there was a small torch anchored behind a large glass lens. The entire contraption was attached to a brass cradle with a rotating gimbal at the base. The lens moved wherever it was pointed.

The woman turned to run, but Duncan grabbed her arm. "Wait. This is a regular patrol. They'll be gone in a few minutes."

He released her and she sat down again. "What's your name?"

"Mae." Her voice took on a softer lilt.

"I'm Duncan. Why can't the demon follow us into the marsh?"

"It can. Just takes longer to find our scent. That's what massa says," her body trembled for a moment, then she regained her composure. "It does his bidding. Like the rest of his slaves."

Duncan gazed skyward. "The patrol will move eastward in a few minutes. Then we move." He glanced over at Mae. "How long do we have before it can track us again?"

She shook her head. "Not sure. A few hours, if we be lucky. Massa very proud he found this demon. It be smart and strong."

"But why send a demon and not a paddy roller?" He grew alarmed when Mae shrank away from him. "What is it?"

"I be *too* special," Mae bit back her rage. "I be his and no one else's."

When what she meant finally sunk in, he felt nauseous. Unable to express any words to ease her pain or her anger, he checked the position of the patrolling airship. "We can move now."

"To the city?" Mae ventured.

"Alexandria?" Duncan shook his head. "Too far. Besides, there are patrols both in the air and on the ground on the outskirts." He closed his eyes, thinking. "The next safe house is in Fredericktown."

"We should go," Mae insisted.

Duncan nodded. "We'll head deeper into the marsh, go north, then cut westward to Fredericktown. I want to get more distance between us and that thing."

They slogged through more reeds and rushes trying to stay under cover. The water level varied from at Duncan's waist to up to his chest. When it got too deep, they swam. A few times, the vegetation was so thick they had to slow down and use Duncan's knife.

"You said your master found this demon. How?" Duncan asked, while he hacked away at the rushes in his path with his small scraping knife.

"He be an educated man. Said he learned of a way to track where demons be hid. That when he set it free, it had to do 'his bidding' else he could send it back," Mae replied, losing her footing on a slippery stone, but catching herself before falling in. "Talked about finding more demons."

"Where? How many could there be?"

Mae shrugged as they walked into open water. "Don't know. Just follow the road, he said. That man did love to lord his knowledge over anyone who cared to listen." She grimaced. "Not that we had any say."

"Once we get you north, you'll have plenty of choices to make."

Though they tramped through the marsh in silence for a few minutes, Duncan could swear he heard her thinking.

"Is it hard?" she finally asked.

"What?"

"Choosing. You know, day-to-day. Like what to eat. Where to live."

"Sometimes. But you'll get used to it quick enough. And you'll like it." Duncan glanced over his shoulder at her to smile, but it was replaced by a look of alarm. "Lights!"

Distracted by fighting the weeds, neither one of them had heard the propellers of the airship. They dove.

Duncan stared up as a beam of light fluttered through the shadowy water. When it touched his leg, he thought he would be yanked up and exposed but it moved on. He counted to twenty, then raised his head high enough to get a breath of air.

Barely creating a ripple, Mae surfaced a few seconds later. Water droplets streamed down her face to form a small cascade. The moonlight caught the droplets, turning them into stars before they disappeared.

Duncan realized that there *was* something special about Mae. He sensed she was more than what she appeared. As if she carried the weight of history. He almost laughed out loud thinking that he might be one of those Irish who could see the future, but he knew one thing for certain: it was his solemn duty to make sure she escaped.

"They changed their routine. This way isn't safe anymore," Duncan whispered.

Mae blinked in acknowledgment.

The patrol flew back around and swept where they were hiding again, forcing them to dive under the water a few more times. It wasn't until the airship headed in a northeasterly direction that he hoped they were safe enough to emerge from the marsh and head to dry land.

It took an hour, but they made it without running into any more air patrols. As they trudged out of the marsh, dripping wet, Mae gestured for him to hand over his knife. Duncan complied without a word and watched as she cut off the bottom third of her skirt, freeing her legs from the tangle of wet cloth. She handed back his knife.

"We can try to make it to the road. Since we're late, our people in Fredericktown will send a man to find us. But ..." Duncan looked her straight in the eye. "We won't make it, will we."

Mae shook her head. "The demon ain't far off. It'll pick up our scent for sure now. And it moves fast."

"Did your master say how he found this demon? Can you send it back? Or kill it?"

"Don't know. Only there be a magical road to take you to where a demon be hid," Mae tried to explain.

"Or imprisoned?" Duncan pressed her. "Wait. He said 'magical road?' Did he ever talk about faerie paths?"

Mae's eyes lit up. "You know about them?"

Duncan never believed his Irish heritage would be useful until now. "Maybe we can use it to help us."

"How?"

They picked up their pace again.

"The Irish be a superstitious lot," Duncan replied in an exaggerated brogue then fell back into his normal voice. "Faerie lore is passed down among all the families. I always thought they were tales to keep the children from misbehaving. But my Aunt Dara used to talk about 'faerie paths,' and their mystical nature. She fancied herself a Medium. A person who could talk to ghosts and the like. But I never thought they might be real."

"You know where one of these paths be at?" Mae stopped to squeeze more water out from what remained of her skirt.

"Aye. I think so. This way."

Duncan racked his memory for every story his Aunt Dara had ever told him about the power of the faerie path as they leapt over fallen logs and tried not to trip over oak tree roots. He remembered one story of how a faerie path stopped an army from invading. That, once found, it could protect you from evil. All you had to do was find one and possess a righteous calling. Aunt Dara often talked about a path that stretched from south of Alexandria down to the border of Virginia and North Carolina not far from where they were, but whether his calling was righteous was another question.

The good news was that a series of caves ran along that route as well. Every abolitionist who worked the underground railroad knew of at least one to shelter in. Duncan knew of two; both were near their usual route. If he couldn't find the faerie path, Duncan hoped they could hide long enough for one of the other abolitionists to rescue them.

What scared him even more than being chased by a demon was that the head of a Great Southern House knew how to catch and control one. Most Northern Great Houses dismissed the idea of demons, ghosts, and other supernatural beings as superstitious nonsense. If Mae's master commanded an army of demons, the entire North might be enslaved to the South without ever understanding their foe.

Duncan glanced up at the stars to figure out their position. "Another mile or two and we should be there. Start looking for a stick that's shaped like a chicken's breast bone."

"A dowsing rod." Mae's eyes lit up. "I've seen the likes of them before."

The summer leaves had begun to fall, allowing the rays of moonlight to filter through and light their way. His wet clothes chilled him, and he suspected Mae was cold as well. They rummaged through piles of dead leaves and broken branches to find something he could use as a dowsing rod.

When a faint sickly smell assaulted his nostrils, Duncan spun around with his knife in his hand. He studied the darkness looking for any sign of movement. About four cart lengths away the air shimmered like it did before, but he only heard the sound of a light breeze blowing leaves across the forest floor.

"Mae?" he whispered.

She crept up behind him. "I saw it."

"If it is the demon, why doesn't it attack?" he asked, his eyes never leaving the spot.

"Don't know. Maybe these woods be haunted." Mae ventured.

"Gah. Just what we need. Demons *and* ghosts." Duncan retreated, holding the knife out in front of him.

"Here."

Duncan glanced over to see Mae handing him a dowsing rod made of swamp oak. "Aye, that'll do. Let's go."

They set out at a trot.

After a half hour or so, Duncan took a sharp turn to the left and ran straight toward a copse of trees. He sat down on a log and slipped into the darkness below. When his feet hit the ground of the sinkhole, he looked up and gestured for Mae to follow.

She landed next to him without making a sound.

They both turned to stare into a dark maw that opened into the earth.

"Take my hand," he whispered.

Duncan felt her cool dry fingers slip into his. He placed his other hand against the edge of the cave opening and used it to guide them inside. He forced his eyes to find any source of light, but there was none. Duncan inched along, taking one small step at a time. A few yards inside the cave he stopped and slid against the cave wall. He let go of Mae's hand and searched the surrounding dirt until he found what he was looking for: a blackened torch. He reached into his pouch, took out his flint and struck it a few times. Sparks lit up their faces and, after a few tries, the torch flared up.

She gasped as the limestone cave gave off a warm and inviting amber hue. "It be beautiful," Mae murmured.

"This way." Duncan took her hand again. "Watch your step."

Duncan led her down a damp path that curved away from the entrance and into a larger cavern. It always reminded Duncan of a church, but without the adornment.

Water dripped down massive limestone teeth which hung from the ceiling. In some instances the teeth reached the floor creating limestone columns. Ten columns surrounded a murky pond which was continually fed by slow leaching from the stone. The cavern had a serene atmosphere which was only disturbed by the presence of Duncan and Mae.

"I'd never seen such a thing before," Mae proclaimed in awe. "And you think this faerie path be here?"

"Aye, but there's only one way to find out." Duncan took the dowsing rod from her and held the split section of the stick lightly in each hand. He took a deep breath and tried to clear his mind of the terror he had experienced that night. Duncan was going to have to shed all his doubt and misgivings about his Irish forbearers if this was to work.

"Keep a close watch," he told Mae.

The young woman nodded and held out her hand. Duncan gave her his knife, though he knew it would be of little use against the demon. Then he closed his eyes and concentrated on hearing nothing but the sounds of the earth and the forest, like the people in Aunt Dara's stories did. Duncan slowed his breathing, trying to sense the life flow from his hands through the wood and into the soil it was once part of. The bark felt rough even against his calloused fingers, but the wood remained unresponsive and he was distracted by his cold damp clothes sticking to him.

He opened his eyes. "This is useless."

"Try again," Mae urged him. "It can't be far off."

A cascade of dirt and pebbles flowed downward from the cave entrance.

"Duncan." The words escaped her lips like a dying breath.

"I know."

Duncan reached toward the ground and scooped up a handful of soil. He rubbed it between his hands and on the dowsing rod, then closed his eyes again and refocused his thoughts. He shoved all the fear, all the desperation he ever had into an imaginary room with a huge metal door. In his mind's eye, there was a lock made of massive gears and wheels. They spun and clacked until the final click bolted his self-doubt away. With a renewed sense of confidence, Duncan relaxed. The soil grew warm in his palms. It bathed his hands in moisture and the wood felt like it had become a part of his hand. When it flared up, he dropped the rod in alarm and opened his eyes.

Before them a wall of emerald and gold light stretched from one side of the cavern to the other. The colors ebbed and flowed, reflecting off the cave walls. Stars twinkled inside it as if he were getting a glimpse of the night sky. The sight was so awe-inspiring that he thought a piece of the universe had broken off and been sent to earth.

Duncan and Mae were mesmerized until a roar behind them shook a few of the limestone towers, causing one to crumble into dust. They turned to witness the true nature of what had been pursuing them.

Hairless and wearing no clothes, it stood almost seven feet tall with an oval-shaped head and a mouth filled with jagged bloody teeth below glowing molten eyes. It stood on two legs that were thick with muscles like cabled rope. Each foot possessed four talons the size of Duncan's hand. Blood and mud clung to them as they dug into the ground. The demon's skin varied from a slick reddish-brown to the color of limestone as it took on the appearance of whatever it stood near. Its hands were claws with one talon that was larger and darker than the other four.

A wave of putrid breath coursed over them.

"Now!" Duncan yelled.

They jumped through the wall of light.

Duncan's skin tingled as he passed through the faerie path and landed sprawling on the other side. He looked over as the demon took one step and leapt over twenty feet to land across from them.

The force of his landing caused portions of the limestone walls to crumble.

"*Bhfianaise na cruinne* will not protect you, human," the demon's voice rumbled. "Give me the girl and I may let you live."

Stunned that such a creature could talk, Duncan skittered away from the beast until he bumped into Mae.

She dug her fingernails into his arm. "There must be another way out," she whispered into his ear.

Duncan shook his head. "No. The faerie path is all we have." He watched as Mae drooped in submission. "If he could pass through the wall, he would have already done so."

"I don't want you dying for me," she murmured.

In his best playful heavy Irish brogue, he replied, "Lassie, we Irish are a tough lot. There be no dying today. Not with the faeries on our side."

Emboldened by the wall's magical protection, Duncan stood up, stepped up next to it and challenged the demon. "Liar. If this wall cannot protect us, then step through it."

A gargling sound came up its throat. It took Duncan a moment to realize the demon was laughing.

"We are all slaves to something, human. Your masters are pride and arrogance."

The creature lurched forward and thrust his largest talon through the wall impaling Duncan in the gut then lifting him up high into the air.

Duncan screamed. He hung on to the demon's arm to find purchase in hopes of releasing himself, but it was no use.

Both human and demon were awash in the light. It felt cool against Duncan's skin until it reached the spot where the creature's talon impaled him. A searing pain began at that point then moved outward to his extremities. His body shook in spasms as he felt poison course through his veins. Duncan's skin turned ashen and puckered as if being pricked by tiny needles. He gasped for air and hoped his death meant the demon's as well.

As the faerie path surged with energy, sparks flew and the colors shifted from emerald to an orange-red. Flaring white hot over the demon's arm, it smoked and ignited in a blaze of fire. The smell of burnt flesh tinged the air.

The creature had lied; he could not cross.

Heat flooded the cavern as the faerie path ignited then exploded. Air escaped from the cave then surged back in again. Several more of the limestone towers collapsed. Duncan held his breath, waiting for the end to come, when both he and the demon fell into a narrow crevasse, pinning them both inside.

The creature's talon ripped out of his stomach taking a section of intestine with it. Blood spattered everywhere.

"Duncan!" Mae cried out.

When the debris settled, he noticed the faint outline of Mae carrying the torch approach him. As she got closer, he saw tracks of tears on her dust encrusted face.

"Duncan! Give me your hand!"

Unable to control most of his body, he managed to lift his right hand toward her. She grabbed and pulled.

"Argh! Stop!" he croaked, the agony too much to bear.

She ignored him.

Duncan groaned at every bump and pull until she got him out of the crevasse. Then he watched as Mae used his knife to tear off another section of her skirt and part of his sleeve to use to staunch the bleeding from his gut.

"The faerie path be gone," Mae told him. "How long 'til help comes?"

When Duncan could finally focus on her face, he realized how terrified and worried she was.

"Not soon enough." Duncan coughed and nearly passed out.

A rumbling sound emerged from the crevasse. A talon appeared, then another.

The demon lived.

Duncan winced when Mae took his hand and watched the creature heave itself out and onto the cave floor. Even with half the muscle of one arm burned off, it did not appear to be in any obvious pain. Covered in limestone dust, it looked like a living statue of everyone's worst nightmare.

As it lurched forward, the demon raised its head and extended its arms in victory. From deep within its belly came a chuckle that turned into a boom of laughter.

Mae used her body to protect Duncan as more limestone fell from the ceiling.

"I am free!" the demon roared as he stomped around the cavern. "No more doing my master's bidding. I am free again!"

Shocked, they both watched the creature celebrate in its own fashion.

"You knew this might happen. That's why you didn't kill us." Duncan coughed; his throat dry and cracked.

The creature whirled around and studied them. "I'm impressed you still live, human," it declared. "And yes, once I discovered you could find the *Bhfianaise na cruinne*, I waited to see if you spoke the truth."

"*Light of the Universe,* is that what you call it?" Duncan's body shuddered as he tried to rise, but failed. "You've got what you wanted. Leave us in peace."

Mae tensed up when the creature crouched next to them.

"I have no interest in taking you back, girl." The demon flicked his claw as if to shoo her away. "Once the bond was broken to our master through your companion and the *bhfianaise na cruinne,* my life became my own again. As is yours." He leaned over Duncan and sniffed the wound. "You, however, will die."

"No!" Mae screamed at the demon. "His people will come. They will save him."

He waved a talon to silence her, but Mae clutched Duncan's hand and refused to move.

"If what you say is true," Mae took a deep breath, "you owe him a debt. Save him. Or are you too weak?"

The demon tapped one of his talons on his cheek in thought. It was such a human gesture that Duncan believed he might help him. That idea was quickly obliterated.

"He will die," the demon said matter-of-factly. "That talon releases a poison that will either kill him or turn him into one of my kindred."

Mae gasped and stumbled back while Duncan tried to grasp the enormity of what the creature was saying. Failing that, he had only one answer. "I will not be one of your kind, Demon. Take my life now and be done with it."

The creature shook its head. "You humans always look at life in absolutes. It's a pity most of you have such small, narrow minds. I was hoping you were different."

"I don't understand," Duncan muttered.

"Even death is not an absolute." The demon stretched his neck as if to relieve some tension. "Since you have freed me, though accidentally, I will give you a gift. You will die, but I can make sure your essence, or what you call your spirit, lives on. The only choice you have to make is where you will die, because that is the place you will haunt forever."

"Will I make it back to Boston? It's four days' ride." Duncan asked.

The demon nodded. "If you wish."

Duncan heard quiet sobbing nearby. "Mae?" There was a rustle, then he felt her take his hand again.

"I be here, Duncan," she murmured.

"You must go with the other abolitionists when they come. They will take you to Canada."

She shook her head. "No. I choose where I go."

Without another word, the demon brought forth his right hand and breathed upon it. The palm glowed. As the creature pressed it on his open wound, cauterizing it, Duncan screamed and passed out briefly. When he awoke, Mae was bandaging him again.

The demon stood a few feet away cleaning its talons with its tongue.

"You have done me a great service, human. Since you two taught me how to find the *bhfianaise na cruinne*, I will use the knowledge to seek out others of my kind that have been imprisoned by it," the demon declared. "For that, I will allow your family to live and serve me once my brethren are free."

"And you call me arrogant." Duncan grimaced in pain. "You need us. Otherwise you would have used the dowsing rod and found the *bhfianaise na cruinne* yourself."

"Perhaps, but I'm sure I can find humans who will serve me in exchange for their lives." It gave him a grotesque grin. "My kind will reclaim this earth for ourselves no matter how long it takes." The demon's head jerked up. "Your rescue has arrived."

The creature leapt across the crevasse and paused. He turned to look at Mae. "If someone attempts to take your freedom away again, girl, kill them."

Duncan and Mae watched as the demon shimmered, turning the same hue as the surrounding limestone, and then, without a sound, vanished.

"Hello! Duncan! You be in here, boy?" An older man's voice shouted.

"Here!" Mae yelled back.

"Mae," Duncan grasped her hand to his chest. "Promise me that you'll go to Canada. Start a new life." He coughed; blood-tinged spittle lingered on his lips.

"I best get you home first. Where you can be with your kin before you pass." She smiled through her tears. "Besides, I hear Boston be a right fine place for a free woman."

# 100  Some Time Later

# COCK OF THE WALK

*By Dover Whitecliff*

INTELLIGENCER:

"There are those that use shadows,
And those that cast them."

*Kyree's Profound Aphorisms,*
as dutifully transcribed by Kenna Wolfesdaughter

"That is not your path, Kenna Wolfesdaughter. Find another."
Duncan Sarn, Ruler of All Istavara, my liege lord, had spoken.

*Not my path?* I swallowed everything I wanted to shout but couldn't. *What do you mean* not my path? *I've been busting my backside training and studying night and day, apart from healing time, since the day Ciaran Wolfe pulled me out of the burning wreckage of the* Indestructible Luxo *and adopted me. Turns out I was the only indestructible thing on the whole bloody airship, mind you. Five and a half years of blood, sweat, and tears. How could this* not *be my path?!*

I bowed and stepped back one precise pace. My brother, Briar, risked leaning to the right to brush my shoulder in sympathy as he stepped forward to take my place in front of the dais. I stayed long enough to stand for him and hear him take his oath of service before the Sarn. No jealousy there. Briar was a born Intelligencer, and I was glad for him, but we'd always dreamed of working together, sneaking behind enemy lines, watching each other's back, being the legendary stuff of the penny dreadfuls.

No sense whinging about life not being fair. Pointless waste of time. Briar would learn to make do without me as a minder, and I'd read about his exploits while I—while I what, exactly? I needed to think. Nothing like denial of a life dream as encouragement to make a fresh start. I left the hall, feeling the eyes follow me out and ignoring the murmurs of the toffs watching the aftermath of the ceremony.

I made my way out of the palace to the usual stares. A ready fist (sometimes Briar's, but usually mine) had stopped the snickers and comments long past, but the stares? Nothing for it. Eyes are always drawn to the different. That's the way we're made, and I got used to it, after a fashion. My arm worked fine. It just looked like shite. The mottled grafts of wyvern flesh that repaired the burns didn't make for the most elegant appearance, but I'd take being alive with them over being dead or armless without them any day or night.

Kyree found me in my usual spot on the roof of the watchtower. He sat next to me for a while and we watched the clouds chase each other in silence. Though Fa had adopted me after the crash, it was Kyree that had sorted me out, the cub with no voice and no memory. A lot of our early time had been spent in silence, and we were good with that. "Double Tet is coming up in a fortnight. Sixteen. Big day. You'll be of age. An official adult. Void help us all."

I couldn't help but smile.

"You have a decision to make, little lupa."

"It must be world-ending if you're calling me 'little she-wolf'."

"World-ending is just another way to say world-beginning."

"Find another, he said. That's it. Nothing more. Duncan Sarn didn't even think twice. Didn't even let me get past saying I wanted to serve."

"It was a long shot. Your Fa thought it might convince him when he saw your scores."

*Your Fa thought.* Interesting. "But you didn't. You knew he'd deny it."

"From a cold, hard spymaster perspective, you're a liability. You have the brains and the skills, but a shadow hand has to blend in, go unnoticed."

"My arm."

"Your arm would either be visible or have to be completely covered no matter the climate. Either way you'd be marked. And useless."

Kyree let me mull that over. It wasn't much of a wrench hearing him say it out loud. It wasn't anything that hadn't niggled in the back of my brain in the barracks lying awake in the dark, listening to Briar snoring in the top bunk. Having a signature drink and being on a first name basis with every super villain and casino owner on three continents is all well and good in the dreadfuls, but I'd always known that Agent Triple Aught Six was a character and not a real shadow hand.

I turned my attention back to the clouds, and I realized I was missing something. Were my career for the crown over before it started, Kyree wouldn't be here. It would be Fa sitting next to me with his arm around my shoulder, consoling, encouraging, talking about University, maybe other types of intelligence work that involved sitting in a box reading reports instead of working in the field. The fact that he wasn't meant something. Two somethings, since whatever path Kyree was about to offer had to be a hard enough choice that Fa wanted it to be mine alone with none of his influence.

"What am I missing?"

"What, indeed?" Kyree stood, all six and a half feet of him, blocking out the sunlight and throwing me into shadow. "There are those that use the shadows, little lupa, and those that cast them."

Epiphany. Kyree couldn't exactly go unnoticed either. He was marked in his own way, taller than most, striking features, and charisma that made soldiers stand taller and toffs drool. Pieces clicked into place. All those times when Fa would disappear during my junior exo-suit bouts. Kyree fanning the crowd, keeping all eyes on us. "The dreadfuls. Triple Aught Six. Mr. Look at Me. He's you."

"Maybe in the next aithercast." Kyree gave me a rare smile. I stood and leaned out between the crenellations, watching the Tamra River plunge down the cliff and into the lake far below. I knew what Kyree would suggest in that moment and I felt like the river, ready to take a leap of faith. "Triple Aught Six *is* based on someone you know. I'll give you that."

"Fa?" Somehow, I knew that was wrong. Fa could disappear in a crowd like nobody's business, hide in plain sight.

"Other way round. Before the Dragon Sword called your uncle to be the Sarn of all Istavara, the Wolves were the best shadows-for-hire on three continents. Your Fa worked the shadows that his brother cast."

These epiphanies were starting to hurt my head. *Not my path.* Duncan Sarn knew I couldn't follow Fa's footsteps. Instead, he saw me following in his own. No pressure.

"So, this is where Fa wants you to tell me how dangerous it will be so I can make a solid decision? That sort of thing?"

"Not exactly. This is where I tell you that you will be assigned to me, and I will kick your arse and wipe the floor with you if you don't take it seriously. You will listen and follow orders because those orders will keep you breathing as long as possible. From this day forward, you will stand in the spotlight; all eyes will be on you and you will keep them there. There is no slipping away in the night if you cock it up. There will be pain, and slow death at the hands of people that enjoy that sort of thing. Do we have an understanding?"

"We have an understanding." I did a piss poor job of keeping my voice from shaking, but Kyree seemed satisfied.

"Good. We have a fortnight to get you ready."

"Right then. What's first?"

"Hardest lesson of all: how to be civilized. Meet me in the barracks after you give your oath. We're going shopping." I could feel the color drain from my face. Maybe I had been too quick with my decision.

The fortnight passed with blinding speed. Having to go to the occasional court dinner with Fa, I had a grounding in the etiquette for most countries: how to meet and greet, which fork to use for what and how to eat without slurping or embarrassing myself. But what Kyree taught was different. My new catchphrase was *Attitude is Everything*. How to turn it on and how to turn it off. How to expect and demand respect and get what I wanted or needed without being a jackass.

My first runs through the high-end shops and parties were disastrous. I might as well have been invisible for all I was noticed for the right reasons. After a quarter turn of the glass, Kyree would walk in with a minimum of attention, other than the nervous stares at his height and physique, and then just, just, I don't know, flip a switch, and all eyes would turn. He commanded attention without saying a word and with a graciousness that put them all at ease. I studied every nuance. It had nothing to do with his looks. It was just *him*. Attitude is everything.

Each day started well before dawn with training followed by a whirl of events and shopping, building a wardrobe and a persona: exo-suit fighter, soon to be champion. As a fighter just out of juniors, albeit in the top of my weight class, I hadn't earned the recognition, and had to learn to pull the eyes to me on sheer guts, each time feeling a few breaths short of a panic attack. I learned to wall off doubt, shyness, fear. Took them all and stuffed them in a little hidey-hole somewhere behind my naval and brazened it out. A crash course in personality.

Nights, we watched aithercast after aithercast of royals and toffs, military commanders and diplomats, how they held themselves, how they commanded attention. The difference between the rude tossers who threw gold around but had no class, and those that deserved the respect. Where the line was between assertiveness and aggressiveness, and how to dance right up to the edge without crossing over. Nowhere near enough time to make it instinct, but enough to lay the foundation. And then the time was gone.

"Double Tet is sun-up after next. We leave for Te Raro tonight."

I don't remember much of the flight from Istavara to Qin-To. Not because I had a fear of airships; any nightmares of the crash were of falling through fire, and I hadn't had one for a while. But most of the time in the air was spent with Kyree drilling me on the mission and the mark, not staring out the windows of the gondola. By the time we touched down near midday, I could barely think straight, my head was so stuffed with details and back up plans. Fortunately, the first stop after checking into the Gratia Artis Resort was the buffet.

"Not that I'm complaining, mind, but is there a reason you're encouraging me to stuff myself silly, with the fight tomorrow?" I set my second near-overflowing plate down. It was a wrench not shoveling everything in as fast as I could. Even on feast days, I'd never seen such a variety of food all in one place at one time. I reckoned they must have at least one chef from every country on staff just for the entrees, never you mind the three heaping tables of desserts that I had yet to sample. I could swear I heard a steamed custard bun calling my name.

"Even you can't stuff that much down your gullet in the time we have before your appointment, and you need to go on a full stomach."

"Appointment? What appointment?" It came out more like, "Ammrphmnph? Mrph *apptmntph?*" but I was fairly sure Kyree could translate round a mouthful of roast pork and cheese toast.

"A shame the adverts for tomorrow's fight are already printed. She-Wolf is the wrong arena name. You should be Squirrel Cheeks. Yes, appointment. It's at the other end of the Kodo, so *wolf* it down if you want dessert."

I swallowed, fortunately, before I laughed, else Kyree would have had a shirt full of spew. "Wolf it down. I see what you did there."

Within a half turn of the glass, I demolished the plate, relentlessly tracked down and inhaled the seductive custard bun, along with a half dozen of his closest friends, and found myself in a private steam carriage doing my best not to gawk at the wondrous chaos that was the city of lights, vices, and guilty pleasures.

At the far end of the Kodo, past resorts and street displays of pirate ships and volcanoes, fountains and street performers, in the older part of the city, the steam carriage pulled over in front of a well-kept shop. The sign that lit the corner of the building in red, white, and black read QIN-TO TRADITIONS. I hopped down after Kyree and looked through the windows. The walls were covered with ink designs to choose from.

"Time to turn the liability into an asset. If they're going to stare, let them stare at art. D'Juno is waiting for you." Kyree nudged me toward the door. "Call it an early birthday present."

"But Fa." I had visions of Fa seeing ink on my arm and skinning me alive.

"Who do you think pulled the strings to get you in a day early? Go."

I stood up straight and walked in. Attitude is everything.

When D'Juno was through with me, not a soul in the Void could tell the grafts from the ink. A She-Wolf stalked down my arm surrounded by flames that looked real enough to cook on. Her tail curled back round my shoulder and a front paw covered the back of my hand, claws extended out onto my fingers. The shading and background were just as detailed as her fur, and I could see shadows of girders and fabric dancing in the fire. The *Luxo*. Where I came from to what I was becoming. Good thing Kyree wasn't there to see the silly grin dripping with tears when I realized what I was looking at, but D'Juno understood. He gave me a pocket handkerchief to wipe up with while I stuck my arm in the aitheric chamber to heal.

The change was near immediate. Passers-by that would have stared in pity or revulsion now stared in appreciation. I heard "nice ink" at least a dozen times before I found Kyree in the pachinko parlor down the street. For the first time, I didn't have to work to put a swagger in my walk, and I might as well have been on top of the world.

The next morning, Kyree came through the door to the adjoining room to find me still grinning like an idiot and staring at my arm in the looking glass in the washroom. That lasted about two minutes. Nothing like a training session with Kyree to take you down a notch, but I still grinned when he wasn't looking. At least there was no one in the gym to see the carnage.

The jitters had already started. If the intelligence was right, our mark rarely left her penthouse suite, but she loved the exo-circuit, especially out-of-class fights. So not only would all eyes be on me for my first professional bout, they would be on me for taking on a Middleweight with years of experience and a suit half again as big as mine. All this to bring her down to the arena and out into the open. Losing wasn't really an option, but I needed to keep the bout going for the full twenty matches to give Fa the time to get into her suite and get back out again with no one the wiser. And, like Kyree said, no slipping away into the night if I cocked it up. No. No pressure at all.

The arena, all 17,000 strong, were mostly waiting for Stinger Rhodes to take the ring with Feydra Kwan. My bout was the equivalent of the opening band, but it was the one our mark was here to see, and she found me after Kyree finished seating the aitheric battery on LUPA's back.

"You will wear my token, yes." She pulled the silk scarf from around her neck and tied it to my shoulder strap, running her finger over the ink on my arm, following the she-wolf's back as if she were petting it. "And you will win for me."

"Consider it done." I inclined my head in respect, it being awkward to bow formally once I was strapped in.

What the announcer said, I couldn't have told you. My eyes were on my opponent and how to get him out of the ring without doing it too quickly. He stared back, belligerent, the fact that he felt I was beneath him in skill and prestige writ large all over his sneer.

I met the Cock of the Walk in the center for the ritual start to the bout and scattered salt and sand to the five elements.

"Puppy." He murmured when the Justicar was out of earshot. "I'll make you run home with your tail between your legs for trying an out-of-class fight with me."

"I will give you all the respect you deserve." I stared him straight in the eye as I backed out of the circle to Kyree to await the start of the first match.

Kyree checked my straps one last time. "Remember who you are, She-Wolf." I nodded, eyes locked with my opponent.

The Justicar struck his staff against the bell and I charged.

# THE DESCENT

*By BJ Sikes*

Nassau, 1903

Theo squinted against the brilliant sunlight glaring off the water below. No words could have prepared him for the intense blue of the Caribbean sea. He breathed in the warm air, his face flushing. Sweat trickled down from under his new pith helmet and his waxed mustache drooped against his cheeks.

The steamship slid into Nassau's harbor. At last he had arrived in the Bahamas, free from the demands of English society, free from his wife, Clara, with her distant eyes. A vision of his departure flashed across his mind: Clara standing on the London train platform, coolly watching him climb onto the train. She had walked away without a smile before his train had pulled out.

Children, brown-skinned and mostly naked, were diving into the clear water, apparently in pursuit of coins flung by his fellow passengers. Theo wondered what Clara would think of the freedom enjoyed by these laughing children romping in the ocean. Or was it neglect? He was sure she'd disapprove in either case. He smiled down at them, fumbling in his pocket for a coin, but came up empty-handed. He shrugged apologetically at the small boy on the dock watching him.

The ship bumped up against the pier and the horn blasted, announcing their arrival. The stench of a busy tropical harbor assailed his nose: the smell of salt spray, rotting fish, pineapples, and jasmine, underlain with sweat and open sewers. A humming flurry of activity began on the dock below. Men, lightly dressed, their skin dark and glossy, tied off ropes and rushed to secure the gangplank. No automatons unloading ships here. Perhaps the Igbo-Carib Federation opposed use of the French machines. Theo spotted scores of people, instead, mostly men, shifting bales of sisal and sponge, ready to load onto the steamship for its voyage back to New York. They were all dark skinned. He hadn't expected such a sharp contrast. The few white people seemed to be milling about aimlessly, perhaps waiting for arrivals.

Theo tried to spot the British ambassador, but the crowds were too heavy for him to pick out anyone in particular. At the far side of the wharf, the crowd of laborers parted to let a procession through. A tall dark man in colorful robes led the group as it made its way between the ranks of workers and across the wharf to the ship. The captain hurried down the gangplank to greet with a deep bow what appeared to be dignitaries. Theo watched them. They talked for a moment, then the captain bowed again and the procession departed. The captain gestured to one of his crew on the deck, and the sailor opened the gate.

A stream of passengers made their way off the ship. Theo sauntered along the railing towards the gangplank. Other passengers, more eager than he to disembark, jostled him and pushed past him on their way. Two women sashayed by, their pale faces, slim dresses, and wide hats reminding of tall white *Amanita* mushrooms. He gazed after them, admiring their unapproachable beauty.

He dabbed a handkerchief to his flushed face and walked down the gangplank, trailing behind the women. As soon as he touched ground, the noise of hundreds of voices overwhelmed him. People, towering bundles of sisal, chickens, and goats crowded the docks and children dashed between it all. The men loading the ship sang loudly. He still couldn't find the ambassador or anyone in an official uniform. The ship's crew departed on their own missions and the captain seemed deep in conversation with a local man. Perhaps that was the harbor master? Would he know where Theo should go?

At last, Theo spotted white ostrich plumes bobbing above the crowd. attached to the cocked uniform hat of a member of the British diplomatic corps. Theo shoved through the crowd towards the man, apologizing profusely as he stepped on feet and knocked people aside. He had no luggage to slow him down, and he soon reached the officer's side.

"My good man! A fellow Englishman, I presume? You're here to meet me? I'm Theophilus Cooke," he said. The man grimaced before responding with a strong Scottish brogue.

"Nay, I'm no Englishman but I am here to meet a Mr. Cooke from England. You'll be the mycologist; I expect?"

Theo winced at his faux pas, but covered it up with a chuckle and an extended hand.

"Oh, I do beg your pardon, ever so sorry, it had slipped my mind that the Queen's Highlanders were stationed here."

The Scotsman shook his proffered hand.

"Aye. Well, 'tis an honest mistake, Mr. Cooke. I am pleased to make your acquaintance. I am Lieutenant McLachlan. And a Happy Christmas to you, sir. I am afraid that His Excellency is unable to meet you today. It being Christmas Eve, he has family duties."

Theo blinked. Christmas? He had completely forgotten about the holiday. He supposed Clara would be celebrating with the children, indulging them with too many sweets and non-sensical entertainment. He breathed a sigh of relief that he was spared this year. Perhaps this assignment would be extended and he'd miss next year too.

"Ah, yes. Christmas. I completely understand. Would you be so kind to show me to my hotel, then, Lieutenant?"

The Scotsman nodded and led Theo through the crowd.

"Ye'll be staying at the new hotel." He gestured towards a large building dominating the waterfront. "They're calling it the British Colonial; a bit *pawkie*, I would say, since the Bahamas hasn't been a British colony since the Afro-Caribs took over back in '98. Most of His Majesty's subjects in Nassau congregate there. The new government prefers it that way. Come along. The porters will bring along your luggage."

The main road leading from the harbor was unpaved, dusty, and dazzlingly white. Masses of people walked alongside Theo and the lieutenant, swirls of loud conversation surrounding them. Horse carts bearing goods passed by, stirring up the dust as they clattered along the sandy track. Theo noticed that the buildings of Nassau were, for the most part, diminutive wooden structures painted pastel shades. Lieutenant McLachlan pointed out Nassau's noteworthy landmarks as they walked:

"Ye see the ridge above the town there? That's Government House. It was built by the British but the Afro-Carib government occupies it now. The British ambassador's home is up there too."

Theo nodded without really listening, not able to take it in, feeling overwhelmed with all the people and noise. He needed to get away.

"Would it be possible to take a tour of the countryside?" He interrupted his guide mid-sentence.

"What? Today? 'Tis Christmas Eve, Mr. Cooke. Can ye no wait a few days, settle in before you go jaunting off?"

Theo pulled a sad face, careful not to overdo the dramatics.

"Yes, it is Christmastime and I'm far from my family. I was hoping a brief outing into the countryside would cheer me up a bit. I could poke about and look for some of the native fungi."

Lieutenant McLachlan pulled at his mustache, frowning. Theo pressed on.

"I wouldn't need company, just one of these people with a cart."

The officer shrugged, defeated.

"Well, I suppose it canna harm anything. I'll arrange for one of the tour guides to take ye on your outing. Don't expect to stay out long. Christmas Eve is taken quite seriously here in the Bahamas."

CRSO

Theo sat on the back of a rickety horse cart. Or rather, a donkey cart. He tried not to think about how ridiculous he looked perched on the wooden platform. He shook his head, questioning the wisdom of his decision to go out to the countryside without even a cup of tea to fortify him. He would've killed for a nice cup of Darjeeling, despite the heat. It had to be at least 80° Fahrenheit and humid on top of that.

A young boy ran alongside the slow-moving cart, calling out to him, begging for money perhaps. Theo couldn't tell; the child spoke some kind of island dialect that he couldn't follow. The boy threw a ball at Theo. Ducking to one side so it wouldn't hit him in the head, Theo put a hand up and caught the ball only to realize he'd caught a piece of rotten fruit. He dropped it to the ground but the funky juice leaked over his hands, staining his gloves. The child shrieked with laughter at the success of his trick on the foreigner. Theo scowled in return. He peeled his gloves off with a sigh and shoved them in his pocket. His hands were sweating anyway. He was a little envious at the boy in his sparse linen clothing and straw hat. The driver, his tour guide, remained silent. He hadn't said more than two words to Theo since picking him up.

The cart traveled down a dirt track through some kind of pine forest; trees towered over them on either side. Low bushes filled in between the trees. He could hear birds shrieking and squawking in the woods. Mosquitoes buzzed around his head. He slapped at them, cursing. The track wound around the side of a small lake, dank and overgrown with underbrush and reeds at the shore. Clouds of gnats rose from the surface of the lake.

"Hold on, my good man, I'd like to take a look at that lake."

The driver didn't respond. Theo growled under his breath. "What kind of tour is this, anyway?"

He shuffled on his knees forward and tapped the driver on the shoulder.

"I say, can we stop and take a look?"

"Nothin' to see."

Theo huffed and scooted back to the end of the cart, legs dangling off. He looked at his dust-covered shoes and sighed. His clothing had already taken a beating on his first day on New Providence. Perhaps he should have worn his walking boots. He would need to remember them next time he went on an island tour.

The woods gave way to fields of spiky plants, probably sisal. Workers tramped up and down the rows, hacking the leaves off with cutlasses. Theo's driver halted the cart and waved to one of the field workers, calling out in his incomprehensible dialect. The men began an animated conversation, something about cows? Theo couldn't follow their conversation, but there *was* a cow in the field and they were gesticulating at it.

Bored and hot, Theo climbed out of the cart to take a closer look at the plants. He spotted some interesting speckles, possibly bacterial, on a leaf. Drawing out his knife, he cut off a section and placed it in his collecting bag. He wandered farther into the field and stopped short before stepping in an enormous cow patty. Theo glanced down and smiled a little, noticing some mushrooms growing in the manure.

"Coprophilous mushrooms; smashing," he murmured and they, too, went into his collecting bag.

He walked back to the cart, eyes on the ground. He heard a pop and something tapped his hand. He looked down, spotting a tiny black lump. Bringing his hand to his face to more closely examine the object, he realized what it was and grinned. He approached his tour guide.

"This is fantastic. I didn't realize that *Sphaerobolus* grew here. Did you know that it projects its spores into the air like a tiny trebuchet?"

The tour guide looked blankly at him. His companion snickered.

"Time to go, Mistah."

ᘓᘔ

The cut-glass decanter of liquor beckoned Theo, although it was far short of the cocktail hour. He looked across the hotel room at the mantelpiece clock. Three o'clock in the afternoon. He shrugged. It had been a long, exhausting day since he arrived in Nassau, and he needed a drink. He poured a long measure and sniffed. Rum? That would make sense, given that he was in the Caribbean. Sipping the sweet liquor, he winced. A nice whiskey would have been better, but this would have to do. Warmth filled his stomach and spread to his limbs. He poured another shot and sat in a cushioned chair by the window.

The view of brightly colored buildings, coconut palms, and bustling dark-skinned people reminded him how far he was from home. He remembered again that it was Christmas Eve and he wasn't in his usual spot at the head of the table. He didn't care much for the holidays, so hadn't objected to leaving the chilly shores of England in December. Still, he was very much alone here. No one seemed anxious to hear his words of mycological wisdom. No one hung on his words at all. He had thought they would be more interested; after all he was a lecturer of mycology from Cambridge University. He drank the rest of his rum and got up to get another. He teetered then staggered.

*Steady on, old man. This tropical elixir is a bit stronger than I thought.*

He poured another and threw it down. It was quite tasty once you got used to the sickly-sweet medicinal flavor. His eyes fell on his collecting case and he remembered the odd little blue-grey mushrooms he had found on the cow patty. Opening the case, he pulled out the paper bag containing his find. He dumped it onto a wooden desk. There were three little mushrooms, already starting to shrivel. Theo tore open the bag and saw blueish spores collected on the inside. The mushroom stems were also staining blue.

He pulled out one of his mycology references and flicked through the pages, sipping more rum. Finding the correct page, he read the description quickly. It appeared to be a *Psilocybe*, probably *P. cubensis*. One of the hallucinogenic fungi. Said to be a euphoric drug.

He contemplated the little mushrooms. *Why not give it a try? Who's going to know? And it could be quite enlightening.*

He took a fortifying sip of the rum and popped a mushroom into his mouth. Chewing it, he almost gagged at the earthy, almost rancid, taste. The rum was useful to wash the taste out of his mouth.

His reference didn't mention dosage. Would one be enough? *Ah, well. In for a penny, in for a pound.*

He shrugged and ate the remaining two, washing them down with more rum.

The effects of the fungi came over him slowly, subtly. First his body grew heavy and cold. It became an effort to move, and when he did an electric tingle spread from his hands, up his arms, and deep into his trunk. Theo shuddered at the sensation—part pleasure, part nausea. His legs seemed distant from the rest of him. He breathed in, almost gasping to get enough air. Rousing himself from the torpor, he stood and walked to the window overlooking Bay Street. The sun had set while he sat brooding and the street appeared dark and empty. The top of the window was partly open, and a warm tropical breeze caressed his face.

He placed a hand on the window, marveling at the cool, slick surface of the glass. He wanted to lick the glass but clamped down on the impulse.

*Get hold of yourself, man.*

As he stood there, a dull calm came over him. His body felt impossibly heavy and distant.

*I'm just a spore. Insignificant. Small. Meaningless.*

He squeezed his eyes closed. A train whistle blasted in his ears. Clara receded into the distance on the train platform, not looking back. He opened his eyes again and stared into the darkness outside his window.

*What's the point? None of this is important.*

He slumped against the window frame, his hand still stretched against the glass.

A cacophony of sound erupted from the street below, shocking Theo out of his stupor. Metal clanged on metal in an uneven beat, rising and falling. Horns blasted a monotonous rhythm along with the thump of drums. He squinted and caught sight of a swell of movement, shadowy figures moving in time with the noise—*was that meant to be music?* His body vibrated with the strange rhythms and he wrapped his arms around his torso, squeezing tight trying to quell the disturbing sensations.

Theo closed his eyes but the feeling intensified and he grew dizzy. Opening his eyes, he spotted a huge bobbing head, rising above the crowd. Its mouth gaped, full of teeth: a monstrous shark, gyrating down there in the street. Long, sinuous tentacles appeared, waving around the shark's head. Theo moaned, unable to keep quiet.

*Dear God, what is that thing?*

His vision kept slipping out of focus. His knees locked and his feet seemed frozen to the floor. Torches flared below and he spotted smaller figures cavorting around the monster, pale shaggy ape-men, with enormous eyes and gaping mouths.

More giant figures came into view ... a dragon, red and green, writhing above the street; or possibly a grinning sea serpent? An owl with glowing red eyes and human hands but with only three fingers ...

*Am I dead? Am I in Hell?*

He glanced back at the hotel room, its wooden furniture looking distinctly solid.

*No ... I don't think there are hotels in Hell.*

Horrific beasts, mouths full of sharp fangs, and unnatural animals with too many limbs appeared out of the darkness, heralded by the constant drumming and clanging. They gamboled to the rhythm then faded back into the shadows. The apparitions remained at a distance and Theo clamped down on his terror, hoping they wouldn't draw closer to the walls of the hotel. He remained motionless, watching, sweat pouring down his face, fearing they would drag him to Hell if they spotted him. He gripped the window frame, its sturdiness keeping him from feeling that he would fly off into space.

*Why did I come to this horrific place? Was home really that bad?*

Theo's legs trembled with fatigue; and waves of sensation broke over his body, distracting him from the horrors on the street. He dropped his forehead to the window and closed his eyes, but that was worse: visions of the monsters ripped through his eyelids, into his mind.

He opened his eyes with a start and stared straight down into the hotel gardens below his window. Was there something moving down there? Were they getting closer? He peered down, willing the fiends away. Theo caught a flash of white, but then it was gone. He stared unblinking until his eyes watered, but saw nothing more in the garden.

His vigil lasted for what felt like hours, until at last, in a climax of sound and motion, the monsters in the street disappeared into the gloom. Theo sagged with relief. Stumbling to his bed, he dropped into it and fell asleep almost instantly, but his dreams were all of gaping teeth-filled mouths and tentacles dragging him into the ocean.

# THE CANNONEER'S TALE

*By AJ Sikes*

No, I was not always a cannoneer. I used to make pastry for the House of Haimlin. Yes, *the* House of Haimlin. There's just the one, you know. Sitting up there on the hill back in beautiful Vainla, in their pretty rooms with their pretty things all around them. Meanwhile we're in the trenches, mud up to our knees and cold rain down our necks. And with an angry nun behind us waiting on her chance to shout. Thank you, Your Majesty, King Joszef.

—

I suppose you're right. It's not all the king's fault. The armorers could have designed these helmets better. Then the rain wouldn't get down our necks. But no art goes into war-making, does it? No, none at all. Ah, here we've a target coming over the wire. Hand me the powder bag now.

—

That's it, yes. Toss it here. Good! Well, you're definitely more the sort we've needed. The last fellow could barely keep his bowels in when the sisters started shouting. Cover your ears.

—

Loud, aren't they? I like it. Reminds me of the kitchens at the palace.

–

Oh, indeed. Never a more raucous affair than the royal kitchens at the Haimlin Palace. Here, we've another target. Must have missed. Yes, they say to correct right twenty. Right twenty. Next they'll be asking for *left thirty*. Fire in the hole!

–

More on the wire. You get it. I'm sick of correcting corrections to their corrections.

–

Direct hit? Well that's good news, isn't it. Just rest your voice now, Sister Krupfer. You've taught those naughty children well enough for today. Here, let's open that bottle you brought. I'll pour.

–

How did I end up here? Same as any other man too close the royal family. They worried I could be a spy, so they sent me off to fight. Makes sense, eh? My entire staff were released from duty and conscripted in the same breath. My, but this is fine Zvock. Where did you get this bottle?

–

Aha! The Old Quarter. Of course. They may as well live in the palace for all the time they spend there. I used to know a few of them. Their sons and daughters were the wine stewards and food servers—not the tasters, mind you. No good poisoning the rich when the poor die just as easily and won't be missed.

–

Oh, it started with a bowl of chocolate. A big one, the copper kettles like you'd see in paintings. I was a pastry chef, like I said. I owe my place here in the mud to that one night. That noisy, busy, messy, beautiful night in the kitchens. A princess of the House of Chambourd—

—

Yes, from the Morraine-Broscht region just behind you there. She was to marry into the House of Haimlin. That would have stopped this whole bloody business with the trenches and cannon, don't you think?

—

Indeed, it would have. Yet here we are, at war. And why? Because on her wedding night, the last night my hands touched chocolate, the princess eloped with a rogue with a violin. Who could believe such a tale? But it's true! Pour yourself more of the Zvock, friend. I'll tell you of this rogue, Rigó Jancsi, and how he wove magic with his instrument.

—

Oho! No, not *that* instrument, my friend. A real one. The kind that carries a spell on its strings when wielded by a sorcerer like Jancsi.

It was late autumn. I remember it well. Overhead, a flotilla of airships carried His Majesty's son, the prince who they shot so they could start this whole charade. Below the airships, two carriages clattered across the Bridge of Chains toward the palace on the hill above the Darnibe. One carriage bore a foreign inventor. A millionaire. The other held Cynthia Dewair, the princess of Chambourd, and her father, the duke.

—

Oh, I speculate a bit, of course. But you see, in the kitchens is where you hear the truth. Always it is the servants and the cooks who know the real story about what happens in houses of wealth and circumstance. Yes, so take what I tell you with a grain of salt if you must, but think whose spoon the salt falls from. A cook! You'll learn something before the night is through.

"Did you not find the music lovely, father?" the princess must have asked. "The violin especially. He simply sang to us with his music. I have not had chance to feel so … inspired … by musicians in the chambers or opera houses of Prise."

The duke, of course, would have turned a smart eye to the princess. "Watch that you do not convey such ardor in public, my daughter. These people are vulgar enough without their tongues wagging with gossip about your virtues. Your wedding is in three weeks' time now. Do not spoil this alliance!"

In the theater, the princess would have watched, entranced by the violinist's music. Meanwhile, her father would be leaning in to speak hushed secrets to another gentleman who had joined them. He'd have been from the palace. The man was twice the princess's age, at least, and scarred on one side of his face. She thought it a war wound.

In the carriage, her father told her the man was an advisor to the prince. A military man of significant standing in the House of Haimlin. The princess silently expressed her relief that he was not the man she'd been promised to. Still, she sulked beneath her father's admonitions and her fear of the coming marriage. Would the wedding feast be like those she'd heard of in Prise? Would *chocolate* be served?

—

Yes, *chocolate*. You see, the ambrosia that we—that *I* would produce, it is a rarity on this continent, a secret held by only a select few royal houses. The princess, you must understand, was both frightened and fascinated by the prospect of tasting it, and found she could only recover her calm by bringing to mind images of the rogue with the violin. His enchanting music. His thick mane of black hair. And his green eyes, flecked with gold like the brocade adorning her gown.

But the princess did not see the rogue again. Not until her wedding night. He came with the cooks, carrying sacks of flour into the palace. She did not recognize him at first, I am sure. But when she heard the music coming from the kitchens, she stole away, likely under pretense of needing the washroom. Her handmaidens accompanied her and made no protest when she detoured down the stairs to hover on a landing above the kitchens.

In the basement rooms, my staff ran to and fro carrying boards laden heavy with fruits and meats of every kind. You have never seen such bounty. Great wooden bowls full of eggs, loaves of bread, strings of sausages and cured meats draped across broad shoulders and around necks. Fowl and fish aplenty, and such wheels of cheese as you can only dream of.

In the middle of it all sat a heavy wooden table, and there sat I, surrounded by my cooks. Our white aprons were smeared with dark stains. And what was on the table before us?

A giant copper bowl. The very one. Down the side ran a single bead of a dark brown substance. And to this bead the princess sent her startled eyes. *Chocolate!*

She had heard of the delicacy, and I must assume you have as well.

–

Yes, yes. I knew it! Everyone is told of chocolate as a child, and the luckiest may have eaten small tastes of it. But only the Haimlins knew the secrets of its creation. And how to infuse it so as to inspire the passions. To see the ambrosia itself, can you imagine it? Before it had been turned into cakes and confections, pastries, creams, tarts and tortes—

–

Oh, I apologize. My belly, too, grumbles for want of a mere crumb of old bread. But you know, the mind can inspire more than suffering. Let yourself dream, my friend. Imagine the room, the smell of it. Aromas of smoke and fruit, flowers and musk. The noise and bustle. The *action!* And in the copper bowl, the richest of beverages, the drink offered only to the gods and those they favored.

*Of course the gods favor these people,* the princess thought to herself as she spied on our industry in the kitchens. She had seen up close the majesty of the House of Haimlin and now, in the kitchens, seeing the rich brown liquor stirred in a copper bowl, gleaming with the promise of ecstasy ...

The stories that had come to her ears, though. Stories from those who had tasted the beverage. The things people had done after drinking it. Would she be expected to do such things on this night?

The strains of the violin came to her ears, and her hand-maidens swooned beside her. From behind me and my cooks, the rogue emerged, his eyes glinting golden fire that illuminated the chocolate. A glow like off a crown rose from the silken brown surface. I and my cooks, and the princess, too, sat entranced until one of the fools beside me ruined the moment and spoke.

"You will have them fleeing the dance floor, Jancsi, my boy."

Another cook, as much a fool as the first, said, "They may start up before the dancing has been done." The others all laughed. But not I. Not I. For I knew what our Jancsi was about. He was playing an old tune, one that you are too young to have ever heard. And even those men around me, all trained in pastry just as I was, they had never heard this tune.

If they had, they would have silenced their laughter in an instant.

Jancsi's face had gone dark at their silly taunting words, and his eyes darkened further as they laughed. His playing changed, as I knew it would. First sweet and melodious, like a spring morning, the song became a winter's stormy night. Jancsi's eyes flashed crimson beneath the gold, now.

"Jancsi! Jancsi!" the cooks all cried, terrified now. Some stepped back, shielding their faces as if the music might burn them to ash. But not me. For I knew. I knew what Jancsi was about, and I quietly celebrated the coming future. We would not be harmed. We who would never in a thousand years be invited to sample so much as a crumb of the confection we would prepare.

In the corner of my eye, I spied the princess creeping forward on the landing. She leaned out, as if to reach the notes from Jancsi's violin as they came to her through the air. To grasp the music swirling from the instrument held by the raven-haired musician whose skin shone like bronze in the light of the kitchen fires.

The touch of a handmaiden's fingers on her arm brought the princess to a halt just as she teetered at the edge of the last stair.

I heard the girl say, "My lady, we shall be missed. We must return."

The girls fled up the stairs, not one of them aware that Jancsi had noticed the princess, nor that he smiled with sadness as he played.

—

We made the dessert, of course. What cause had we to shirk our duty? And what if we had? I'd have been executed. Maybe that would have been better. Instead they sent me to war. Still, it's better than having to clean up after the Haimlins and Chambourds. That dinner, and the mess they made …

—

Eh? Oh, yes. The dinner. The princess must have been nervous. It was her first meal as a member of the House of Haimlin. Her husband, Prince Rolf—

—

Yes, yes, the one they shot, like I said. That's him. He'd spent the dinner talking to other men. He leaned around the princess to see the man to her right, some other prince or an advisor. The princess did not know their language and so ate quietly, communing with her food as all women were expected to do. Looking around the room, she saw other wives and ladies of the court eating as she: in silence and regarding only the utensils in their hands or the wine glasses that my stewards kept at least half filled.

Prince Rolf turned to face the princess only once during the meal, when his father and hers proposed a toast to celebrate the occasion. Her father again described it as an "alliance", earning great applause from every corner of the room.

When my cooks and I entered with the dessert, a hush spread across the hall like a wave from the door to the kitchens. Whispers followed us on our path to the royal table at the head of the room. Recalling her father's stern warnings, the princess kept her eyes from seeking too much for her violinist. She needn't have looked, though. He did not stand among us, for he had taken his leave of the kitchens as quickly as he had arrived, playing a final note that even I, who knew the tune, had not expected.

And such desserts we prepared. Each one a feast for the eyes and the tongue. Small enough to be eaten at once, but demanding patience, forkful by forkful, to finish. Little square cakes of chocolate and white, dressed in a shimmering sheet of chocolate glaze. But I go off track, pining for my former life.

We were in the royal dining hall. A room covered in gold. Tables all around a dance floor, drapery and lace, and heavy doors in each wall. The royal table was at the far end, so we had to parade our confections and concoctions through the room, for all to see and admire before the royal family were served.

Finally, a plate was set before the princess, gold rimmed and ornately decorated with lions and flowers. It held a single square of cake. This dessert was no bigger than the cup you hold in your hand there. The princess drank from a cup just as small, but of course worth more than you and I shall ever see in our lifetime. Steaming dark coffee poured from a copper carafe into the cup as the chef—that's me—now dressed in a clean set of whites, described the chocolate creation.

"Your majesty," I said. "For you and your bride, we make this special delicacy. A cake divided into three layers to symbolize your glorious houses, and the bond formed between them this night." The room exploded with applause, of course. The rich love it when you remind them of their importance.

When the prince gave a look that had them all sitting on their hands again, I went on. "Between the first and second layers of cake, a mousse of chocolate so fine, so smoothly blended with the purest vanilla, sugar, and cream, it will melt upon your tongue and diffuse through your palates with the sensation of true ecstasy."

The prince grew uncomfortable at my emphasis on passions, or perhaps at how I had looked at the princess as I uttered those final words. Seeing his majesty's discomfiture, I altered my speech accordingly.

But clearly the damage had been done, else why would I be leaning against an angry nun with my feet sunk in the mud, eh? Well, I managed to get the rest of the dessert explained, for what good it did anybody.

"Your majesty," I went on. "Above the middle layer, a filling of cream infused with the essence of rose. A perfume to match as close as can be done the sweetness we all now perceive from this most splendid and blessed union of the House of Chambourd and the most royal House of Haimlin!"

The room exploded again, laughter and cheering, hands clapping and glass clinking. Some of it breaking. The princess raised a forkful of the cake to her mouth, no doubt thinking of her happiness that I had not used the word "alliance". I could see it in her eyes.

She will recall the experience of that first bite until her death. Slipping the fork from between her lips, she felt her tongue flex, pressing the morsel of chocolate against her palate. Instantly, music and images of firelight and gold flashed into her mind.

—

Well, I lied. I tried some, like I always did. I had to, you see. They never allowed me to serve food I would not eat myself. So I know what the princess saw and heard when she ate that first bite of cake. Singing, laughter, and the sound of her rogue's instrument. And more. An orchestra of them, his people who live in the wood or the edges of towns. Warbling strings and thumping percussion, as though rhythms were beat upon the floors of wagons or upon crates used as seats.

Beneath it all, a violin sang a plaintive melody. She saw spinning, twirling figures cast in silhouette before a bonfire. Others danced before a stand of mighty oak trees. The forest swam in her mind, the trees swaying in some great wind that threatened to sweep all aside.

And then all were swept away. The dancers, the fire, the trees. Gone. But the violin remained, its melody singing now of loss and sorrow, of love dashed against the cold heart of war where it shattered, never to reform.

—

You see! Good for you. You have been listening. And that look on your face, just the same as the princess had. Like you do now, she stifled a scream as scenes of battle replaced the dancers in the forest. She saw armies in ranks, men dying in waves. She saw us. Us! Hiding in trenches of mud and wearing masks that give us faces like machines. She saw bombs falling and exploding, sending mud and bodies into the sky.

—

Now you understand. And so did she. Her bile threatened and she quickly washed the cake down with a swallow of coffee. Looking around the room, though, she noticed none suffered visions like hers. Every face had turned upwards, chins and brows lifted in joy. Eyes closed as each guest, her new husband included, reveled in the magic of the chocolate dessert. Across

the hall she saw a group of guests from her native Prise beginning to disrobe. Prince Rolf had come out of his reverie and had
his hand around the wrist of a serving youth. The boy twitched as
if to flee and then relented. Other guests began to take liberties
with serving girls.

—

Oh, my staff and I retreated. I stayed to watch through a
curtain, but once the buttons began to pop, I departed. I know of
these events for having heard the stories about previous nuptial
feasts. And yet what I saw when I entered the dining hall after
all was said and done …

—

No, I shall not describe it. It is all I can do to keep myself in
one piece as I recall what must have occurred on that night.

In the dining hall, a platter clanged to the marble floor and
the pitch of voices rose to cover it with a din of lust. The princess
spun from her chair, knocking it aside as she fled. Her husband
took no notice of her, nor did her father who, though he'd seen
her, was too occupied with her handmaidens who descended
upon him, ripping at his clothing with their teeth.

—

We found him under the table. Like many of the others.
Sated, yes. And bloodied. But what of the princess, eh? She'd fled
upstairs, to the royal bedchamber. She settled against her pillows
and attempted to sleep. The activity in the dining hall had died
down, but only to a dull roar. Then, hours later, it was only meek
whimpers and a sparse few cries of pain that came through the
flues and vents to disturb the princess from her rest.

Then the prince arrived, stinking of wine and a perfume she
did not recognize. Was that blood on his collar and hands? He
struggled with his jacket, getting tangled in the sash he wore
and finally stumbling forward, falling into bed beside her. His
snoring kept her awake into the small hours.

The princess got up. She stood and went to the windows, looking at the gray-green lawn and topiary of the palace garden. Moonlight made the gardens cadaverous in the cold autumnal night. She turned to go back to her bed, back to her husband. And stopped when she heard the violin.

Spinning, she saw her rogue on the balcony, playing for her. His music came into the room, muffled by the window glass. She went to the doors and stood with her hands against them, smiling at him as he played. Should she open the doors? Would the prince awaken? Doubtful. She now knew the stories about chocolate were true. She had heard the screams of pleasure and agony, and the cruel laughter.

Unlatching the doors, the princess let the musician's gift enter the room, fill her senses, and enthrall her anew. He stopped playing and drew her to him, kissing her gently. Drawing back, she stared into his gold-green eyes and saw a storm there. Fear darted into her heart and left again as the rogue smiled at her.

"You should not fear. You are safe. I saved you."

"But how," she asked.

"With my music, princess. I played into the chocolate as I always do. But tonight, I added something special. Something for you to see. Would you stay and wait for that day to arrive? Or would you flee, and find freedom in the arms of a man with no flag to wave?"

The princess must have smiled, or nodded, or even kissed her rogue a second time. For we know that she left that night.

—

That may not be exactly how it happened, no. But it's as close a guess as any man can make. How much of the Zvock is left? Enough to last the night? Good.

—

No, no. You go ahead. I'll rest here with my head in the sister's lap. Wake me if the wire chirps. Otherwise let me sleep. And let me dream.

—

What do you think I would dream about? Of the life I used to know. Before the royal ones and the rich ones decided they could make money by killing off the rest of us. And who will make their chocolate cakes? Those stupid bastards. We who know how to make such delicacies, we'll be the ones to enjoy them, eh? More for us! Haha! Whatever they have that passes for cake in the palace now, they're welcome to it. And long may it rot in their stomachs.

# FLOWERS OF LONDON

*By Sharon E. Cathcart*

*Author's Note: I was fortunate enough to find an 1882 book by US Navy Lieutenant Frank Sprague that discussed the sights of the Electrical Exhibition. Many thanks to Disney Imagineer and friend Myles Cupp for his willingness to explain what the equations meant.*

1882

Thaddeus Flowers awoke in a bed not his own, head pounding. He'd definitely taken too much ale at the White Horse last night, and was not entirely sure where he was. The pub was in the Seven Dials, but he might be anywhere from there to Chelsea.

Raking his fingers through his dark hair, Thad sat up slowly. The dull light filtering in through the curtains showed a respectable enough room; his clothes were draped across a chair … on top of what looked like a petticoat.

Oh, dear God.

Thad looked at the sleeping figure next to him. The young woman's auburn hair was spread across the pillow, her face serene in sleep.

A pretty girl, Thad thought. I wish I remembered her name!

With movements that were far too practiced even for his own liking, Thad slid out of bed without disturbing the redhead. All clothes except for his boots were donned quietly. Once outside the room, and the house, he would put on his boots and walk away.

As he'd done so many times before.

Of course, that had been in America. Thad had promised himself that he'd be better behaved once he moved to London. But the women all seemed to adore his handsome face and charming accent … and so, here he was again.

Tiptoeing out of what seemed to be a respectable boarding house, Thad paused to slip on his boots and get his bearings. There was Covent Garden, and Drury Lane. So, not far from Seven Dials at all.

Very well, then.

Thad hailed a cab to take him back to his own boarding house in Baker Street. During the ride, he reflected on how he came to London in the first place.

Thaddeus Bartholomew Flowers was born in Placerville, California, on July 4, 1861. His father, William, had successfully struck gold on his claim after many years' effort and, upon doing so, promptly married a young woman with aspirations toward social climbing. While William was plain, with a long face and thinning brown hair, his bride was a lively blonde girl with a quick laugh, sparkling eyes, and a lush figure. She had caught his attention some while back, and when he asked the girl's father for permission to call, it was given quickly. William was 26; his bride was ten years younger.

Martha Jane Flowers' insistence upon giving Thad what William called a "high-falutin' name" was born of those aspirations. She was determined that her son would not grow up in what the locals called Hangtown, a rough frontier sort of place with a single main street comprised mainly of saloons. The local constabulary was greatly aided by the kind of rough justice that saw vigilantes throwing rope nooses over tree limbs and taking matters into their own hands. This was not, Martha Jane, proclaimed regularly, the kind of environment in which one might raise a gentleman.

It must be said that Martha Jane's concept of what constituted a gentleman came directly from the pages of her favorite romance novels; she had a subscription to Placerville's tiny lending library, and devoured books like *Pride & Prejudice*, *Five Weeks in a Balloon*, or *Miss Marjoribanks* almost as soon as they were available.

Thaddeus was not much inclined toward school; he was more of a dreamer. He wanted to have adventures of the sort he read about in the dime novels. He greatly admired the soldiers he saw strolling in and out of the Presidio of San Francisco, and entertained the idea that the army might be a ticket to adventure one day. He didn't seem to notice the number of veterans of the War Between the States, only six years past. His child's eye thought only of the glamour of seeing new places.

This was Martha Jane's greatest legacy to her son: an ambition to see bigger and better things, and to leave the whole idea of small towns behind.

During Thad's eleventh year, William and Martha Jane welcomed a baby daughter to the household. Lavinia Clementine Flowers was the apple of her parents' eye, and Thad alternated between feeling like a proud older brother and as though he were completely invisible. So much focus was on the new baby, who was somewhat unexpected. Thad was old enough to understand that Martha Jane had thought she could not have another child. The little girl's blond curls and blue eyes seemed to enchant everyone who saw her.

Then the measles came to San Francisco. Miraculously enough, neither of the children caught the disease. Martha Jane, who had gone to help nurse a neighbor's child, came down with it. She stayed with that neighbor in order to avoid exposing her own children.

She never came home.

After Martha Jane's death, William Flowers didn't spend much time mourning. With two children at home, one of them a baby who still needed the bottle, he needed to find a wife. There was one young woman who decided that William's wealth was more than adequate inducement to put up with what she privately called "an ugly face attached to a couple of brats"; Melanie Carson Dennis was entering her second season and about to turn twenty. With her glossy black hair, willowy figure, and brilliant green eyes, she could not have been more different from the late Martha Jane in appearance if she tried. She also differed from Martha Jane in that she never cared for books; they required too much effort.

Thaddeus hated her.

On his eighteenth birthday, Thaddeus left home. William gave him an advance on his inheritance and wished him well. Thad chose London as his destination, working his way across country on the railroads until he could get a ship. During his time on the rails, he became interested in mechanics, and he had an idea for an airship. In his spare moments, he created drawing after drawing of the device.

Thad's sketches showed a ten-person gondola, painted white and trimmed with gold around the top and on the rudder. The gondola was painted with beautiful creatures from mythology, like Pegasus and Unicorn, and was suspended from three large balloons in shades of pink and blue to match the other decorations. The idea behind the airship was to lighten the traffic of London streets; it didn't have to go very high, Thad reasoned; just above the buildings. Notes on the side of his first drawing indicated that lap rugs and warm drinks would be provided to passengers, and that eventually a fleet of the ships would parallel the routes of the horse-drawn omnibuses that covered the city.

Thad kept up a correspondence with his younger sister; Vinie was the only one he wrote to anymore. Vinie confided that she kept his letters secret, her ten-year-old's enthusiasm making a game of the whole thing. She also told him that she thought that his flying machine idea was "just grand," and that she hoped one day to see it in action.

As the cab drove past the Tower of London, Thad envisioned his beautiful airship sailing overhead to dock there. Perhaps even Her Royal Majesty would ride in the painted gondola, traveling quickly through the sky instead of stuck in a carriage! She could take the airship from Buckingham to the Tower and be there in a trice!

Right now, Thad needed to worry about the present instead of either the past or the future.

His landlady, Mrs. Hudson, had introduced him to a fellow boarder. That peculiar chap was interested in all manner of science, so Thad showed him the sketches he'd made. Young Mr. Holmes had drawn a circle around the three balloons and written "This won't be practical; how will you heat them equally?" in a tidy hand. That led to a lengthy discussion about the practicalities of engineering the airship, as well as what fare to charge ("How will you beat a half-penny seat on the omnibus," Holmes had asked). There was so much more to it than Thad had first thought.

In the end, Holmes recommended that Thad visit the Crystal Palace to see the electricity exhibition. That might be just what he needed to get his concept off the ground, both literally and figuratively. And that was the plan for today.

But first, Thad needed to take care of his hangover.

He paid the cab driver and went into the boarding house, hoping against hope that Mrs. Hudson would still be abed.

His prayers were dashed when the formidable lady met him in the hallway.

"Breakfast is waiting for you on the sideboard, Mister Flowers. I was rather concerned when you did not come home last night; your meal went to waste."

"My apologies, Mrs. Hudson. The time got away from me, you see, and I stayed with a friend."

"A friend. Is that what you call those women, Mr. Flowers?"

Thad wasn't sure, but he thought he saw a hint of a smile on the woman's face.

"In any event, sir, please do break your fast. And let me know if you'll be, er, staying with a friend again this evening so that I may plan supper accordingly."

"Yes, ma'am," he said, daring a little smile of his own.

After bolting his breakfast, Thad went up to his rather messy room to change clothes and shave. He hoped to talk with someone like Thomas Edison or Nikola Tesla at the exhibition; surely one of those greats would give him the information that he needed to set his idea in motion. He grabbed his plans from a precariously tall stack of books, put them into a portfolio and ran out to hail yet another cab for Hyde Park.

Inside the Crystal Palace, there were more exhibits than he could ever have imagined: nine different kinds of lightbulbs, just for a start. To his chagrin, though, neither Edison nor Tesla were actually present; they were represented solely by their inventions and an assistant here and there showing off the various devices.

An exhibit showing an electric motor caught Thad's attention, and he looked around for the man who had invented it. Surely this would be the answer to at least part of his problem. There was no scientist to be seen ... but there was a young woman, dark-haired and wasp-waisted in a fashionable gown of celadon green and wine brocade. Perhaps she was the inventor's daughter. Thad put his most charming smile on his face, and addressed her.

"Excuse me, miss? Hello, I'm Thaddeus Flowers. I would like to speak to the man who invented this engine."

She turned to face Thad, and he was struck silent by her beauty. She had the most amazing eyes he'd ever seen: they sparkled like emeralds in a high-street jeweler's window.

"I'm Arabella Abingdon," she replied. "And I am the 'man' who invented this engine."

It took Thad a moment to recover from his surprise. Trying to behave as though a female scientist were the most natural thing in the world, he took out his design to show her.

She examined the drawings and began making notations along the side: equations that Thad couldn't even begin to follow. After a moment, she stopped and spoke.

"Your idea is an interesting one, Mister Flowers. I would like to discuss it with you further. Perhaps over dinner."

It was as bold a proposition as any man might have made. After a second's hesitation, Thad accepted.

"There is a public house nearby, the Three Tuns," Arabella continued. "I will meet you there at six o'clock this evening. And now, I must return to my work. I can hardly sell my engine design if I don't publicize it, you know."

She extended her hand, and Thad bowed over it. Afterwards, she turned her back to him, and gave her attention to another man who was examining the engine with great curiosity.

Thad would be counting the hours until six o'clock.

CRSO

When Thaddeus Flowers awoke the next morning, he was in his own rooms on Baker Street ... with no recollection of how he got there.

The drawings of his airship were gone.

She couldn't have. Surely not. Could she?

# Seeking Atlantis

*By Michael Tierney*

The pirate airship stalked its prey, prepared to attack.

"Mr. Jenkins, decrease buoyancy and keep them dead ahead of us." Captain MacNee scanned the enormous passenger airship below them in the twilight. He could see no evidence that the other ship had detected them—no evasive maneuvers and no sign of a watch in the observation dome at the top side of the envelope.

A great amount of misunderstanding exists about how airpirates attack another airship. In the popular "penny dreadful" stories, the tale is often told about how a pirate airship comes alongside its target, fires a shot across the bow, and boards her to remove everything of value from her cargo and passengers.

Captain James MacNee wished it were so easy.

Because an airship's envelope is so much larger than the small gondola at its keel, the gondolas of two airships flying next to each other are still very far apart. A boarding party under fire would never have a chance of crossing from one ship to the other.

"Helmsman, bring us down right on top of them. Set elevator flaps to 10 degrees down," he cried. "Prepare the boarding party."

The pirate airship slowly closed in on its prey from above and behind. MacNee believed this method had the advantage of stealth unless the opposing captain had set a watch at the top of his ship's envelope, a rare event during normal operations. MacNee ordered the main guns constantly trained on the upper envelope of their victim during the approach, should the need arise to shoot first and board later.

"Buoyancy to neutral. Ready boarding pikes." The grey skin of the airship was now only a few feet from the open hatch at the bottom of the gondola. Two pirates stabbed their pikes through the skin and hooked the boarding pikes onto the airframe, firmly attaching the two ships together. Some quick cuts to the fabric of the envelope by an airman's knife and they gained entry to the *Sussex*, one of the big Transatlantic airliners, full of wealthy passengers and cargo that could not wait to reach Canada by steamship.

The captain picked up a speaking tube. "Miss Leigh, set engines to idle, but keep them ready in case we need to make a quick escape."

A woman's voice answered, "Aye, Captain." While a widely-believed superstition usually prevented women from serving on airships, Miss Leigh was the daughter of the previous captain of the *Daedalus*, and MacNee had promised her father he would keep her on. Besides, she was a damned good chief engineer.

MacNee ordered the suitably armed boarding party down onto the narrow gangway between the *Sussex*'s gas cells, commanded by his first mate, Mr. Sherman.

Sherman called up the ladder to the bridge "There doesn't seem to be any watch set anywhere at all, Captain. The envelope is deserted." MacNee had started to question his choice of first mate, of late, and Sherman's seeming inability to properly board a ship was not helping his case.

"What do you mean 'deserted'? Isn't there any crew about?"

"No, sir. There's no one as far as I can see fore and aft."

The captain shook his head, wondering why his attacks never went smoothly. He looked out at the immense envelope of the *Sussex* curving away from him in all directions. In frustration, MacNee considered ordering a shot fired down through the bow of the ship just to attract their attention. He risked completely destroying his prey though, which made plundering it considerably more difficult.

"Well then, go straight down to the gondola and demand their surrender." Sherman had come with good recommendations from the Air Pirate Employment Guild, so the captain generously gave him another chance to prove himself. If not, he would be out at the next port, or sooner.

CRISO

Sherman led his men down the ladder from the spine of the airship through its duralumin airframe towards the keel, stopping at each level and furtively looking around. They had almost reached the gondola and had still not encountered any crew.

The first mate raised his index finger to his lips and whispered, "Listen …"

Barely above the noise of the wind and the engines, they could hear the sounds of celebration: raised voices, clinking glasses, laughter. The boarding party crept down the ladder until they were one level above the gondola. The sounds seemed to come from behind a frosted glass door at the bottom of the stairs, labeled "Main Saloon."

"The crew must be having a party. They won't be expecting us. All right, men. Follow me, guns at the ready", said Sherman.

Sherman shoved open the door and rushed into the room, pistol in one hand, short sword in the other. "Surrender or be killed!" he cried.

As he entered the room, he stopped short, and his men collided into him in the doorway. Facing him from the room was not the crew of the *Sussex*, but another band of pirates, with flintlock pistols in one hand and drinks in the other.

"Oy! What do you think yer doing?" said one pirate, who seemed to be the leader.

"Ah, um," Sherman briefly hesitated, then stiffened. "You lot! You surrender as well!"

The leader fearlessly stepped forward, squinting. "Who are you? Who's your captain? What ship are you from?"

Sherman quickly decided that to answer these questions was not a smart move. Yet the pirates facing him seemed to think otherwise. Best to get on their good side, he thought. "My name is Sherman, Will Sherman. More I will not say at this time."

"You don't have to say anything, Mr. Sherman, Will Sherman, or should I say, First Officer Sherman. Oh, yes, I know of you, and your captain, and your ship, the dread pirate airship *Daedalus*," he chuckled, and his men laughed with him. "How's yer first voyage going, Mr. Sherman?"

Sherman raised his eyebrows.

*How did he know about my joining the crew of the* Daedalus*? I haven't even told my wife yet.*

"You seem to have me at a disadvantage, Captain ..."

"Oh, yes, at a disadvantage in several ways. As far as I know, there's only one ship flying the North Atlantic with a First Officer named Will Sherman, if that is your real name. No, don't tell me. I don't need to know. We are pirates after all. What would be the fun if we all used our real names? Be that as it may, I have agents in many places sending me all manner of information that might prove useful. So, please send for Captain MacNee, if that is, in fact, his real name, and let him know that his men are interfering with Captain Redbeard's bounty."

"Redbeard?" Sherman knew the infamous name well, and the tales that were told of his exploits. "Wait a minute … your beard is brown!"

Redbeard stroked his luxurious brown whiskers for a few seconds thoughtfully. "Now, Brownbeard just doesn't have the same fearsome ring to it, does it? Your captain, please?"

Sherman had spent the last two months aboard *Daedalus* carefully observing the captain and crew, all the while playing the part of a less-than-able first mate, disguising his ultimate goals, and even changing his speech to sound more like a fellow airpirate to the crew. He knew Captain MacNee's weakness— that while he may be an able air pirate captain when the plunder was easy and plentiful, he lacked the dedication to be truly ruthless. Sherman drew near to Redbeard. "Just between you and me, Captain, we won't be needing to bother Captain MacNee. I think I can come to an agreement with the crew. They'll follow me. I'm sure we can strike some bargain," he said slyly, hoping that Redbeard wouldn't see through the slight exaggeration.

Redbeard smiled slightly. "Let me get this straight. You're on your first voyage and you're already plotting mutiny? I think Captain MacNee needs to find a different hiring agent to crew his ship."

Sherman wondered if he had pushed the point too far. Redbeard was obviously a tougher mark than MacNee—a better judge of character and less gullible. He had quickly seen through Sherman's ploy.

Redbeard stepped up to Sherman nose-to-nose, "Let me tell you plain, Sherman. I'll talk to your captain, and no one else, especially not a would-be mutineer."

CR80

Sherman nodded to one of the men still crowded in the doorway behind him, and the pirate clambered up the ladder to fetch the captain. Less than a minute later, the captain barged into the room.

"I'll take over from here, Mr. Sherman," said the captain. He turned to the pirate with the lush brown facial hair, "Redbeard! Get your men off my prize!"

"Your prize, MacNee? I think not. We had already taken the *Sussex* and were well into celebrating when your lot spoiled the party. Look," he raised his glass, "we've already almost finished our celebratory drinks. By the way, how in hell did you manage not to notice that the ship you were attacking had already been taken?"

"We used the Rheinbach manoeuvre, staying in *Sussex*'s wake and dropping down from above."

"Ah, yes. A bit old-fashioned, but effective, I suppose. I prefer the Santos-Dumont gambit, coming up quickly from below and boarding the gondola from our dorsal platform. Much more direct especially when the target is unarmed. And, as you have just proven, invisible to ships trying to attack the same ship from above."

"Enough!" cried MacNee. "There was no trying about it. We attacked, and we succeeded. Now take your scurvy crew and get off our prize."

Captain Redbeard let out a hearty laugh. "You're actually threatening me? Captain, let's be honest here. You have no right to the *Sussex* because we were already in control of the ship when you attacked. You can battle us for her if you really want, but I assure you that the *Daedalus* is no match for the *Demon's Scourge*. If it came down to an air engagement, you and the *Daedalus* would go down in flames.

"Then we can rename her the *Icarus*," added Redbeard. MacNee sighed at the not-so-clever joke.

Redbeard lowered his voice so that the others in the Main Saloon could not hear him. He put his hand on MacNee's shoulder. "Captain MacNee, I am certain that I do not have to remind a man of your experience and learning what the Pirate Code says about stealing another man's bounty," he paused, "but I will anyways. 'No pirate shall steal bounty or prize from another pirate or crew. Usurping another crew's treasure will result in forfeiting said treasure, permanent banishment of the captain and crew for a distance of 1000 miles, and other punishments as may be deemed fit by the Airpirate Tribunal.'"

MacNee blanched, "Surely, Captain, you can see that this is a simple misunderstanding, and that we would be only too happy to relinquish any plundering rights from the *Sussex* and be on our way."

"I'm not sure that will suffice, Captain. We cannot treat the Pirate Code as mere guidelines. No, while I do believe that your interference in our capture of the *Sussex* was inadvertent, and a result of incompetence rather than malice, you and your crew must bear some consequence. We've found the North Atlantic to be fairly lucrative hunting what with the commercial airships to and from British Canada, and the French and German ships to the United States. Competition would only reduce our plunder. Let's say that you and your ship stay out of our way for a couple of years. Maybe relocate to the Mediterranean. Or the West Indies. You could become an airpirate of the Caribbean. Weather would be nicer too."

"And if we refuse?" MacNee held out one last scintilla of resistance.

"Captain, I know you're an educated man. Maybe too educated to be a pirate. Should it be decided that you and your ship have broken the Pirate Code, the punishment would be much stricter and much more, let's say, lethal, than what I have offered you. I will make sure of that. I'm giving you a fair, and let's be honest, generous offer. So you'd be wise to accept it, you see."

MacNee knew he was beaten, but just when he despaired of receiving any sort of mercy from his foe, Redbeard leaned in and spoke quietly but firmly, "And mind you keep an eye on that first mate of yours. He's not one to be trusted."

CR80

A light Mediterranean breeze wafted past Captain MacNee, who was now dressed somewhat inappropriately for the weather in a heavy leather coat and high boots. Despite the pleasant weather, or maybe because of it, the man gazed out onto the horizon with growing unease.

"What's the matter, Cap'n? You don't seem excited about reaching Athens." MacNee had taken Redbeard's warning about his first mate to heart and he considered everything Sherman said in its light.

"We've been prowling the Mediterranean for over a month now and not an airship to attack or a village to plunder." The Captain looked down from the glare of the horizon. "Tell me, Sherman. How are the men? Are they content?"

"The men have naught but respect for you."

"Oh, yes, of course, I'm sure they have fond memories of plundering the regular Transatlantic trade, when the profits were flowing. But being banished from those rich targets, I'm not sure how long the crew will abide not getting a regular bounty. I shouldn't have agreed to Redbeard's compromise. We should have stayed and fought! Not let him bully us around!"

"With all due respect, Cap'n, we never would have had a chance against their ship. I took a good look at their armaments. Their guns were loaded with incendiary Dragon Fire shot. They could've taken us out along with the next three ships and not blinked an eyelash. You made the only choice that made sense, Cap'n. The crew understands this."

"If we only could find some plunder." The Captain looked out at the dry brown lands below. "What kind of land has no riches, Sherman? Oh, sure, that village in Sicily looked promising, with an ancient castle and all. Until the villagers started shooting at us with their fowling pieces. They would never have damaged the ship, of course, but it just seemed like so much work for so little reward—just a couple of jugs of olive oil and a basket of tomatoes."

"Well, the cook did make some nice meals with them." The Captain glowered back at his first mate. "Surely there must be some more tempting targets, Cap'n. The Mediterranean Sea is literally the center of the world—the word itself means 'middle of the land'! The Greeks, Romans, Egyptians, Phoenicians, all their civilizations rose and fell in this area. They must have left behind some treasure."

"How do you know so much about ancient history, Sherman?"

"I wasn't always an airpirate, Cap'n. I read Ancient History at Oxford before the Air War."

"Really? I read Classics at Edinburgh! My interests always did lie more in literature rather than history."

"What a coincidence—two educated men ending up as airpirates!"

*An Oxford man. That's probably why he's so eager to have the ship. Thinks himself above doing actual work and wants quick advancement. Well, he doesn't have my ship yet.*

"I don't think our university learning will help at all, Sherman. Redbeard said that I might be too well-educated to be a pirate. He might be right—both of us." The Captain stepped over to the rail and absentmindedly peered through the spyglass mounted there. "If only the stories of Plato were true, then we could just fly over to Atlantis and plunder to our hearts' content."

"Wait, who's to say they're not, Cap'n?"

"Excuse me, Sherman, just what type of ancient history did they teach you at Oxford?"

Sherman jumped up from leaning on the rail and paced excitedly around the gondola. "No, hear me out, Cap'n. Plato's description of Atlantis has inspired legends for centuries, right?"

"Yes, but Plato's stories are just allegories ..."

"Spoken like a true Classics student, Cap'n. You understand that Plato's story of Atlantis is an allegory concerning the hubris of nations, but I doubt the crew will. Legends of treasures of lost civilizations have tempted men for hundreds of years. Look at the Spanish Conquistadors and their search for El Dorado, the legendary city of gold, and the Fountain of Youth. Men are easily led to believe in such tales."

MacNee squinted. "What exactly are you proposing, Mr. Sherman?"

"We tell the crew that we're going after the legendary treasure of Atlantis. It'll give them something to look forward to, a goal. And who knows? Maybe we'll find some real treasure along the way. You'll look like a hero. Any thoughts of mutiny will vanish."

As Sherman spoke, MacNee wondered just how much he could trust him. He would have to keep a sharp eye on his first officer, lest he cut him off at the knees.

"Are you sure we don't have any more classics students amongst our crew?"

"Pretty sure, Cap'n. What are the odds?"

The next day, the crew assembled in the gondola. The Captain, generously assisted by his first mate, informed the crew of their new destination.

"The legend says that Atlantis lies past the Pillars of Hercules, the ancient name of the Strait of Gibraltar. We'll want to give the Air Service patrols from the aerodrome in Gibraltar a nice wide berth, so we'll be heading south over Morocco and out into the Atlantic."

Although they were operating legally at the moment and outside their usual territory, Captain Sherman did not want to take the chance that the crew of a British airship might have heard about a few less legitimate jobs for hire they took on in their past.

"We'll search for Atlantis off the coast of Africa."

"Africa!" said one of the younger pirates. "I've heard of ivory and rubies from Africa. Diamonds too!"

"And spices!" another youngster contributed.

"Spices? Who are you? Christopher Columbus? Let's just stay with easy to transport gems and precious metals—gold and silver. No spices!" said the Captain.

After a day of making their way southwestward, off the port bow appeared the coast of Africa. A thin green band near the shore quickly faded to the pale beige color of the desert. Twelve hours later, the *Daedalus* had passed over the northwest corner of Africa and headed out to sea, the men in search of treasure, MacNee in search of a way out of the risky gamble his first mate had gotten him into.

As the ship flew over the blue Atlantic, the crew manned the rails, brass spyglasses trained on the horizon, in search of the fabled Atlantis, and riches unimaginable. Sherman helpfully explained what the legends told of the land—a mighty country that dared to oppose Athens for domination.

"But, sir, don't the stories tell that Atlantis was destroyed?" asked young Jenkins.

Sherman looked at him skeptically, "Ah, they say that Atlantis was lost. Whether that means destroyed, or just lost to memory, has been argued for ages."

"Hasn't anyone else gone looking for it?"

"Oh, many have. Some have not returned. Others sailed back with tales scarcely to be believed. The exploits of others have become part of the legend of Atlantis itself."

"Captain, land on the horizon, off the starboard bow. It looks to be a fairly large island."

MacNee strode over to the large brass telescope mounted on the rail and looked through it in the direction the crewman was pointing. Yes, he was right. There was an island there. Mountainous, and of good size. And not on his charts. Not that he had accurate charts of this area of the ocean anyway. MacNee now regretted not stopping to find some more recent charts of the Mediterranean when they flew past Marseilles.

"Helm, change course. Turn thirty degrees to starboard."

"Weather looks to be changing, Cap'n." MacNee looked out and noted thunderclouds in the distance building up.

"Can we make it to that island before the storm hits?"

Sherman did some quick calculations. "I think so, Cap'n, if we push the engines."

MacNee pushed the engine telegraph to the "Ahead Full" position. A few seconds later a bell rang—the engine room acknowledging the order. He felt the airship gradually accelerate. "What's your estimate of the distance to that island, Mr. Sherman?"

"Without charts, it's a guess, but about thirty miles. At our speed, we should be at the Atlantis coast within an hour. That should be right when the storm hits."

MacNee paced the distance between the front rail and the helm, checking the horizon and the airspeed indicator at each trip.

*How have I gotten to this point? Any sensible captain would have turned around and tried to outrun the storm, or at least sought a safe aerodrome with a nice unoccupied wind-proof airship hangar.*

*Now I'm deliberately flying the ship into the teeth of a building storm, just to look good to the crew.*

On his next orbit around the bridge, he stated, "We're encountering headwinds, Mr. Sherman. I don't think we'll make it to that island in time."

The first mate picked up the speaking tube, "Can we get any more speed, Miss Leigh?"

"The engines are almost to their limits, but I'll see what I can do."

As the headwinds increased, their speed dropped to a crawl. The coastline seemed to come no closer. "Decrease buoyancy, go into a shallow dive." MacNee hoped to increase speed, but the ship only rose.

"We're caught in an updraft ahead of the storm, Captain," said the helmsman. "It's no good."

The airship jerked violently upwards as the outlying winds of the storm hit them. Suddenly, they were in the clouds, and the island disappeared. The ship shuddered as the gusts became erratic.

"Make the ship ready for storm conditions," MacNee cried over the increasing noise of the wind. "Try to keep our heading steady, Jenkins. We'll try to ride it out. This is probably just a regular thunderstorm. It can't last too long."

At least he hoped not. *Daedalus* had never encountered turbulence this violent before. He glanced at his first mate, who sat calmly to the side of the helm, seemingly unconcerned.

*Pompous Oxford ass. I should never have listened to his crazy scheme. I should have heeded Redbeard's warning and pitched him overboard.*

# WHEN JOHNNY CHIMES CAME TO TOWN

*By Richard Lau*

The town of Snakebite lay coiled in the desert sand about two hundred yards from where the covered wagon had stopped on a shallow hill.

For the forty-six-year-old Gustaf Hoffman, the American West was too hot for his charcoal suit, but all he had left from his former home were his clothes and European etiquette. He lifted his bowler hat and wiped his sweating brow.

The heat didn't seem to bother Hoffman's companion, sitting on the buckboard next to him. To be sure, the companion's body of yellow metal was hot to the touch and shone as a tiny twin to the gold sun beating down from the cloudless sky. For Hoffman, it was like sitting next to a lit stove.

"At least you're dressed for this weather," Hoffman panted, nodding to Johnny Chimes' grey Stetson, the metal man's only item of clothing, present more to satisfy Hoffman's sense of humor than for practical function.

As usual, there was no reply.

Still holding the reins with one hand, Hoffman reached into his vest pocket with the other and withdrew a three-inch brass key.

Hoffman inserted it between the fourth and fifth ribs of the wooden exoskeleton surrounding Johnny's chest cavity. Hoffman paused, thinking of the trade-off he had made in Johnny's design. While the wood cage offered less protection than a metal casing, the lighter frame enabled Johnny to move faster and farther.

"Well, Johnny Chimes, today we bring in the Rutger Brothers," Hoffman said, turning the key and winding the metal man's mainspring. It wouldn't do to have Johnny run low in the middle of a gunfight.

Experience had taught Hoffman the exact tightness to turn to, but still he checked the tension gauge above the key slot.

When he removed and re-pocketed the key, Johnny obediently turned his back to his inventor, exposing a small crank with a short handle located between his shoulders.

Hoffman slid aside a safety tab and turned the crank, adding tension to a trigger spring attached to levers and pulleys in Johnny's arms. The inventor's hands still shook, remembering, in Johnny's earlier prototypes, how the spring had stretched out to uselessness from being under constant tension, or even worse, snapped. Hence, the crank was left unwound until a gunfight was imminent.

After a prescribed number of turns, a repeated set of notes chimed softly from Johnny's mouth grill. The tune was "Für Elise," and the spinning of the unseen perforated metal drum let Hoffman know that all was ready.

He pressed the button behind Johnny's neck, making sure he didn't slide the gunman's hat forward over his visual receptors.

As the metal man stiffly climbed down from the driver board, Hoffman leaned heavily in the opposite direction, his corpulence counterbalancing the disembarking mass of the metal man.

Tipping the bowler, he said, "See you in town, Johnny."

Hoffman flicked the reins.

Johnny chimed back and began his walk to town.

०380

Moments of relative calmness were a rarity in Snakebite. An act of violence was noted as much as a wind-blown tumbleweed. Shouts, screams, and gunfire, as natural as the raptor's cry.

Yet, when Ed Bishop burst through the barbershop door, his sudden appearance sent the barbers' razors stampeding like buffalo across a plain of shaving cream, cutting across one dangerous jaw in particular.

"Ed," growled Big Bart Rutger, leaning forward in his chair, rubbing the trickling red nick on his chin with the thumb of one hand and lowering the other hand to the pistol slung on his waist. "You'd better have a good reason for coming in here like your pants were on fire."

Ed stopped dead in his tracks, realizing he was moments away from being stopped dead permanently.

Big Bart was not misnamed, and the only thing short about him was his temper.

Teetering back on the heels of his boots, Ed stammered, "Ter-ter-terribly sorry, Mr. Rutger! But there's a metal man callin' you out!"

Jeremy and Hank, slightly smaller mountains in the Rutger range, grabbed Ed's arms and prepared to lift and throw him like a bale of hay.

Big Bart waved them to stop. "What the hell are you talkin' about? Is there another tin star in town?"

Ed laughed nervously. "Tin star? Heck, all of him's tin! Or some sort of metal."

Bart toweled off his chin and neck. "Let Ed go, boys. Sounds like we got somethin' better to kill."

Metal or not, for making Bart bleed a little, this new stranger was going to bleed a lot.

The Rutger Brothers stepped out onto the barbershop porch, squinting eyes adjusting to the sunlight, and heard a strangely monotone voice coming from down the street repeating, "Bart Rutger. Jeremy Rutger. Hank Rutger. The law has come for you."

Sure enough, farther down the wide, dusty path that served as main street, there was a golden man standing stiff as a signpost, comically nude except for two crossed gun belts and a Stetson.

It would take more than a little anatomically incorrect nudity to intimidate the Rutgers. With long-practiced pacing and spacing, the outlaw brothers approached their challenger, unafraid and unconcerned. They solved their problems with their guns and their number, and this was just another problem. Still, they weren't blind or drunk, and they realized the novelty of the situation.

The brothers were so focused on the stranger and his strangeness that they didn't notice a covered wagon on the side of the street, nor its portly driver in the damp black suit and funny round hat. If they had, they would have recognized the annoying perfume and aftershave salesman who had risked his life spraying them with a sweet-smelling sample right before they had entered the barbershop.

Hoffman had taken advantage of Johnny's slow walk to scout ahead in the town and identify the men they were after. Now he waited, their wanted posters in his hand. Good thing he had sprayed them with an invisible paint that was only luminescent to Johnny's receptors. After their visit to the barbershop, the Rutgers didn't resemble the rough drawings on the posters. Johnny could compensate a little but was still far from perfect. Hoffman liked to be on hand in case something went wrong. A sharp whistle from his lips would serve as an override.

"… Rutger. The law has come …" Johnny's message cut short as the Rutgers moved within twenty yards of him. Hoffman was always amazed how different his voice sounded through Johnny's mouth grill. Perhaps he had hammed it up a bit when recording the wax cylinder. Hoffman viewed his recordings as largely disposable. The fragile cylinders were recorded specifically for each bounty and, once the rough stuff started, they were no longer needed. Johnny Chimes literally became the strong, silent lawman of the West who let lead do his talking.

Still, the Rutgers advanced, closer than they normally would, curious at what stood before them. They were fearless by nature, number, and numbness.

Now that Johnny had stopped "speaking," they could hear the chimes still echoing from inside the metal man. That stopped them.

"Wha?" started Bart. "The thing's a goshdurn music box!"

Hank, commenting on Johnny's brass coloring, "Or a spittoon."

Jeremy, the youngest of the three in more ways than one, added "He's more spittoon than man. Like a spittoon, he doesn't even have a …"

Jeremy made a motion with his hand toward his groin that Johnny misinterpreted. The crank on his back spun into a blur.

Up came Johnny's guns, down dropped Jeremy, dead.

Bart and Hank drew their pistols a split-second later, more out of instinct than will.

The thunderous roll of gunfire rebounded off buildings and in ears, until only silence remained. Even the sound of Johnny's chimes had stopped.

CR80

Hoffman grunted as he loaded each dead Rutger into the wagon. Johnny stood guard. In these small towns, one could never be certain if outlaws had friends.

The inventor wasn't pleased at the way Johnny drew first, but the brothers' fate was sealed when they stepped into the street.

The wanted posters fluttered under one of Johnny's spare gears, currently serving as a paperweight. Hoffman intentionally chose to go after the worst outlaws and the ones wanted dead. It was a brutal decision, but Johnny's inelegant mechanics fit the brutality. The collected bounties would help him make improvements and hopefully some fine-tuning to his metal lawman.

Farther down the street, in the shadows cast by a jutting hotel balcony, two Sioux and a poorly chiseled cigar store counterpart had witnessed the showdown.

"How do we approach the warrior without getting killed?" asked the younger of the two, his knife hand twitching after what he had seen.

The older one, a chief, shook his head. "We do not approach the warrior." He pointed to the round, little man in the dark suit. "We approach the chief."

# SOME TIME LATER

# THREE MEN AND A WEREWOLF

### *By Harry Turtledove*

Harris and I stood on the corner smoking our pipes for at least twenty minutes before George deigned to honor us with his presence. We would have been more annoyed had we been more surprised. George, I expect, will be late to his own hanging. And, should he somehow evade that fate, the *Times* will surely commence his obituary with the unvarnished truth: "The late George—passed away yesterday at the age of ..."

He did bring it off well. He commonly does, but then custom hath made it in him a property of easiness. Most men who inconvenience their relations or friends by coming late to the ball (or the supper, or the rugby match, or ...) will act, and may even feel, flustered and embarrassed. Not George. He assumes you will be glad to see him when at last you do see him, and never mind when you should have set eyes on him.

"Hullo, gents!" he said, saluting us with his umbrella. It had rained the night before and was still drizzling when we set out, so we had ours as well. The sun, sliding between clouds, shone off the bright, pointed tip of Harris's. George went on, "Seen any vampires lately?"

167

"Not this past year, thank heavens," I replied. Harris nodded and looked sober—not the most common look for his face to wear, I know, but I am trying to tell the truth here, however unlikely it may sound. George could have hit upon no better way to make us forget whatever pique we might have felt at his tardiness. Our one brief encounter with the undead was plenty for a lifetime; no, an eternity.

To help ensure I have no more such encounters, I've mounted a small, none too noticeable crucifix above the door to my room. I am not of the Romish persuasion, but why take chances? I keep bulbs of garlic on the window sills, and sometimes even remember to change them. I haven't asked my friends if they take similar precautions, but they would have to be a kind of fool they are not to fail to do so.

"Jolly good," said George. "Let's find this eatery, then. We can tell everyone we know we've tried things most people have never even heard of."

We went down Flamborough Street towards the Thames and into Limehouse. That is a peculiar district, and one less well known than it might be. Though lying just east of the City, it might as well be a different world—several different worlds, in fact. The City runs the Empire; Limehouse is where its dregs wash up. Lascars and Chinese and Lord only knows who all else doss there and drink there and eat there and sometimes even pray there—we passed the Chinese Mission as we walked. It says its name in common English letters and again, lower down, in the peculiar characters the Celestials favor (or at least I think so, being sadly illiterate in Chinese).

Smaller places also showed their names in both the alphabet we use and Chinese, Indian, or Arabic scripts. Some of them—generally the smallest of the small—omitted our letters altogether: you had to belong to the folk they served to know what they were serving.

"Suppose there's a fire," said George. "How do you tell the station which place is burning up?"

"You say which street it's in, and between which two," replied Harris. "If they can't find it after they know that much, the fire's not very big."

"I wonder how we'll find the place we're looking for if it has no English sign," I said. "It won't be on fire, or it had better not be."

"Leave it to me," declared George.

"You're learning Chinese?" asked Harris.

"Not a bit of it." George tramped up to a ragamuffin hawking newspapers. They were so new, I could smell the ink coming off them. The headline screamed OLD WOMAN MUTILATED LAST NIGHT! Ignoring it, George held a silver shilling a foot in front of the boy's eager eyes. "Here, pal, this for you if you can tell us how to get to Lee Ho Fook's."

"You're almost there. Turn left next time you can. Two doors down, on the left." The newsboy snatched the coin from George and made it disappear. Then he went back to crying up his lurid papers. I wouldn't have given him so much. People lie as naturally as they breathe—I should know—and all the more readily with so much to earn by quick invention.

But the place was where he claimed it would be. It did boast a tiny sign in English, with a bigger one above it in Chinese. I opened the door. A bell rang. I waved George and Harris in ahead of me.

It smelled good in there, meaty and greasy and spicy—not the same smells you'd find in a meat pie shop, but the same kind of smells. What you get here will be cheap, but it will taste fine, they promised.

People shoveling rice and chopped bits into their mouths with chopsticks paused, morsels suspended in midair, to gape at us. They were all Orientals, with golden skins, narrow black eyes, and flat faces. Most of them wore gowns with odd collars; the rest had on cheap Western clothes. Never before had I felt so much a stranger, a foreigner, in my own country.

Harris, now, might become an ambassador if only he could stay sober. He nodded to the pigtailed bloke behind the counter, who was wielding a fat cleaver with might, main, and considerable skill. "May we take a table, sir?" he asked.

"'Elp yourselves, mates." The cook may have looked like a Chinaman, but he talked like any other East Ender. He shoved a badly printed sheet across the counter. "An''ere's a menu for yer."

I picked up the menu while George and Harris sat down. Then I joined them. The table held a cruet of the liquor from fermented soya beans (I'd hoped for Worcestershire, but a sniff left me disappointed), a shaker of salt, one of black pepper, and one of red pepper that I eyed with wary respect. We passed the menu back and forth. It was in both Chinese and English, the latter almost as incomprehensible as the former. Chow mein? Egg foo yung? Egg I recognized; the rest was gibberish.

"You want forks or chopsticks?" asked the counterman.

As I've mentioned, the Celestials were conveying food to their gobs with those bits of wood. Some Englishmen who go out to the Orient come back with the knack, but none of us possessed it. "Forks," said George with decision, while Harris and I nodded.

They were mismatched and cheap as can be, but they were forks. "What you gonna eat?" enquired the fellow.

Again, George had his mind made up: "We must have some fried shrimp. I don't see how anyone can go wrong with fried shrimp."

"And some fried rice with pork." Harris pointed to the item on the menu. "That sounds exotic."

"Some kung pao chicken, too," I said. "I like the noise of it."

"That's a spicy one," warned the counterman.

I glanced at the red pepper flakes again, but then shrugged. "We'll live dangerously. And may we have some tea while we're waiting for the victuals?"

"Comin' right up." The man set a china pot and three handleless cups on the table. The tea poured out green and thin, not black, and neither milk nor sugar seemed on offer. The Celestials in the place took the style for granted, poor souls. We looked at one another and wordlessly decided to rough it.

A sensible choice: however much I preferred good old Breakfast or Earl Grey, I could drink this stuff. "It will go well with the food, I hope," said Harris. I held the same hope, though I dare say more gingerly than he did.

The door flew open. The bell clanged. In strode a large, dapper chap, an Englishman, perfectly coifed—not a hair out of place—in a sack suit of such striking pattern and cut that it might have come from a lifetime in the future, not these mundane days of the nineteenth century drawing to a close. I wouldn't have liked to meet his tailor.

"Hullo, Lee Ho, you old crock!" he said cheerily. "How about a big old plate of beef chow mein, and some steamed rice to go with it?"

"You'll have it in a jiffy, Mr. Warren, sir," said the counterman, proving himself to be the eponymous Lee Ho Fook.

"You're famous, you know?" said the newcomer—Mr. Warren. He brandished a menu all wrinkled and teary, probably from the rain the night before. "I found this all the way over in Soho."

Lee Ho Fook's grin showed a gold tooth or two. "The more people 'oo know about us, the more 'oo'll want to eat 'ere."

We got our grub before Mr. Warren, as we should have, standing in front of him in the queue, so to speak. I've had fried prawns at fish and chip places now and then, but Lee Ho Fook's outdid them. The rice fried with pork tasted of the fermented soya beans and had bits of egg and scallion and I don't know what all else in it besides. It was strange, but it was good. And the kung pao chicken? I was enjoying the meat and the cashews and the strange spices of the Orient until I made the dreadful mistake of biting down on one of those peppers.

Spicy, the counterman called them. Good heavens, I thought the top of my head would blow off! My mouth might have been full of the hydrogen flame from the Döbereiner's lamp Professor van Helsing carried. That green tea did go well with the food, but it made a painfully—*le môt juste*—inadequate fire extinguisher.

George started gulping his at almost the same moment I did. Whilst gasping and spluttering and perspiring, I noticed Mr. Warren tucking into his luncheon with chopsticks. He used them as readily as the Chinamen, eating rice and beef and odd vegetables with easy aplomb ... and at least as fast as I could feed myself with my ordinary utensil.

George noticed something I failed to. "That's quite curious," he murmured.

"What is?" I asked. Harris's coughing fit said a kung pao pepper had just introduced itself to him.

"He's got hair on the palms of his hands," said George.

And so he did; his palms were almost as hairy as the backs of his hands, which says a great deal. I must confess, I let out a schoolboy snigger and whispered, "Maybe he practices the solitary vice to excess."

George chortled, to use Mr. Lear's lovely coinage. But Harris's bony visage took on a thoughtful—even a sorrowful—aspect. "That may not be the only thing troubling him," he said, also in a low voice.

"How d'you mean?" asked George. But Harris bit down on another of those infernal peppers just then. Smoke might have spurted from his ears. A tear ran down his cheek, but could not douse the flames in his mouth and gullet. George went without an answer.

Mr. Warren set half a crown on the table and went on his way. As none of the meals in the place went for more than one and six, that left a goodly gratuity for Lee Ho Fook. I must confess that we, while not niggards, showed the counterman less generosity.

"Well," I said as we also made our exit, "what do you think?"

"Not bad for the money, but I could have eaten more," said George. But then George must carry around inside him a steam boiler in place of a proper stomach. By the way he stokes it, he should tip the scales at twenty-five stone, not his actual twelve, yet somehow he doesn't.

"I'm glad I tried it once, but after those dynamite sticks in the chicken I'm not sure I care to go back," said Harris.

"Oh, come on," I said. "You'll be telling stories about those peppers for the next five years." They wouldn't grow milder in the telling, either. Having braved them myself, I was already sifting phrases that might convey at least a trifle of their inflammatory nature.

"Where now?" asked George as we mooched along. The newsboy had a fresh edition of his paper. The headline on this one compared the old woman slain the night before to the Ripper's slightly less recent victims. Headline writers will compare anything to anything else if it makes readers part with pennies. A scribbler myself, I know whereof I speak.

Harris pointed. "That pub serves up a better than decent bitter. And, should we find ourselves peckish later, the steak and kidney pie is first rate." I don't frequent Limehouse; I felt myself slumming when we went there. So far as I can tell you, it's not one of Harris's usual haunts, either. How did he know, then? There is a mystical, even a magnetic, attraction between Harris and pubs: that is as much as I can say.

And the bitter was better than decent, and the steak and kidney pie everything steak and kidney pie should be. Chinese,

Lascars, shaggy-bearded Russians, Armenians in peculiar caps, Scotsmen in different peculiar caps—the whole world stopped at that pub. George and Harris and I stopped there for quite a while.

When we came out, it had got dark. Not many gas lamps in Limehouse, I fear. But the sky had cleared, and the full moon, big and bright as a golden sovereign, shone in our faces. Then again, it had looked much the same the night before, until the clouds masked it and the showers started.

No sooner had I remarked on the similarity than George said, "It's the harvest moon, of course," in tones implying that anyone who didn't jolly well know it was the harvest moon had to be too great a ninny to live. Worse, he went on, "It has to do with the autumnal equinox, you see. The moon's eastward path across the heavens looks more nearly parallel to the horizon than at any other time of the year, so it rises only slightly later night by night. Almost the same phenomenon will occur a month from now—hunter's moon, the countryfolk name that one."

Harris and I gaped at each other, astonishment no doubt writ large across both our faces. George so seldom seems to know anything whatsoever, yet now we heard him discoursing learnedly of astronomy? "How on—or rather, above—earth ...?" said Harris, beating me to the punch.

George coughed a couple of times and made a small production of lighting his pipe. After he'd got it going and tossed the lucifer to die a hissing death in the wet gutter, he answered, "I've made the acquaintance of a clever young lady who works as a computer at the Greenwich Observatory. I've learned a good deal from her."

"So it would seem," I said in portentous tones. "But what has she learned from you? Or is that a question better left unanswered?"

"Better left unasked, I should think," said Harris.

George glared from one of us to the other. He has a temper, George does; the moonlight was plenty to show the flush mounting to his cheeks ... and to show his hands folding into large, knobby fists. Then, with what looked to be a deliberate effort of will, he relaxed them. "I nearly forgot what cuckoos the two of you are," he said, as if he were indeed reminding himself.

I was about to tell him that, however far the line of cuckoos should extend, he would always head it. I was about to tell him any number of witty and insulting things. I had them queued up on the tip of my tongue, ready to salvo one after another.

Then we heard the scream, and every one of them flew straight out of my head.

Anyone who lives in London will hear screams of startlement and rage. Anyone who visits the theatre will have heard screams purporting to be of terror. I have done more than visit the theatre; I have lived there. And I have heard a great many such screams. Never until that evening, though, did the genuine article show how counterfeit they were.

As any proper terrified scream should, it burst from a woman's throat. Queer how the fair sex's fright turns members of the unfair sex to tigers, isn't it? George, Harris, and I dashed towards the horrid noise without a second thought—or, as best I could tell, even a first. Had we thought, we surely would have run away from danger, not into it. Any animal surely would have. Great Scott! Perhaps George is human after all! Perhaps I am, myself.

Running, I wondered whether the soiled doves the Ripper slew screamed like that, and yes, I wondered whether this was another one. (This also made me wonder whether a bad paper's headline writer knew what he was talking about, a flight of improbability I should have been incapable of under smaller stress.)

And I wondered what in blazes we'd do when we got to where the scream came from—this, as we rounded a corner and tore into a dark, smelly alleyway. We still carried our umbrellas: their sails furled, as the night was fine. In my pocket I had a clasp knife with a two-inch blade suitable for despatching almost any infirm cockroach I might come across (oh yes, and with a corkscrew, in case I needed to bleed a wine bottle instead). My friends were similarly armed.

George struck a match. The dim, sputtering light showed—briefly—a huge, dark creature with slavering jaws all full of teeth crouched over a motionless woman. Wolf? Man? Some unhallowed hybrid of the two? Before I could be sure, the blasted lucifer expired.

George's oaths were frightful things. Harris and I were yelling, too, as loudly as we could, as much to keep up our own courage as to intimidate the monster. It gave forth with a hideous snarl, for the moment balked of ripping the lungs from its defenseless victim.

"I'll teach you!" shouted Harris as George lit another lucifer. Its glow let me see Harris rushing at the great hairy thing (no, not George—the lupine one), his bumbershoot thrust out before him like a knight's lance in days of yore. I rushed after him, not that I felt much hope for either one of us.

This match died just as Harris and the creature came together. They both roared at the same time, Harris in something like triumph and the beast-man (to my amazement) in something like anguish.

Then I scratched my own match against the sole of my shoe, which luckily was not too damp to fire it. In the flickering flame, I saw Harris pulling his umbrella from the chest of a naked man—a man whose nakedness, and whose deceased status, made me need a moment to recognize him as the diner who'd chopsticked his way through that plate of beef chow mein at Lee Ho Fook's eatery half a day (or was it half a lifetime?) earlier.

As the match went out, Harris said, "My brolly boasts a silver ferrule. I never looked to use it for a weapon against werewolves, but there you are. And there he is." He sounded almost as excited as he would have after squeezing the last trick from a difficult hand of bid whist.

"What about the lady?" I asked, though even then I suspected I was giving the female in question the benefit of the doubt.

There was a thump and a wriggle in the darkness as the woman pushed the werewolf's corpse—now in human form once more—off herself and scrambled to her feet. She gave forth with a passionate, consonant-clogged paragraph: Russian or Polish or some such tongue. When we could not answer in a language she understood, she darted out of the alley past us and disappeared into the night.

This time, Harris lit a lucifer. Staring down at the body, he murmured, "What on earth do we do now?"

"We take a powder, same as the gal did," answered George without a moment's hesitation. "Bobbies and law judges, all they'll see is a dead man. They'll clap us in straitjackets if we start babbling of werewolves. My own solicitor would have me committed if he heard me going on that way."

He hadn't finished before we were all hurrying to the alley's outlet. A plump man saw us in the moonlight and asked, "Did you hear a screech, like?"

"Not us," we chorused together, and decamped before he could decide to disbelieve us. Looking back over my shoulder, I saw him take one step towards the alleymouth and then visibly think better of venturing in by his lonesome.

Three days later, I discovered a small item on an inside page of the *Times*. Warren Z. Wolfe, aged thirty-one, was founded stabbed to death in a Limehouse alley, it read. Robbery is suspected, as he was despoiled of his valuables down to the skin. The decedent was identified by a cook. He has no known kinfolk.

I didn't mention the squib to my friends when next we fore-gathered. While neither George nor Harris mentioned it, something in their eye told me they'd seen it.

Harris raised his glass of cheer on high. "Here's to Three Men well out of the supernatural!" he said.

"Amen!" said George and I together, and the three of us drank the toast.

# DEATH STALKS CLOSER

*By Kirsten Weiss*

*From the Journal of P. LaPorte*
*October, 1849*
*New York City*
*The Medium*

The vision rushed toward me, and my hands trembled on the dressing table.

I saw a tall, stork-like man with an uneven face and a broad smile. Leaning on his walking stick, he was unaware of the man in black striding up behind him. Unaware of the gleaming revolver drawn from his murderer's waistcoat. Unaware, until he heard the click of a hammer being drawn back. And then he turned, too late.

Hot pain pierced my side, and I gasped. I pressed my hand to the whalebone ribs of my corset and closed my eyes, waited for the vision to subside. I can't control when the visions come. But they come for a reason, and I'm duty-bound to honor them.

I'd never stopped them from coming true, though.

The pain stopped, and I opened my eyes. In the mirror, my smooth brown skin had gone a trifle sickly. I rose from my dressing table and staggered to the wardrobe. I let my silk dressing gown slip to the rough, wood floor. Hastily, because the room was cold enough to see my own breath, I dressed in a plain ginger skirt and bodice. In the room next door, a child wailed. His mother shouted a rebuke.

I've heard tell we live in a clockwork universe. I can't say if there's a guiding hand behind it all. But I do know the only accidents in life are those moments we don't pay attention to, those instants when the gears click into place and we turn away.

So I paid attention.

I'd rescued the future murder victim, Mr. Crane, only weeks before from an unpleasant situation. The native folk believe that if you save someone's life, you're responsible for them for the remainder of yours. That never seemed quite fair to me. If you save someone's life, shouldn't they be grateful? Shouldn't they feel compelled to make sure you stay safe? Nonetheless, an unpleasant sense of obligation hung over me like a sticky miasma.

The man could have exposed my innocent trick. He'd every right to. If he had, my mama and I would have lost everything. But something had stayed him, chivalry maybe.

I smoothed my collar. Well, he hadn't exposed me. I had to try and help the man. I might not be able to stop the vision—*could I this time? Was it possible?*—but at least I had to bear witness. Still, futile hope spun inside me. Perhaps I could staunch his wound and keep him alive? But no, that had been a killing shot.

Grabbing my sturdy parasol, I hurried onto the roof where my mama hung laundry.

"I'm going out, Mama," I said. The pungent scent of boiling cabbage drifted from one of the neighboring apartments.

"You'll do as you please, like always," she said in her soft, slow voice and clipped a petticoat to the line.

I smiled. I knew my mama was proud of me. She was less proud of the tricks I sometimes had to play when the visions didn't come, but she was proud I'd bought her freedom and my own.

The *peculiar*—vile, disgusting, horrible—institution of slavery was even more peculiar in the City of Washington, where men could hire out their slaves and take a cut of their earnings without having to feed or board us. The man who'd bought me had figured I'd hire myself out as a washerwoman, like my mama. I'd had other ideas, and once I'd bought our freedom, we'd left the cruel South behind.

I squared my shoulders and let a stern expression settle across my face, then strode down the stairs and onto the dirt road.

Laughing Germans tumbled out of the beer hall next door. No one bothered me. The Germans weren't as superstitious as the Irish, but it was no accident my neighbors had more than their share of hex signs above their doors. Still, I gripped my heavy parasol and hoped I wouldn't need to wield it.

I walked down the narrow lane and turned the corner. The sky was iron gray, hinting of snow, and for once I was glad for the thick, woolen stockings beneath my ginger skirts.

The vision had shown me the brownstone where Mr. Crane and I had first met. But my visions, when they came, were oblique. The brownstone could have been a reminder of *who* the doomed man was rather than hinting *where* the murder was to happen. And the visions never told me *when* things were coming. It was like looking down through a glass of murky water. I couldn't gauge quite where the bottom was. But the vision was all I had, so I walked to the brownstone and prayed I was not too late.

A man shouted something crude, and my shoulders twitched beneath my fringed shawl. I lengthened my strides, my skirts brushing my ankles.

The city changed, tenements giving way to more gracious buildings, until I reached the Manhattan park across from the brownstone where I'd rescued Mr. Crane. The buckeye trees had turned the color of sunset, a welcome splash of color against the dreary brownstones.

My heart gave a jump. Mr. Crane sat smoking a cigarillo on a bench at the far end of the park, his long arms spread across its back. He was here, and fear dried my mouth. If Mr. Crane was here, the shooting would happen soon. But maybe, just maybe, this time ...

I crushed my optimism. I'd never stopped a vision from happening. Never.

Dodging a rattling carriage, I hurried across the road and into the park. "Mr. Crane!"

He turned his head, and his eyes widened with surprise. The gentleman rose and swept his stovepipe hat from his head, bowing and smiling. "Miss LaPorte. This is indeed an honor."

Tall and angular, the man was ugly as a Sunday sin. His brown-checked trousers and ill-fitting frock coat did not improve the portrait. But there was something in his nature that could not keep me from smiling in return. Besides, I owed him a debt of sorts.

"Mr. Crane, I have had a vision—"

"Oh?" Disbelief scrawled across his face. "A vision, is it?"

Cold dread formed in the pit of my stomach. "Yes, sir, of a man in black with a revolver. He intends to kill you, here, in front of this house."

His brows rose. "Does he, now?"

"Sir, this could happen at any moment." My gaze darted about the street. Three men in black strolled in our general direction beneath the buckeye trees.

"Forgive me if I am less than credulous about your vision. I have the greatest esteem for you—"

I began to argue, but he raised his hand. "No, let me finish. I do respect you. You are, as they say, some pumpkins. You're smart and you're resourceful, and if you play with the truth now and again, well, what of it? I don't think you harm anyone. You might even help people, putting their minds at ease."

My hands clenched in their calfskin gloves. "But Mr. Crane—"

"And that device—"

"Which you confiscated," I said tartly, then shook myself. That was not why I was here. "Never mind that. We have to leave this park at once."

He leaned on his walking stick. "Why do you really want me gone? Are you planning another table turning at that Queen Anne? I thought we'd agreed you'd leave that one alone."

My heart galloped like a runaway mule. Why would the man not listen? "Mr. Crane, I assure you, I would not be here if it were not urgent."

He laughed. "Oh, I'll bet it's urgent."

"My vision—"

"We both know how your visions work." He grinned. "You're a humbug. An elegant and ingenious humbug, but a humbug nonetheless. Now what is it you're really after?"

The men were getting closer and we were running out of time. And the good Lord forgive me, but it flashed into my head what might happen if I, a colored woman, were found in the company of a murdered white man.

Anger stormed through me. He didn't know what I was risking. And yet I couldn't force myself to leave. "Mr. Crane, we have to go. *Now.*"

He tucked his walking stick beneath one arm. "There are still some things I don't understand about that séance of yours. Now, I understand how you created that ghostly wind and made the instruments play, but how did you know that Mrs. Smythe had lost a brother named Benny?"

Two of the men in black crossed the street and strode directly toward us. A trap rattled past.

My jaw clenched. "It doesn't matter!" He considered himself a man of science. If he would not trust me, perhaps he'd believe his own reasoning. "Who wishes you dead? You must have some inkling you are in danger."

"I reckon there's plenty who'd like to stick me." He quirked a brow. "I hope you are not among that company."

Good lord. Was the man flirting? My gaze darted to the two men in black. I'd known all along I would fail, and yet I could not cease trying. "And are any who might wish you ill on this street, now?"

"You know, I did my own search for Mrs. Smythe's brother and couldn't find a single reference to the boy. How'd you figure out a brother even existed?"

"How can a man of such obvious intelligence be so dense?" I snapped.

"Obvious intelligence?"

"The good Lord must have given you some intellect to compensate for your visage."

He barked a laugh.

I tugged at his arm, but he was unmovable. "Now let's go!"

But it was too late, as it was ever too late. One of the approaching men, tall and cadaverous, drew back his frock coat, exposing the handle of a weapon holstered in his belt.

Mr. Crane shoved me roughly behind him.

A gunshot cracked the crisp, autumnal air.

Mr. Crane grunted and fell atop me. His elbow rammed into my side. The hot pain made me gasp. And then the pressure lifted, Mr. Crane rolling off me.

I scrambled to my knees and gazed at him in horror.

Mr. Crane stared sightlessly at the sky, a red stain spreading across his fawn waistcoat. Men shouted.

"Mr. Crane? Mr. Crane!" It was too late. I knew it was too late. But I pressed my hand to the wound like my mama had taught me and felt …

I cocked my head, confused. I felt …

Fury spooled through me. The vision had been real, but it had only brought me here to play witness. Why? What was the point?

I could hear the men coming closer, their footsteps heavy. But I couldn't tear my gaze from my hands, covered in blood—it was real blood and warm. My hands pressed against his waistcoat and beneath that what could only be a device that had …

Mr. Crane winked, and resumed staring blankly upward.

… stopped a bullet.

# ALL WARFARE IS BASED UPON DECEPTION

*By David L. Drake & Katherine L. Morse*

Erasmus felt another bead of sweat run down his neck and further dampen his perspiration-soaked collar. He shook his head to flick off the bead forming on the end of his nose. The silence was killing him more than the stifling heat of the small, enclosed room or the pain in his wrists from his restraints. He took a minute to watch the play of shadows on the wall coming from the single candle flame that was stationed near the half-height door. He decided that he should work with his beloved rather than let her stew.

"Do you want to talk about it?" he asked Sparky.

"Which 'it' did you mean?" she snarled. "Being shackled together in this fetid, airless toilet of a root cellar? My claustrophobic reaction to being in a room in which I cannot stand up? How about your inability to enquire about a potential suspect's activities without getting us … what's the best term … *taken prisoner?*"

"No, I meant that you insisted that we sail all the way to Brazil to ascertain whether there is a real threat to the British Empire by a mad person in Lincolnshire. I think it was …"

"What!?" she spat out. "This was all your idea! Queen and country and all that rot. You really know how to show a girl a good time." She rolled her eyes, but since she was sitting back-to-back with Erasmus, the gesture went unseen.

"If I may get the whole sentence stated, I think it was incredible that there was something to this story. I got a glimpse of the laboratory next door when they marched us in here. I recognized the containers of wet cells for electrical storage, but I can make neither heads nor tails of the ceramic pylons with wire wrapped around them. And what is the purpose of the small room with the door that looks like a ship's hatch? I do believe I glimpsed someone, or at least their shadow, inside that little room!"

Sparky wrestled against her restraints for a second. "Okay, you've distracted me from our horrid circumstances for the moment. What do we know? Thomasin Trent spoke of the future and time travel. All the hints that we found led us here to São Paulo, Brazil, to another sanatorium, where we found two patients who spoke of traveling through time, wearing clothing styles that are oddly out of step with current fashion, both of whom were reportedly entirely sane mere days before they were committed. And then your clumsy enquiries got us dragged to this barn-lab-thingy building on the outskirts of São Paulo. Ironically, you may have gotten us to the location where the scientists are performing these temporal experiments."

"You could not possibly think there is actual time travel involved? We discussed all the impossibilities on the way here. There is a host of complications, not the least of which is that the earth spins and orbits the sun. To travel in time and stay on our planet, one would also have to travel to a pinpoint location, which is currently out into the ether! That capability to just jump from place to place would be highly valuable, and would have been developed and sold long before the invention of time travel."

Sparky couldn't sit still. She wiggled in her chair and even tried to stand up, immediately reaching the end of the chain that tethered her to her seat. She cursed under her breath, sitting back down with a grumpy sigh. "You're just goading me into conversation. As your monarch would say, I am *not* amused." She shook her chains and continued. "In your police work, you must have been introduced to William of Ockham's philosophy of efficient reasoning."

"Yes, I am familiar with it, and have used it for simplifying the deductive process. It states that when given a choice, the simpler explanation is the better one. It eliminates complex conspiracies as the reason for why things happen, and usually replaces it with gross stupidity or bumbling luck."

"Well, when I was taught it, it was for diagnosing medical issues. It leads the physician to treat the most obvious cause first, before considering much more complex maladies. And it applies to science just as well. We should find the easiest explanation for what we've observed."

Erasmus tried to relax his shoulders and arms, hoping to reduce the effect of the manacles cutting into his wrists. "Using efficient reasoning, we can deduce that there must not be time travel, or we would have seen many people popping into existence. Since we have not, then at no time was time travel invented. Or no one considers our present day interesting enough to visit. There must be more interesting times ahead of us."

"Ha, ha," Sparky dryly retorted. "How could our current period of exponential scientific growth not be interesting to a scientist who was intelligent and curious enough to invent time travel? Maybe physics only allows time travelers to go forward, into the future. Well, I guess we're all going forward into the future, but boringly enough, at the rate of one minute per minute. A real time traveler would go faster or slower. Hmm, I just realized that wouldn't be enough. The traveler would not only need to perceive the time rate change, but they'd also need to not age as quickly. Otherwise, you could describe the effects of opium smoking as a form of time travel. Time just passes by without notice."

Erasmus allowed himself to get lost in the thought. "Well, that is all very possible, but it is not the case we are investigating. The real challenge is traveling back in time with knowledge of the future, being able to discover what happened in the past, and using that knowledge to their advantage. If the traveler went back and lost all their memories, then they are not much use to whoever is funding the venture."

Sparky stopped struggling for a second. "That's true, unless the traveler kept a written ..."

A loud ZAP-BANG erupted from the direction of the laboratory; both Sparky and Erasmus went limp in their chairs.

ᘓᘖ

Sparky groggily came to first. She noticed that the candle had burned down a half hour's worth. "Drake! Wake up!" She shook their chains.

Erasmus lifted his head and groaned. He let his tongue wet his mouth and lips, making sloppy moist noises, and finally he uttered, "What was that ...?"

"It came from the laboratory! Whatever they're doing, it knocked us unconscious through the wall! I don't even know what could do that from such a distance."

The door slammed open and a stupefied man in a laboratory coat staggered into the room. He mumbled something in Portuguese and started to unlock Erasmus's shackles. Halfway through the endeavor, he stumbled backward and fell down in a heap.

Erasmus watched his unmoving body for a few seconds before he felt around with his fingers. "He left the screw key in the lock! Give me a second to unlock this hand ... there we go!" With his left hand freed, he leapt up and released one of Sparky's hands. "Did you understand anything he said?"

After releasing his right hand, he handed the key to Sparky to release herself completely. She replied, "It may have been, 'you are next,' but that's just an educated guess."

Holding his shackles in his hands to aid in defending himself, Erasmus nudged the unconscious scientist with his foot. The man did not respond to the prodding.

Erasmus looked to the door. "Let us get out of here," he offered in a low tone.

They gingerly stepped through the door and proceeded carefully and quietly down the hallway, watching the doorway of the laboratory closely for others who might come out. Erasmus took the lead as they approached the door. He held the shackles in his hands as he had done before. He looked quickly around the jamb of the open door and surveyed the lab again. The hatch to the small chamber was open; its interior was empty. The three men in the room, all wearing laboratory coats, were still woozy from the event half an hour ago that had rendered Drake and McTrowell unconscious. One had his head down on his worktable; another was sitting on the floor; the last was wearily twisting some control knobs on an apparatus. Erasmus signaled Sparky to look in, but immediately followed with a *stay close to me* wave as he proceeded down the hall. Sparky snuck a peek into the lab and followed the Chief Inspector.

As they exited the building, the red of the evening sun filled the sky. Erasmus and Sparky tried to get their bearings as they looked around the exterior of the building. Another building was nearby, and the white puffs of smoke rising from it hinted that it might be the building that generated the power for the laboratory. Erasmus whispered, "There may be others in that building. Caution is warranted."

The two of them hugged the building to see what else they could determine without raising notice. Having assumed their relative safety, Sparky spoke up. "Doesn't that laboratory indicate that they may have had some success? That chamber was empty! Outside of stupefied lab-coat-wearing scramble-brains, we may be the first to witness this modern miracle!"

Erasmus shook his head. "Do not forget that there is the darker side of William of Ockham's philosophy, the one used by illusionists and swindlers. They fool you with your own efficient judgment. If the easiest explanation is that someone can really perform magic or communicate with the dead, then that is what you believe. It may be possible that what we just witnessed was an incredible ruse to make us return to Her Majesty with stories of time travel and future battles! And that the Empire should invest in obtaining this technology. Do you really think they did not set up our escape just now?"

"But we were knocked unconscious from a distance! And those scientists looked like they had been through multiple exposures to that ... I'll call it a blast, for lack of a better term. They were exposing their minds to something that may have inched them closer to insanity. I know I'm as guilty as any scientist of experimenting on myself," Sparky continued, "but this is going too far!"

"Do you think they send almost insane people through their machine? That would explain why they come out thoroughly deranged," Drake posited.

"Or the temporal trip itself makes them insane. Or they use insane people as test pilots until they think it works properly. Or they have one machine for sending and another for receiving, and the receiving one is in Lincolnshire! I don't know; there are so many possibilities!"

"Or all of these explanations are too wild to believe, and this was all a sham to fool us. All of those folks in the White Hart may have been in on the deception."

"Now who's buying into the complex conspiracy, Chief Inspector? Of the two of us, I thought you were the logical one."

The engine in the far building roared up to a full head of steam, which billowed out of the smokestack. Sparky and Erasmus took a few cautious steps forward to get a better look at the building and noticed an arc of miniature lightning erupting from the spire at the top of the laboratory building behind them. The blue-white dancing chain of electrical power, hissing and crackling at every gyration, discharged over twenty feet into the air.

Sparky wondered out loud, "Do you think they're sending another person out?"

A large, bull-nosed guard dog rounded the building, hell bent on protecting the grounds, its metal chain clanking behind it. The animal had the look of madness in its eyes, probably from the same exposure to the experiments. Without hesitation, Sparky and Erasmus sprinted away from the beast, straight toward the engine building. When the dog's chain pulled taut, the cur yelped with pain at hitting the leash's end. The runners turned just in time to see the electrical discharge leap from the spire to the dog's chain and out to the engine building with a bright flash, explosively incinerating both buildings and the cur.

"Well, that's the end of that," Sparky observed with relief.

Drake stared into the conflagration, mesmerized. "Perhaps not."

"What?!"

"So long as I am playing the role of the conspiracy theorist," Drake postulated, "it is possible that this explosion was also a piece of fiery, but convincing, theater. Perhaps we are intended to think the scientists and their invention are destroyed so we will stop investigating. I think it is time for us to return to the sanatorium."

CR&O

"*Bem vinda* ... oh, it is the two of you again," said the receptionist dryly. "Do you want to talk to our patients again? I must say that you upset the two you talked to earlier today."

Sparky felt that as a doctor, she should take the lead. "Madam, we are not here to disquiet this institution's ... charges. We are on a mission from Her Maj ..."

Drake jumped in, not wanting to tip their hand too much. "We are on an enquiry that only these two patients can resolve. We will only be a few moments. And I must say that your English is exemplary." Erasmus smiled pleasantly.

"¡Obrigado! Thank you! We have patients from many places. I talk to them as best as I can, and I pick up pieces of this and that. Let me bring Josephine and Simone out to you." The receptionist curtsied before leaving the front desk.

Sparky scrutinized Erasmus. "What?" he asked in surprise.

"Did you ... give her a *look*? She went from prickly to amiable in a very short time."

Erasmus smiled. "I have no idea what you are talking about. I felt complementing her on her English would put her in a better mood."

Sparky weighed his simple explanation for a few seconds. "I think I'm beginning to understand how you do your police work. Just save some of those compliments for your fiancée."

Erasmus took his beloved's hand and kissed it. "My heart is all yours."

The receptionist returned and reintroduced the patients to the two adventurers. They settled into private conversation on the porch overlooking a well-trimmed garden.

"Have you had discussions with the scientists that work nearby?"

Josephine and Simone glanced at each other before answering. Josephine replied, "We really should not say anything, but we have had conversations with them. They promised us an overseas trip."

Erasmus nodded. "Why should you not discuss this?"

"We'll get in trouble with the doctors here. We're not supposed to leave."

Simone chimed in, "Yeah, we're not supposed to leave." She looked around to make sure no one heard her.

Erasmus asked, "Have they given you a trip before? From their laboratory?"

Josephine said "Yes!" at the same time Simone said "No!" They looked immediately at each other as if they didn't have their story straight.

Simone rubbed the side of her head, messing up her long black hair. "It's so hard to remember. We went to the lab; I fell asleep. I dreamed we visited a far-off place."

Josephine looked at her. "That's not right. I wasn't with you. I was with … what was his name … Thomas! That's his name. I was traveling with Thomas."

Sparky wanted to cut through the fog. "What country are you in?"

Josephine said, "Brazil." Simone looked at her, dumbfounded. "How do you not know this is England?"

The women started to say nasty things about each other, some in English, but mainly in Portuguese. Nearby nurses came over to quiet them and asked Sparky and Erasmus to leave.

The couple stood, recognizing that they weren't going to make any further progress with the discussion. Sparky rolled her eyes and had started to leave when Simone grabbed Erasmus by the sleeve, leaned close, and whispered, *"Toda guerra é baseada na decepção."*

After thanking the receptionist, Drake and McTrowell left the sanatorium and headed in the direction of the shipyards. Erasmus asked Sparky, "Did you catch what she said, right near the end of the conversation?"

"Yes, I did. 'All warfare is based upon deception.' What warfare could she mean?"

"A time war?"

"If you had time travel, why would you need deception?"

"Perhaps to keep others from realizing that you had time travel and trying to steal or replicate the technology," Erasmus posited. "They could be faking their insanity to fool us into believing that time travel is not viable because of its terrible consequences. They may have actually made time voyages."

"They could be the real scientists pretending insanity to convince us of that. Or it could be a war *of* deception. I'm back to considering the possibility that this whole thing was a charade to convince us that time travel is possible to get Her Majesty to … do … something. I don't know. My head feels like it's going to explode like that laboratory. You know, I only have one more thing to say."

Erasmus smiled. "No need to tell me! You do not ever want to speak of this again!"

They both laughed, hugged, kissed, and walked hand in hand towards the ship that would take them home.

# THE WHEEL OF MISFORTUNE

## Part II

### *By Lillian Csernica*

Dr. William Harrington sat at his desk, in his study, feeling like an utter fool.

The housemaid Akiko stood before him, tidy and correct in her brown calico work dress, white bib apron, and little white cap. Madelaine stood beside her, holding the small journal where she kept her notes on the Japanese language. That, her single braid, and her blue wool dress made her look like a small schoolteacher.

"Akiko-*san* is very grateful for your offer, Papa," Madelaine said. "She doesn't understand why you would want to help her family. You're here to take care of the Abbot."

"I see him once a week, more often if I believe there's reason to do so. That leaves me a considerable amount of time to see other patients."

"Yes, Papa."

"Did you make it clear to Akiko I won't charge for my services? That I am happy to do whatever I can for her family?"

"Oh yes, Papa." Madelaine frowned, turning pages in her journal. "At least I think I made that clear. The verb forms are rather complicated."

"Very well. Tell Akiko she can go."

Madelaine spoke a few words of Japanese to Akiko. With visible relief, Akiko bowed to Harrington and fled back to the kitchen.

"Perhaps we'll have more success with the head gardener." Harrington didn't believe that, but he had to keep trying. "Madelaine dear, would you go and find Mr. Tanaka?"

A few minutes later a soft tap at the French doors announced Mr. Tanaka's arrival. Harrington rose to open the doors. Mr. Tanaka stood there, hat in hand, his overalls grubby with dirt and grass stains. Madelaine stood beside him.

"*Konnichiwa*, Tanaka-*san*," Harrington said.

Tanaka bowed. "*Konnichiwa*, Harrington-*sensei*."

"Papa," Madelaine said. "Mr. Tanaka says he's sorry, but he should stay outside. He has dirt on his clothes."

"Please thank him for his consideration, then ask him if I can be of any assistance to his family."

"Yes, Papa." Madelaine spoke to Tanaka, now and then referring to her book.

Tanaka looked at Harrington in some confusion. "*Arigato gozaimasu*, Harrington-*sensei*. *Domo arigato gozaimasu*." He bowed, backing away from the door.

"Mr. Tanaka is very grateful, Papa, but it's most likely going to be the same with all the Japanese on staff."

Harrington beckoned Madelaine into his study. He closed the French doors, took his seat behind his desk, and let his head fall into his hands.

It had seemed like such a good idea. The Abbot had told Harrington he must care for the "forgotten people." In a British household, apart from giving the daily orders, one affected not to notice the household staff. Rarely, if ever, did one have cause to inquire after their families. The death of a parent or the birth of a close relative might merit a day off, but other than that, such people did not exist in the regular interaction of master and servant.

"Papa? May I make a suggestion?"

"I wish you would, Maddy. All I want to do is help them."

"I know, Papa. Perhaps I should explain why the Japanese people don't understand your offer."

"You know?" The Japanese servants adored Madelaine. Thanks to that, she'd picked up quite a lot of the language and no small amount of cultural understanding. "Tell me, darling."

"Here in Japan, who you are is defined by who is above you in rank and who is below you." Madelaine laid her hand on his arm. "Here in Japan you are the Abbot's personal physician. That is your position in this society."

"That doesn't mean I'm not allowed to treat anyone else."

"You have that freedom, Papa. The Japanese people do not."

"Why not?"

"People like Akiko wouldn't dare take a moment of your time away from the Abbot." Madelaine's sweet features took on an adult gravity. "You see, Papa, that would be like disobeying the Emperor himself."

Of course. Harrington kissed Madelaine's forehead. "You are my little genius, darling. I rather wish you could go into diplomatic service. You'd be brilliant at it."

Madelaine smiled. "Thank you, Papa."

Mrs. Rogers, the housekeeper, appeared in the doorway. "Pardon me, Doctor. Miss Malloy is here."

"Thank you, Mrs. Rogers. Please show her in."

Julie Rose Malloy stepped into the study. The daughter of Augustus Malloy, Miss Malloy had large dark eyes and sweet smile suited her demure, generous nature. Harrington was pleased to see Miss Malloy, dressed in purple silk trimmed with black lace with a modest bustle, a charming bonnet with lavender ribbons, and a parasol in hand. The picture of propriety, she was a wonderful "big sister" for Madelaine.

"Good morning, Dr. Harrington."

"Good morning, Miss Malloy. Where are you ladies off to today?"

Madelaine hurried over to Miss Malloy and clasped her hand. "Mama says we shall go walking in the park to see the cherry blossoms. I asked Mama if we might have tea at the tea house near Nijo Castle."

"An excellent choice, my dear. Do enjoy yourselves."

Harrington turned his attention back to the task at hand. Who were the people the Abbot wanted him to treat? If such people were too humble to come forward and make their ailments known, how was he to seek them out? Twice now the horrible flaming wheel monster had attempted to run him down. The third time might well be the charm, deadly and final. For the sakes of both Constance and Madelaine, Harrington had to find these forgotten people. He picked up the brass bell on his desk and rang it twice.

Mrs. Rogers appeared in the doorway. "Yes, Doctor?"

"Please send a message to Mr. Fujita. Ask him to meet me at Kiyomizudera in one hour. The matter is urgent."

CRSO

Harrington knelt on his cushion before the Abbot with Fujita at his side.

"I thought I could find these 'forgotten people' on my own," Harrington began. "I started with my household staff. I offered to treat them and their families."

"Where did you go when you made this offer?"

"Go? I couldn't go anywhere. None of them were willing to let me treat them."

"Then how did you present your offer to them?"

"I was in my study, at home. Madelaine helped me. Her ability to speak Japanese is a godsend."

Fujita translated. The Abbot replied.

"The Abbot does not understand why you began looking for the forgotten people under your own roof."

"We have a saying, 'Charity begins at home.' It seemed logical to me to start with my Japanese servants."

Fujita relayed that to the Abbot. They spoke back and forth several times.

"This saying is a western saying, Harrington-*sensei*. You cannot hope to find the forgotten ones by searching for them as if you were still in Great Britain."

"Then please, show me where these people are."

Fujita spoke to the Abbot, who studied Harrington. At last, he spoke.

"Harrington-*sensei*," Fujita said. "You hope to right a wrong committed out of arrogance, thoughtlessness, selfishness, and negligence. The Abbot wishes to know what you believe will remedy these four causes of your wrongdoing?"

Frustration left Harrington's head aching. What was the key to this riddle? Madelaine understood the nuances of the Japanese culture far better than Harrington himself did. She'd pointed out the need for considering the Japanese people's side of things. How would a Buddhist answer the Abbot's question?

"Humility, mindfulness, selflessness, and diligence."

Fujita translated Harrington's answer. The Abbot spoke.

"The Abbot congratulates you on such an insightful answer. If you will follow me, Harrington-*sensei*, I will take you to your guide."

After the formal farewells, Fujita led Harrington to the enormous red *torii* gate that marked the entrance to Kiyomizudera. A single monk stood there. He was younger than most, perhaps twenty or so. His head was completely shorn of hair. He wore the black *kimono*, white *kimono*, and gold sash of the monks of Kiyomizudera.

"Harrington-*sensei*," Fujita said. "This is Sanada-*san*."

"*Konnichiwa*, Sanada-*san*."

"*Konnichiwa*, Harrington-*sensei*." Sanada bowed.

"Sanada-*san* will see to it everyone knows you act with the Abbot's blessing and you are under the protection of Kannon herself."

"What exactly is the Abbot sending me into, Fujita-*san*?"

Fujita stepped back and bowed. "I wish you success in your efforts, Harrington-*sensei*."

"But—surely you're coming with me?"

"My instructions from the Abbot are very clear, Harrington-*sensei*."

"Fujita-*san*, how am I to follow the Abbot's instructions without someone to help me speak Japanese? Does Sanada-*san* speak English?"

"Harrington-*sensei*, please bear in mind your answer regarding the remedy for the four causes of your wrongdoing. Those four virtues are essential to your success."

Harrington watched Fujita walk back toward the Abbot's private quarters. He didn't know where he was going, he didn't know if his guide spoke any English, and he had the distinct feeling the whole situation was about to get much worse.

രജ്ഞ

Harrington straightened up, hoping to relieve the ache in his back. He stood in a two-room shack built from pieces of scrap lumber along the banks of the Kamo River. The makeshift infirmary reminded him of battlefield conditions. The stench of the outdoor latrines made him ill. Night had long since fallen. Inside the shack three small lamps burned, adding the reek of fish oil. Six hours' exposure left Harrington's sense of smell deadened to it. Eight people lay on futons under precious few ragged blankets. Pneumonia, pernicious anemia, borderline starvation, bones broken and badly set … at Harrington's request, Sanada had sent runners to Nurse Danforth with a list of necessary supplies. Under no circumstances was she to join him.

Still more people lined up outside the shack. Infections. Skin diseases. Dental problems. At least four women in dire need of proper prenatal care. Harrington mopped at his brow with his stained handkerchief. These *burakumin* were the butchers, the leather workers, the gravediggers, the people who did all the worst and dirtiest jobs. For centuries, such contact with death had left the *burakumin* unclean in the eyes of other Buddhists. The poorest of the poor, cousins in misery to those desperate wretches inhabiting the slums of Bombay and Delhi. Here in Kyoto Harrington never thought to see such squalid lean-tos jammed together with nothing but a stretch of mud separating the two sides of what only just qualified as a street.

"Harrington-*sensei*." A woman approached him, bowing so low he could only see the top of her head. In her hands, she held a chipped mug of inferior ceramic filled with some dark liquid that sent up wisps of steam. "*Dozo.*"

Tea. Knowing the water had indeed been boiled, Harrington accepted the cup. "*Arigato gozaimasu.*"

"*Do itashimashite*, Harrington-*sensei*."

The tea was hot and strong, bringing warmth and renewed strength to Harrington's weary body. Sanada stepped in through the thin cotton hanging that covered the doorway. In his arms, he carried more boxes of bandages.

"*Arigato*, Sanada-*san*." Harrington's command of Japanese had improved considerably in the past few hours. "*Ju? Ni ju?*" Were there ten, or perhaps twenty, more patients waiting outside?

Sanada set the boxes of bandages aside, then held both hands up, crossed at the wrists. Harrington recognized the Japanese sign for "no more" or "finished."

"Really?" Harrington stuck his head out through the doorway. In the flickering light of more oil lamps and one fire burning in a rusty metal drum, the long line of people stood or sat, waiting.

"Harrington-*sensei*." Sanada beckoned to Harrington, then gestured out through the doorway.

"It's time for me to go home?" Harrington struggled to come up with the right word. "*Uchi?* Home?"

"*Hai.*" Sanada picked up Harrington's coat and held it out for him. Harrington rolled down his sleeves, buttoned his cuffs, and settled the coat across his shoulders.

"*Wanyudo?*" he murmured.

Sanada slipped his hand under the golden sash tied across his torso. He pulled out a long, rectangular strip of parchment covered in brush strokes of black ink. "*Ofuda.*"

Harrington knew that phrase. The Abbot had written down a *sutra* that would protect them against the *wanyudo*. Harrington picked up the bundle of fresh clothing that sat waiting for him in one corner. As he stepped out through the doorway, all of the people in line or waiting nearby bowed. Those who'd been sitting struggled to their feet. Cries of thanks rang out on all sides. Along with his own name, Harrington recognized the name of Kannon, Goddess of Mercy. These poor people must have thought he'd been sent to them straight from the hand of the goddess herself.

"Please, Sanada-*san*," Harrington said. "Tell them I'm coming back. Tomorrow. Er, *ashita? Ashita, hai?*"

"*Hai*, Harrington-*sensei*." Sanada spoke to the people.

More cries of thanks echoed off the broken, piecemeal walls as Sanada led Harrington toward the expatriate section of Kyoto. Harrington's immediate priority was finding a bathhouse where he could give himself a good scrubbing before returning home to his wife and daughter. Tomorrow he would make arrangements to provide the *burakumin* with more regular and long-term medical care. Something had to be done.

CRSO

Harrington arrived home long after Constance and Madelaine had gone to bed. Fortunately, Mrs. Rogers was accustomed to the irregular hours a physician kept. She had a plate of cold meat, bread, and cheese waiting for him. Dressed in her nightgown and shawl, she bustled around the kitchen putting the kettle on for tea.

"Can I get you anything else, Doctor?"

"You're a treasure, Mrs. Rogers." Harrington gave her a weary smile. "You go along to bed now. I can look after myself."

He made a cup of tea, set it on a tray along with the plate of food, and carried it all into his study. As tired as he was, Harrington wasn't sleepy. He wanted to ponder the events of the day while he ate, to sort out the stunning variety of contrasts between the splendor of Kiyomizudera and the ghastly filth where the *burakumin* lived.

A knock at the front door interrupted his thoughts. Much to Harrington's surprise, he opened the door to discover Alexander Thompson, Undersecretary for Technological Exchange, Harrington's de facto supervisor.

"Good heavens, Undersecretary! Do come in."

"Sorry to disturb you at this hour, Doctor." Short, stout, and balding, dressed in drab tweeds: as always, Thompson reminded

Harrington of a banker facing an audit. "You look like you've just come in."

"Indeed I have. It's been a rather long day." Harrington led him to the study. "Let me pour you a brandy."

"Very kind of you. I'm sure we could both use one."

Something in Thompson's tone, a mixture of sympathy and disapproval, raised Harrington's hackles. He handed Thompson his brandy. They touched glasses and drank.

"See here, Doctor. It's quite late, so I'll come straight to the point. I know where you've been and what you've been doing."

"I beg your pardon?"

"It won't do, Doctor. It just won't do." He took a large sip of brandy. "In Bombay and Delhi, the untouchables are a recognized caste. That isn't the case here."

"I'm sorry, Undersecretary. I'm afraid I don't understand."

"The people in that slum are not part of Japanese society. You cannot be seen in such a place."

Harrington was beginning to get the idea, and he didn't like it at all. "Tell me, Undersecretary, how did you come to hear about my visit to the slum?"

"It was hardly a secret, given the way you had those boys racing back and forth with messages and supplies." Thompson huffed. "Really, Doctor. I would expect more discretion from a man in your position."

"Perhaps it would help matters if you knew I went to the slum under the direction of the Abbot of Kiyomizudera. I'm sure your source must have told you a monk accompanied me?"

"Making the situation doubly dangerous!" Thompson thumped one fist on the arm of his chair. "Who knows what diseases run rampant there? Good God, man! What on earth were you thinking?"

Real anger flared up, threatening Harrington's composure.

"Those people are human beings, burdened with the most loathsome tasks. They've lost fingers due to accidents butchering meat. Cuts and scratches that would be minor to us result in immediate infection due to the filth they clean up and carry away."

"Yes, yes," Thompson said. "Your outrage does you credit, Doctor. You must understand that while such people need assistance, you are not the one to provide it."

"Then I will see to the organization of a field hospital. Medical supplies. Proper staff. At the very least, a trained nurse who can teach the mothers what they must do to have healthy, strong children."

"William, please. At this point we enter into the realm of diplomacy." Thompson drained his brandy. "I can pass your ideas along to the appropriate department, but I cannot allow you to have any further contact with those people."

Harrington's patience snapped. "Let me guess. Someone in the Japanese government has made it clear nobody wants more of 'those people'? That they should be left to suffer and starve, just as they are?"

"Think of your wife and daughter. You've shown great loyalty to the Crown, moving your entire household all this way. When your time here is done, you will return to England with your future success assured."

"All I have to do is turn my back on the Hippocratic oath."

"Doctor Harrington." Thompson stood up. "If you cannot conduct yourself in a manner which puts the health and safety of your patient ahead of all else, then I'm sure there are many other physicians in England who will be only too happy to take your place."

Harrington found that highly unlikely. Even so, he could not risk returning to England under a cloud of disfavor. That would cripple his practice and ruin Madelaine's chances of making a good marriage.

Now Harrington knew why the Abbot had called those poor creatures in that slum the "forgotten people."

"Yes, Undersecretary." Harrington bowed his head, hating himself and the society that had brought him to this moment. "I'm sure there is much in what you say."

Thompson reached across the desk to lay a consoling hand on Harrington's shoulder. "You're a good man, William. That is beyond question."

Harrington saw Thompson to the door, then stood there staring out into the midnight darkness. He faced an impossible choice. To help the *burakumin* meant risking social and professional ruin. If he turned his back on those people, knowing what he now knew, he couldn't live with himself. The wrath of the Wheel Monk might almost come as a relief.

CR&O

Harrington settled his head more comfortably on his pillow. His bed was soft and warm and absolute paradise after all the trials of the day. The pleasure of sleeping late was a rare treat for a physician. He planned to enjoy every minute of it.

What seemed like only moments later, a fist hammered at the front door. Harrington stirred, raising his head and looking around through bleary eyes. He dismissed the sound as a dream and settled down again. Another round of hammering brought Mrs. Rogers out of her room. The front door opened. A woman's voice spoke in frantic Japanese.

"I'm sorry!" Mrs. Rogers said. "I don't know what you're saying!"

The pleading note in the Japanese woman's voice made Harrington throw back the bedclothes.

"You'll have to come back tomorrow," Mrs. Rogers said.

"Mrs. Rogers! I say!" Harrington seized his dressing gown and strode through the house while he tied the sash. "Let that woman in."

"Doctor, I really don't think that's wise. No better than a beggar, covered in soot and ash—"

"Bring her in. Feed her, if she'll eat."

Harrington eased open the door to Madelaine's room. As he'd expected, she was sitting up in bed.

"Papa? Does someone need help?"

"Yes, darling. Come and help me talk to a Japanese woman."

Harrington found Mrs. Rogers in the kitchen. A thin Japanese woman sat hunched at the kitchen table, every bit as grimy and ragged as Mrs. Rogers had said. A plate of tea biscuits sat before her. She took a handful and tucked them away in her sleeve, then stuffed two into her mouth.

Madelaine stepped forward. "*Watashi no namae ga* Madelaine *desu.*" She gestured toward Harrington. "*Otoo-san.* My father."

"Harrington-*sensei!*" The woman slid off her chair, landing on her knees and bowing down until her forehead touched the tiled floor. "*Tasukete, kudasai!*"

That much Harrington understood. The woman was begging for help. She said more, too quickly for him to keep up.

"Papa, this lady is talking about her mother. I'm not quite sure why she needs you, but it must be serious."

Harrington stared down at the back of the woman's head. Her thin shoulders shook with sobs. Had someone wept like this for Mrs. Carmody when she died because the doctor hadn't bothered to come when he was called?

"Maddy, ask the lady how she found me."

Madelaine spoke to the woman, who replied.

"Sato Mariko is her name, Papa. She said something about her son and Nurse Danforth."

The son must have been one of Sanada's runners. For this woman to come alone, through the midnight streets of Kyoto, all the way to the expatriate section of the city was an act of supreme courage.

"Maddy, get her to eat something more substantial. Mrs. Rogers, call for the carriage. I shall dress and get my bag."

When Harrington turned to leave, Mariko let out a desperate wail. Madelaine soothed her, guiding her back into her seat. In the master bedroom, Constance was just pulling on her own dressing gown.

"William? What is it? Is someone in the neighborhood ill?"

"She comes from a bit farther than that, but yes." Harrington gathered up the clothes he'd worn home from the bath house and stepped behind the painted screen to dress. "I must go out, my dear. I don't know how long I'll be."

"William, are you sure this is wise?"

"Why wouldn't it be, my dear? I am a physician."

"I—I overheard Mr. Thompson. Please, think about what you're doing."

"I am doing my duty."

"Surely there must be some other type of medical help for those people? A midwife, perhaps?"

"These people have nothing." Harrington fastened his waistcoat, pulled on his jacket, and sat down on the bed to button his shoes. "No food, no heat, and no regard at all from their fellow countrymen."

"If Mr. Thompson should hear of it, or worse, whoever told him to come here tonight—"

"Constance." Harrington picked up his Gladstone bag. "I will not let another human being die because of the medieval prejudices of some politician."

Harrington strode back into the kitchen. He was pleased to see Mariko finishing a dish of oatmeal. Her hands and face were clean. Madelaine sat there, nibbling a tea biscuit.

"The horses are being harnessed, Doctor," Mrs. Rogers said.

"Thank you, Mrs. Rogers. Pack me the biggest basket you can lay hands on, with all the most nourishing food we have."

"Yes, Doctor."

In minutes the carriage was ready. Harrington bent to kiss Madelaine on top of her head. "Please tell Sato-*san* to come ride in the carriage with me."

Madelaine beckoned to Mariko. The three of them left the house through the front door. Madelaine pointed from Mariko to the carriage and made shooing motions. Mariko backed away, bowing.

"Do you love your mother?" Harrington asked. "Your *okaa-san?*"

Wide eyed, Mariko nodded.

Harrington thrust one finger at the carriage. "Then get inside! Now!"

Tone, if not language, succeeded. Mariko climbed up into the carriage. Madelaine started to follow.

"No, Maddy. Where I'm going is no place for a young lady."

"Papa, you need a translator."

"Once I get there, I'll send for someone. You've been a great help. Now go back to bed."

"Yes, Papa."

Harrington climbed up onto the step. "Dobson, take us to the shanty town on the south side of the Kamo River."

"That's a bad part of town, Dr. Harrington."

"Yes, I know. I spent most of the day there. Now go!"

As soon as Harrington had closed the carriage door, Dobson snapped the reins and urged the horses into a brisk canter. Mariko let out a yelp and huddled on the floor of the carriage, wedging herself into the corner with her arms around her knees. The empty streets allowed Dobson to make good time, but Harrington felt every second slipping past.

A deep shout of anger echoed off the walls nearby. From the mouth of an alley to the left burst the Wheel Monk.

"*Gizen-sha!*" roared the old man's face. "*Gizen-sha!*"

The flaming wheel rolled right in front of the carriage, blocking its path. The horses went mad, fighting to escape the flames. Mariko shrank into an even tighter ball, arms over her head.

Harrington threw open the carriage door and jumped down, walking stick in hand. "Get out of my way!"

The face of the old man sneered at him. "*Gizen-sha!*"

"Bite your filthy tongue!"

"*Gizen—*"

Harrington struck the Wheel Monk across its huge face. The sudden crack of bone sounded like a gunshot.

"I am here, in the filth and the cold and the loneliness of the night to bring medicine to a sick old woman." He drew a long, ragged breath. "If that's not enough for you, then take me! Take me to whatever hell spawned you. But not before I see my patient!"

Flames blazing, eyes glaring, blood streaming from its broken nose, the Wheel Monk rolled inch by inch back into the alley.

Harrington climbed up into the carriage and thumped on the roof with the head of his walking stick. Dobson tamed the horses and drove them to the place where the paving ended and the riverbank began.

"Sato-*san*." Harrington pointed toward the slum. "*Okaa-san?* Where is your mother?"

Mariko climbed down from the carriage. She bowed, then ran ahead, beckoning him to follow. Inside her particular shack, Harrington found a man, two young boys, and a girl gathered around an old woman wrapped in a variety of threadbare garments. Her skin was translucent, stretched like the finest parchment over the bones of her skull. At Harrington's entrance, the family backed away, bowing. He knelt beside the old lady and took her hand.

"I am Dr. Harrington."

The old lady's thin fingers with their gnarled joints closed just a bit around Harrington's fingers.

*"Arigato ... gozaimasu,"* she whispered. The breath it took to speak turned into a coughing fit. The old woman fought for breath.

Harrington pulled his stethoscope out of his bag. "Can you sit her up, please? I need to listen to her heart and lungs."

Mariko must have known how he used his stethoscope. At her insistence, the man and one of the boys raised the old woman upright. Harrington listened to the rhythm of her heart. Too fast. Pain? The struggle to breathe? Heart disease? Congestion in her lungs spoke of a pulmonary affliction.

"She needs a tea brewed with the flowers of the ephedra." Harrington rubbed a weary hand across his brow. "I'm sorry, I have no idea what that might be in Japanese."

"Fortunately, I do." In the doorway stood Sanada. He carried a small wooden chest. Setting it down at the old woman's feet, he opened the lid, sorted through the contents, and pulled out a small paper packet. "Mariko-*san, ocha, onegai shimasu.*"

*"Hai."*

Harrington stared at Sanada. "You speak English?"

"English, French, Italian, and some Russian."

"Why didn't you say so earlier today?"

"You did well, Harrington-*sensei.* You fought hard to learn the words you needed to cure the sicknesses of your patients."

Harrington had fought hard. The old guilt burned away in a glow of satisfaction.

"Forgive me for not arriving sooner, Harrington-*sensei*," Sanada said. "I set out the moment I received your daughter's message."

"How on earth did Madelaine know how to contact you?"

"She sent word to the Abbot, who in turn sent me here with this chest of medicinal teas."

Mariko's husband and sons supported her mother while they coaxed a few swallows of tea down the old woman's throat. By the time she'd drunk the entire cup, her color had improved. Her heart rate settled into a normal range. She breathed easily and drifted into sleep.

Mariko and her husband knelt before Harrington and bowed, stammering their thanks over and over again.

"Sanada-*san*."

"*Hai*, Harrington-*sensei*?"

"Please tell the Satos it is they who have done me the greater kindness. Through them I have been the instrument of Heaven's mercy, and I thank them for that opportunity."

Sanada spoke. Mariko wiped her eyes and called out to her children. They scattered. In minutes, they returned with a small dish of rice, one pickled plum, and half a small bottle of *shochu*. Mariko arranged it all with great care in front of Harrington, then bowed.

"Harrington-*sensei, dozo.*"

"*Arigato gozaimasu*, Sato-*san*."

The rice was rather dry and the pickled plum so sour Harrington was more than grateful for the harsh taste of the cheap liquor. Once he'd eaten, Mariko led him to a corner of the shack where a thin, stained futon lay. Giving not a single damn about fleas or lice or bedbugs, Harrington lay down, closed his eyes, and sank into sleep.

CR&O

The golden blaze of sunlight fell across Harrington's eyelids and roused him. He looked around at the splintered wooden walls. His back ached from a night spent with only the thin futon between his back and the hard, stony ground. His groan brought little faces peeking in through the doorway. A chatter of voices ran off. Moments later Mariko came in and knelt, bowing to Harrington.

"*Ohayo gozaimasu,* Harrington-*sensei.*"

"Good morning, Sato-*san.*"

The old lady lay wrapped in another blanket. She smiled up at him with bright eyes and toothless gums. He checked her pulse, then listened to her breathing. Definite improvement. The old woman spoke several slow words of Japanese. Her gnarled hand came out from inside the blanket. She handed Mariko a small wooden box.

"Harrington-*sensei.*" Mariko held the box out to him with both hands. *"Domo arigato gozaimasu."*

Harrington took the box and opened its lid. Inside lay a worn but lovely shrine talisman made of white silk with gold stitching. Two of the children appeared in the doorway, pulling Sanada along by his hands.

"Good morning, Sanada-*san,*" Harrington said. "Can you tell me what this means?"

Sanada looked into the box. He made a noise of surprise, then bowed to the old woman. She spoke to him, nodding at Harrington.

"Ogada-*san* offers this to you to show you the family's deep gratitude for your kindness. You left your bed in the dark of the night to help those whom many white men would kick away like stray dogs."

"Really," Harrington said, "this isn't necessary. It's my duty to—"

The old woman hushed him with a look. She spoke again, pointing to the box. Sanada bowed.

"Harrington-*sensei*, Ogada-*san* insists you accept this shrine talisman. It is meant to bring the gods' blessings on whatever work you choose to do."

"This must be a family treasure! I can't accept this."

"You must. The *burakumin* are lowly people, but their hearts are as sincere as any others."

Sincerity. Among the Japanese, that was a very important trait.

Harrington bowed. *"Domo arigato gozaimasu,* Ogada-*san."*

He smiled down on the talisman, closed the lid, and tucked the box inside his jacket next to his heart. He would see to it the *burakumin* received medical care, even if it meant Alexander Thompson came face to face with the Goddess of Mercy herself. But there was one other task to be completed first.

"Sanada-*san*, would you please be kind enough to deliver a message to my wife?"

"Of course, Harrington-*sensei*."

"Tell my wife I'm going to pay a call on Augustus Malloy. Mrs. Harrington will understand."

# TIGER, TIGER

## A Miranda Gray Mystery

### By T.E. MacArthur

September, 1892

"Well, of course Franklin's man killed her brother." Miranda Gray snarled. "One does not need to be an inspector with Scotland Yard or a member of the Ipswich Geological Society to have guessed that. I've seen lesser evidence offered in the penny dreadfuls I used to publish." Miranda snapped at the Colonel, far too aware that she was reacting with anger—yet too angry to stop herself. "The question is, why? Why would Franklin send that thug to kill the man who was helping him get his prize?"

The Colonel didn't appear to mind the tantrum, or he'd grown accustomed to her temper. "It'd be too soon, even if he planned on killing Ernst off eventually," he said coolly.

Breathing, in the hopes of calming her fury, she stopped pacing. "What changed? What is it that changed, that drove Franklin to send his man to kill Ernst?"

"You're assuming Franklin sent him. It's not a bad assumption, but we don't know for certain. That Damien chap might have gone ahead on his own."

She sat down with little grace. "All cards up and out on the table." She rested her hands on either side of her teacup. Before she could start, the Colonel dug into his coat pocket. He withdrew a battered flask, removed the top, and poured some golden contents into her cup. "Is that the only other thing that survived Crete?"

At first he didn't acknowledge the question. Slowly, while pouring the whiskey into his cup, he nodded in agreement. "Yes. You, me, and this thing. That's it." He had a little trouble putting the top back on the flask, but eventually closed up the container and re-pocketed it. "I—uh—want to thank you for ..."

Miranda waved him off, almost in fear of the memory as much as not wishing to take too much credit. "It was mutual, I'm sure."

"No." His voice swam in something akin to shame. "I'm not the sort of man who—who ..."

"Who is loyal and protective?" She sat back and watched him. He wasn't willing to look at her, that much she could understand. His pride was as beaten up as his physique. "You were loyal to your last employer—despite what he'd done. You sought revenge for his death. And of course—now you have Crete in your experience. You are precisely that 'sort of man.'"

He shifted nervously in his seat.

Her voice had sweetened, and she knew it was only putting vinegar on his wounded sense of purpose.

"We don't need to go over it in any great detail," he said, not looking at her.

"Agreed. The less I think of Crete, the better. What happened, happened. And we still don't know all of it."

The Colonel sat up. "Which brings us back to your friend's situation."

"Yes. What do we know? That Lucy Mercer contacted me in Vienna and said that she was in trouble. Her father had passed away, leaving his entire estate to her, and bypassing a brother in his will. Her brother is contesting the will—or at least he was—until someone stabbed him to death."

Nodding, the Colonel added more. "Ernst partnered up with Henry Franklin, who wants to buy out the business. One presumption is that Franklin wants to get rid of competition in the market. Or perhaps Ernst owes him money? Drinking and being entirely disreputable are expensive pastimes—trust me."

"No, no." Miranda interjected. "Franklin wanted the inventory of the business, not the business itself. Warehouse and office intact. Then there is a matter of cheques, written supposedly by Lucy, which left the whole company worthless."

"Not so worthless that Franklin lost interest." He sat up, and began playing with his teacup, occasionally sipping. "So, where are those cheques? Weren't they essential to proving Lucy incompetent, possibly even deranged? They were seen at one point, Lucy said so, but where are they now? Locked up in the business office where no one can get to them. Why are they there and not in the hands of lawyers or the court?"

"My guess would be that they weren't supposed to be in the office, but got locked inside by accident. Which brings up another problem—Franklin is a gentleman. Tell me, how many gentlemen wait around in alleys hoping to catch someone breaking into a building?"

The Colonel smiled. "He was there to break in himself, but your Lucy showed up first. Quite a chance he took."

Miranda swallowed her cup of tea in one go. "What is in that office that he would want to keep everyone out, yet risk arrest to break in himself?"

"Assuming Ernst completely supported Franklin's plan, why did Franklin need to break in? Once Ernst had control of the business, he could let Franklin go in at any time. Franklin would be delayed at best from getting whatever it is he is looking for. And we did run into Ernst in that same area, didn't we?"

"With dirty, greasy hands. You did see that, didn't you?" When the Colonel looked at her sideways, she continued. "Ernst had grease and clay on his fingertips."

"He was trying to pick the lock using ridiculous methods. Just how many people are trying to break into that office?"

"Two more, before tonight, I'll wager?"

"And neither of us will be stupid enough to have grease on our fingers."

Miranda stopped and looked at him. "And neither of us will have our own thug to knife someone who shows up inconveniently. We better keep our eyes and ears open."

The Colonel swallowed his cup of Scottish courage and orange pekoe, nodding.

"By the way, Colonel, why are you doing this? Not that I want to question your being here, but ..."

"Call it a need for distraction. After ..."

"Yes, after Crete."

○ॐ○

Picking the lock, unbolting the door—none of that was necessary. The door to Mercer and Van Ruthan was wide open. The office was being ransacked. Miranda raised her pistol closer to a ready position but not foolishly held straight out from her body. The Colonel had shown her how an outstretched arm was not as strong as a bent one. He was close behind her, holding a Webley '87, though he'd grumbled earlier that he disliked not having his air rifle. The Webley was at least more serviceable than the Enfield rifle, he'd groused.

A box of something sounding like loose coffee beans hit the floor. Miranda slipped quietly to the other side of the office door.

A terrible thought occurred to Miranda. What if this was Lucy? They hadn't seen her all day. She had been with her brother's body, accompanying it to the morgue, and then to the police. But that was hours ago. What if it was Lucy ransacking the office? As the Colonel lowered his weapon into a position less handy for firing wildly, she assumed he might be thinking the same thing.

*Crash!* The pillaging of the office was noisy. Objects were being pulled off the wall. What were they looking for?

The Colonel pulled a cylinder-lamp out of his pocket and nodded toward the office. In an instant, the office was illuminated in a fierce green color.

Damien was ripping through paintings on the wall.

Both Miranda and the Colonel stepped in and pointed their weapons.

Damien's knife left his experienced hands with a violent throw. It whizzed past the Colonel and split a hair's space between Miranda's shirt collar and skin. The Colonel turned to see her struggling to pull free from where the knife had pinned her to the door. "For God's sake! I'm fine. Get him before he gets away." He stared at her collar, which showed signs of red bleeding into the cloth. "Go!"

She pulled one more time and everything came free, including the silk tie she'd been wearing.

The Colonel turned on his heel and raced into the warehouse after Damien.

Miranda's own cylinder-lamp brightened the office enough for her to see much of the room. Touching her neck gingerly and cursing softly when she inspected her bloodied fingers, Miranda forced any notion of mortality out of her mind. Her head momentarily spun, and she worried it might be due to the blood loss. Touching her neck again and seeing only a little blood on her fingertips, she decided she would be fine.

Boosting her resolve with anger that she was left behind and had nearly become the damsel in distress, she walked over to where Damien had been standing. Slowly, she turned in place, to see whatever it was he might have seen. Immediately her gaze landed on a set of cheques. From the look of them, they hadn't been moved in a couple of weeks. If he had come in to collect the cheques to damn Lucy with, how had he not seen them? They were right there. He hadn't touched them.

She then turned her attention to the destruction ravaged on the place—in particular, on the wall paintings. Damien had left certificates and photographs alone, and had focused his rampage on works of art. On art ... On work generated by human hands ... On the frames and contents ...

A shot rang out in the warehouse, followed by silence.

CRSO

He'd seen the blood, and the recollection of his actions became blurry at best. The warehouse was dark, dirty, dusty, and somewhere in the shadows waited a man with much skill with a knife. To think that Damien was unarmed would be foolish, but the one assumption—that he had more knives and not a gun— was borne out by the man's actions. The Colonel didn't care what the weapon was, he was just glad he had it.

This might not be as easy as he'd hoped.

It smelled like the jungle in there. He knew the jungle. He knew about scouting for convoys moving through the dense foli- age—defenseless against whatever chose to stalk them. His ears had been sharply searching for the slightest sound out of place— as they were now. Back then he'd been hopeful. Damn the other soldier's lives, he wanted a prize and the glory. He'd bagged a tiger, they told him. He had been proud at the time. Now—the pride was gone?

A scrape on the floor ... too heavy to be a rat or a cat ...

Behind and to the left ...

Ten feet? Twelve?

The tiger.

Damien made his mistake. Rushing swiftly to strike.

The tiger of memory had done the same.

One shot. The Colonel never missed. He simply never missed his prey, whether shooting from the hip or carefully considering a sniper's target.

The tiger had dropped, dying before landing on the ground. There was a brief, inexplicable relief in that his Bengal tiger enemy hadn't suffered. As the Colonel noted that the dead man at his feet was not a tiger or anyone he should feel relief over, he quickly forgot about his strange compassion for the creature of memory. After all those years, he couldn't understand why he cared about the tiger. As for Damien—well, some beasts needed to die.

He left the dead man in the warehouse, equally confused about why he'd been so moved by Miranda's wound or why he had taken such an interest in this case at all.

"I was rather hoping he hadn't changed his weapon to a gun. May I presume we are no longer under direct threat?" She stood with the cheques in hand and not nearly as much blood on her collar as he'd feared.

Nodding toward the cheques, he asked, "Was that what he came for?" His voice squeaked—he hadn't considered how tense he'd been for the past few minutes. It was not like him to be so worked up. Not at all. "Are they?"

"No."

CR80

Lucy was almost hysterical when she was presented with the cheques; a set of rectangular, translucent sheets of paper with her signature. She looked up at Miranda, tears welling up in her eyes. "Oh dear heavens, I *did* sign them."

The Colonel cleared his throat. Miranda would certainly let him explain this part. It was a criminal activity, and—well, he was an expert in this area. "No, you didn't."

"But that's my signature."

He noted Miranda's raised eyebrow and tried not to smile. "Yes, it is. Exactly your signature, each and every time."

"I don't understand."

"No one signs their name the same way every time." He waited while Miranda stacked two of the cheques on top of one another and held them to the light. "No one. See, that's a forger's weakness: unless he's learned how to think, draw, and write like his victim, he's forced to copy each time he produces a signature. Copy—exactly—without errors that might make detecting his crime even easier. Most people won't check for such things. But if there's a glaring difference between a forged and real signature, well then, it's obvious. The trick to succeeding in forgery is not to draw attention to the signature—at all."

"Then, these are all copies of my signature, and I ..."

Miranda handed the cheques to her, and finished her sentence, "didn't write those or sign them. My belief was Franklin had them forged so that you would be discredited. In the morning, we'll ask a gentleman friend to inquire at the bank as to just who owns the companies the cheques are written to. I suspect we'll find your money." Miranda smiled more broadly at the Colonel.

For a moment, he felt as if she'd given him a pat on the shoulder and a *good job*. Why that mattered was going to bother him—later.

"You won't be needing that money if it comes down to it," Miranda said, with a cooing voice.

"Oh, I do believe I'll need it—before they tear down this house for auction."

Here it comes, the Colonel thought, as he leaned back in the overstuffed chair and waited for Miranda—his partner—yes, *his partner*—to explain the last of the mystery.

"Do you have your little painting?" Miranda inquired.

"Yes. Just here. Why?"

"I'm going to have to ask you a favor. You must trust me. I will fix it if you will allow me to open up the whole thing, frame and all."

Lucy looked horrified.

"She'll put it back," the Colonel said, scrounging in his pocket for a knife. He had an idea where this was going.

As the Colonel handed it to Miranda, Lucy leaned in without taking her wide-eyed gaze off of him. "He seems—I mean—how does he know about forgeries?"

"He's very well versed in a multitude of things, and a Johnny-on-the-spot when needed," she added when the Colonel handed her a small folding knife.

Carefully, meticulously, and with Lucy cringing at each step, Miranda opened the back of the terrible little painting. She had to break open the gorgeous gold frame, which brought silent tears to Lucy's eyes.

What Miranda pulled away with the childish canvas was a surprise to him. He'd honestly thought the frame, being so thick, was concealing something like jewels.

Instead, Miranda began carefully pulling a second canvas out from underneath Lucy's painting. Another painting had been hidden behind the other.

"That's what I thought!" Miranda exclaimed.

Lucy was dumbstruck.

"I was counting on diamonds, or such," the Colonel said, leaning forward to see the hidden canvas better. It was dark, crackled slightly, but strong in design. A self-portrait by an older artist. Small and perhaps a little unfinished.

Miranda held it up to the light and smiled broadly. "I don't think gems and jewels can match this."

"What is it?" Lucy asked.

"By the tone, style, and the fact that your dear Mr. Van Ruthan was a collector of old masters, I'm leaning toward this being a Rembrandt. An unfinished, unvarnished self-portrait by the artist." Miranda handed it to Lucy, who took it like a communion wafer. "Now, this is a guess on my part, but that looks like a prototype or practice effort before he finished one of his more famous self-portraits. What you have in your hands is a gift from the rather generous Mr. Van Ruthan to you."

"A Rembrandt?" she whispered.

The Colonel replied, "An unknown Rembrandt. You could be holding something that shakes up the whole art world. And yes, Madame Archaeologist is right—that is worth far more than diamonds or rubies."

He sat back, shaking his head and watching the two women in wonder. Only Miranda Gray would find an old Dutch master's painting under a sow's ear. It was a pleasure to watch her describe all the clues as to why Lucy was now in possession of something so amazing—and how she should present each clue to art experts who would be incredulous at first. Yes, Lucy's worries were about to be over.

What was it about the whole situation that was touching on his feelings? Why did he suddenly care? Four years earlier and he would have snatched the little masterwork out of their hands, threatened them, and gone off to sell it for his debts.

Four long years ago.

Nothing was the same.

Miranda was staring at him.

"You will, Colonel, have a look at those forged payments?"

"Oh, not I. But I will insist that someone who owes me a favor poke around. It might take some time before that painting can be sold or whatever Miss Lucy decides to do with it. I'm sure she doesn't want to lose the house in the meantime."

Did he just say that? Truly! Did he?

Miranda didn't appear to believe it either, but looked at him kindly. There was no love there—nothing tawdry or romantic—but there was respect. He'd forgotten what that was like.

The Colonel left the ladies to their own adventures of art and discovery. He took the cheques, slid them into his wallet, and decided that tonight would be a perfect time to drop in, unannounced, on Reginald Martin. The rotten little cheat owed him money. He'd collect half in cash and the other in Martin's understanding of finances—other people's.

Yes, that would suit him. He'd follow through with his promise to find Lucy's money, and he would have time to indulge in a bit of vice on the cash. He had his reputation to maintain.

With whom?

Turning to look up at the house, with one room still lit, he caught himself asking: with whom did he have to maintain his reputation—and further still, why?

No.

Vice tonight. Tomorrow, introspection.

He pulled his hat down firmly and headed toward the flat of one R. Martin.

# THE DAY OF RECKONING

*By Anthony Francis*

With the great airshark *Prince Edward* soaring overhead, and the stirring drums and trumpets of Liberation Academy's Reckoning Day Parade drawing her forward, brand new Ranger Cadet Jeremiah Willstone marched smartly ahead, stepping high, blunderblast held upright.

In step with her fellow cadets, Jeremiah turned her head, saluting the faculty stands, catching a brief glimpse of her former mentor Dean Navid Singhal next to her new superior, Ranger Commander Oxford J. Anderson, before the march forward swept the stands behind.

It had been a hard two weeks; she had a lot of catching up to do if she wanted to make the midterm cut, just days from now. But as a Falconer, she'd been an outcast, with the stink of *washout*; as a Ranger, she was a minor celebrity for thwarting a Foreign Incursion.

True, she saw less of Erskine now, but becoming a Ranger Cadet gave her a way to overcome her disgrace. Becoming a Ranger Cadet gave her a second chance to achieve her dreams.

Becoming a Ranger Cadet gave her new hope. But beyond all that ...

Becoming a Ranger Cadet gave her access to a thermionic weapons lab.

CR⁊O

High atop the clock tower of Edinburgh Castle, Senior Expeditionary Commander Jeremiah Willstone surreptitiously watched her younger self winding her way towards the gargoyle-encrusted Northern Barracks, home of the Ranger Corps and her destiny.

Jeremiah extended her hand, snatching her buzzing Dorago3 from the air as it returned to her. Pulling out her iPhone, she plugged the tiny supercomputer that masqueraded as a phone into the tiny helicopter that masqueraded as a dragonfly ... and watched the video.

As planned, the Dorago3 had caught herself filming the attack on Dyson with her iPhone, while a still earlier copy of her elder self came to the aid of herself as a cadet, firing in unison upon the clockwork octopus until her doomed lover, Erskine, dove in to save the day.

Two recordings, three memories: all subtly different.

Something was still meddling in time. Her vigilance must be doubled as her young self and lover barreled towards their tragic conclusion—because, even without temporal meddling, the particulars of *this* conclusion were events the elder Jeremiah could no longer remember.

CR⁊O

"You've done spectacularly in your first fortnight, Ranger Cadet," Ranger Commander Anderson said, surveying Jeremiah's *Kathodenstrahl* pistols on his desk as she stood at attention. "Passing every test we had—aptitude, fitness, knowledge. Congratulations."

"Sir, thank you, sir."

"And you've selected your own weapons, just like a true Expeditionary—extraordinary. Two weapons with, together, the fire rate of a blaster—and ten times the ammo. Sounds like a good choice." He steepled his hands. "So … why request a post in the weapons lab?"

"Sir, *Kathodenstrahls* are fragile, sir," Jeremiah lied. The grey-haired, steely-eyed Anderson was a veteran of the War of Realignment, an American from the days when there still was an America, and looked to be far stricter than Navid. "I'd like to investigate alternatives—"

"'Sir, the cadet would like to investigate alternatives, sir,'" Anderson corrected, and Jeremiah stiffened. "Prevarication won't work on me, Cadet. I've run your kind through their paces for twenty years. You're still working with Navid on something, aren't you?"

"Sir, the cadet *is* working on a special project with the Dean, sir," Jeremiah lied. In truth this was on her own initiative; she'd realized she needed a way to tell if Erskine could be trusted … and she could think of only one way to be sure. "Sir, access to the weapons lab—"

"Is denied," Anderson said. "We're right to celebrate throwing Victoria from her throne, and you marched sharp—but you would have been served better the past two weeks drilling for *your* reckoning day, the midterm cut. As a Ranger Cadet, you will give up 'special projects.'"

"Sir … the cadet is afraid she cannot, sir."

"*What* did you say?" Commander Anderson said, standing.

"Sir, the Dean has commanded all inquiries go directly to him, sir."

"You answer to me, *Ranger* Cadet," Commander Anderson roared.

"Sir, the cadet respectfully informs you that the Dean has commanded—"

"Cadet!" Anderson snapped. "Do you want to be a future Ranger, or a future *physicist?*"

Jeremiah clenched her jaw. And she'd thought the *Dean* had an authoritarian streak!

"Sir, I may be a cadet, sir," she said, "but I have been called on to act as a soldier in a war which you well know threatens not just this school, but this planet, sir. With all due respect, sir, I will not violate the orders of my commanding officer to suit the whims of a professor!"

That last bit came out far more impudent than she expected, and she blanched as mottled shock spread over Commander Anderson' face like a growing storm cloud—then Anderson burst out into a huge, hearty belly laugh and sat back down at his desk.

"What spine, Ranger Cadet," Anderson said. "Clearly this is a chain of command issue I will need to work out with the Dean. I'll take the matter up with him as he has commanded of you ... to *request* of me." He waved his hand. "Access granted. Dismissed."

Jeremiah licked her lips, then began to speak.

"If an apology were required," Anderson said, "I'd have demanded it. Dismissed."

"Sir, yes sir," Jeremiah said, and, praising her good fortune, clicked her heels and left. Within the afternoon, she was inside the halls of one of the best nonlethal weapons laboratories in the British Isles ... with a glittering Foreign circuit in the pocket of her cadet blues.

With luck, she'd find a way to destroy the circuit ... without killing its host.

CR๕๏

"You look a bit young," Anderson said, "for a Senior Expeditionary Commander."

"That I am, sir," Jeremiah said, glaring needles at Navid, who'd signaled her to teleport to his office with Dyson *and Anderson* present. "Sir, with respect, when I requested you keep my presence in confidence, I had in mind a smaller set of confidants than *the whole faculty*—"

"We'll hold the line here," Anderson said firmly. "I insisted, but now I understand—and so you have *two* department heads on your side, plus the Chancellor." He shook his head. "Still … not sure whether to be more impressed by the teleportation, or the time travel."

Jeremiah blinked. "Equally, sir. They're, formally, duals of each other." She gave him a quick breakdown of the plague of gears. "The gearwork is a temporal processor, self-assembling if a compatible circuit receives a signal from the future. Worse, some individuals are infested, but the matter is being adequately handled by Navid's agents—contemporary agents, sir—"

"Good God," Anderson said. "You mean, by you? As a *cadet?*"

Jeremiah pursed her lips. "I *am* young for a Senior Expeditionary Commander—"

"Got your start fighting monsters here, eh?" Anderson said, grey eyes as steely now as she remembered them—which, of course, was because this epoch was when she remembered them from. He pressed, "*Adequately* handled? A hedge. Think that third-year's up to the task?"

"Well," Jeremiah said, "My younger self *is* on the case, sir, and she's quite capable—"

"You don't," Anderson said. "God! A Foreign Incursion, and a cadet's on the case—"

"Oi!" Jeremiah said. "I'm here now, and I'm more capable—"

"But *why* are you here now?" Anderson said. "What's going to happen?"

Jeremiah stared at him, then quickly averted her eyes. She didn't need the reminder.

"If I tell you, it changes how you treat me, which changes me, which changes what I tell you," Jeremiah said. "And so on, and so on, until something vital breaks. The center cannot hold, because there is no center—only an ever-widening spiral that can blow history apart."

"And you're willing to risk that?" Anderson snapped.

"To save the world, yes," Jeremiah said. "Believe me, I don't want to meddle in my own history—I suffered in ways you can't conceive to get these brass wings, and I wouldn't trade them for anything. But I promise you, sir, if I decide I must intervene …I will do my duty."

CRSO

"I'm not sure how the Dean convinced the Commander," said Labmaster Stacey Farsight, suspiciously surveying the clipboard with Jeremiah's orders one last time before she unlocked the door to the Thermionic Weapons Lab, "but he *did* grant you all hours' access, Cadet."

"Clearly the Dean knows me too well," Jeremiah said, mouth falling open as she took in endless shelves tottering to the rafters, their mahogany boards and brasslite tubing bowing under piles of tubes and coils and gears and resonators. "My project is on Lorentzian lances—"

"What?" Farsight said. "Those toys? They've proved useless—"

"Against humans," Jeremiah responded.

"But then why—ohhhh," Farsight said.

"Precisely," Jeremiah said, lifting a long, boxy, rifle-like array. She sighted down the lance's length, a long rectangular prism, hard to aim—but holding a row of aetheric coils. She raised a glittering but broken circuit. "Can we find resonators for this, ma'am?"

ᙢᘓ

Scowling from the clock tower, Jeremiah watched her young self skipping across the courtyard, a large, heavy duffel over her shoulder. Events were transpiring as she recalled—on her end—but what was happening on Erskine's side, that was more baffling.

The thing was still in him, eating away. But Erskine had not tried to infect anyone else. She detected no signals, identified no confederates. True, he was engaged in skullduggery, but if anything, he'd become a better soldier in Navid's private little war than even she had, dutifully gathering and collating every scrap of information about the gearwork that he could. And as for *his* secret project—even the elder Jeremiah could see it was of practical use. Baffling.

"I thought I might find you here," Anderson said. "Any progress?"

Jeremiah didn't turn. "The cadet's identified a possible agent, and is—"

"I meant you, Commander," Anderson said. "Have you chosen to intervene?"

"I've … confirmed my identification of the agent," Jeremiah said carefully, "but not their hostility. If anything, the agent's more stalwart than before—"

"*My* agents confirm that report," Anderson said, and Jeremiah grimaced; he'd guessed Erskine was infected, but was somehow refraining from action. Anderson had to be walking an even tighter tightrope than she was. "They describe a … noted improvement in character."

"At first I thought we were facing an in-place takeover," Jeremiah said, staring off into the courtyard. "Now, we face the disturbing possibility that this gearwork is attempting a full assimilation with the host, a—a process which I prove is possible, but—"

"Commander," Anderson said gently. "Please look at me."

Jeremiah hesitated, then looked straight into his eyes, finding herself, despite her best efforts, simply unable to *not see* that aneurysm in his frontal lobes. Not even thinking, she came to full attention, and Anderson's expression grew bittersweet.

"How did I know that you knew, and all that," he said, and she smiled despite herself. "I *have* run soldiers through their paces for decades, yes, even soldiers like you, Commander: greatly accomplished people, filled with regret."

"I," Jeremiah began, momentarily taken aback. "Sir—"

"It's all right," Anderson said quietly. "Clearly you've done well, Senior Expeditionary Commander Jeremiah Willstone. In all my years, I never advanced as far as you have, and I must trust your judgment. Do what you have to do, just ... don't second guess yourself."

"Thank you, si—" Jeremiah began, but Anderson cut her off.

"Thank *you*, ma'am," Anderson said—and came to attention himself.

Jeremiah drew a breath; now, she outranked him. She could give him this.

"Thank you for your counsel, Ranger Commander," she said curtly. "Dismissed."

Anderson clicked his heels and, sharp as if on dress parade, spun and marched out. Jeremiah watched him go; if memory served, this would be the last she'd see of him. Dead within hours, his body cremated before her young self was next released from hospital.

She turned back to the courtyard, just in time to see herself sneak out to meet Erskine.

"One last picnic," Jeremiah said, watching them go ... their "special projects" in hand.

CRSO

Jeremiah hefted her duffel, grinning at Erskine walking beside her with a picnic basket. They'd eluded the proctors and were heading back to the park where they'd had their very first picnic—and made love for the very first time. And wasn't that what this was: love?

But, still, something was off. Erskine hadn't just grown doting and stalwart; he'd grown clever and secretive. His personality had become ... disjointed, his moods changing too quickly. And whatever was that heavy thing in his picnic basket?

They reached the park, skulking along the corners until they found a shaded clearing not too far from the site of their first adventure. Erskine rolled out a Victoria blanket and set down his picnic basket; Jeremiah unpacked her duffel—and pulled out a portable dynamo.

"What is that for?" Erskine asked, opening his basket. "I thought you had a tent—"

"A projecting aerograph," Jeremiah lied, stringing the cable from the dynamo to the device inside her duffel. "I've got the latest Edison cylinder—who doesn't love a spicy little airship romance? Your turn! What's that?"

"Insurance," Erskine said, raising a glowing, lantern-like device.

"Oh, *bollocks*," Jeremiah said, standing, too slow—as Erskine fired. A blue beam struck her amidships, and she juddered back, pins and needles rippling up and down her whole body. But the prickling quickly faded. "B-blood of the Q-queen, Erskine, what—"

"Still on your feet—thank God!" Erskine said. "Quick, now, how do you feel?"

"Like I've been electrocuted," she said, clutching her chest. "What was that?"

"Like I said, insurance—a weapon against Foreigners," Erskine said, scanning her with his astrolathe. "I inverted the energy Dyson detected in the device, creating a resonance that would destroy it. If you'd had any infestation—but no. You're still human, Jeremiah!"

"Oh, am I, Erskine!" she said, stepping towards him, tousling his close-cropped, curly hair. "Remember our first picnic here? We'd met at that study session for the metric algebra—the math needed for your device. As a first year … you never quite got it."

Jeremiah kneed him in the groin and shoved him away, throwing aside with a flourish the Victoria blanket covering the Lorentzian lance. She kicked on the dynamo in her basket and raised her weapon, crackling with power. "Now we find out whether *you're* infested—"

"Jesus, Jeremiah," Erskine said, struggling to stand. "You busted a nut—"

"Erskine, I am so sorry," she said—and blasted him.

A dark purple blast of collimated miasma struck Erskine square in the chest, and he stumbled back. But he did not fall, merely clutched at a black hole scorched into his vestcoat, and Jeremiah gasped at the crater beneath in his *flesh*—oh, God, she'd *burnt* him!

"It wasn't supposed to hurt," she began, lowering the weapon. "Erskine—"

Gingerly touching the burnt crater, Erskine looked up, then swung—

CR80

—decking the cadet, who toppled like a log, weapon falling to the ground. Erskine stood over her, swaying, feeling at the crater in his chest, pain crossing his face; then that expression was rapidly replaced by others in quick succession, as if he was trying them out.

Then, face wooden, he reached, mechanically, to unbutton his pants.

"Not so fast," the elder Jeremiah said, stepping out of the shadows, her great brass dragonfly wings spreading behind her, the oval shields flipping over to reveal four faery membranes that unfurled and glowed … as her hand flared with power.

"Jeremiah!" Erskine said, shocked. "There are two of you?"

"No, just the one," Jeremiah said, kicking Erskine's lantern away. She stepped astride her fallen form, as she had so many times now; how *did* she survive Academy without herself? "Always wondered what happened tonight, and now I know— you *rapist*."

"I … I wasn't," Erskine said, then looked down at his unbuckled belt. "I—"

"I know, it isn't really you," Jeremiah said venomously—then sighed. "Erskine, I *do* know that. I'm so sorry, but you're infected. A Foreign influence has taken control of you, and would make you do horrible things. I'm sorry, but … I must purge the infection."

"How are you going to—" Erskine began; then he took in her insectoid brass limbs, her glowing faery wings … and the crackling power gathering in her hand. "Oh, God. *You're* infected! Please don't kill me—"

"You're already gone," Jeremiah said. "Your head, it's full of gears—"

"*Your* head is filled with … with … bug parts! How are *you* any better?"

Slowly, Jeremiah pulled back her hand. She still could obliterate Erskine—but there *was* a speck of him still in there, and she overcame her revulsion for the machine before her and used every matahari trick she had in the book to reach that last glimpse of the man.

"Oh, my love, I'm so sorry," she said. "Neither of us deserve to die for what we are. But when I merged with myself, I ended up with the host's personality. The thing inside you is using what's left of Erskine like sheep's clothing. Open your eyes and see."

Erskine stared at her curiously ... then looked down, seeing for the first time the stream of mechanical tentacles pouring out of his chest like an unfolding clockwork octopus. His eyes widened in horror, and the tentacles twitched spasmodically.

"God," he said. "It's ..."

"It's *consuming* you," she said. "Already it's running your personality in mere snatches of time to craft its illusion. There's no guarantee there'll be anything left of you—but, *for now*, you can still choose. What do *you* want?"

"Please, Mya," Erskine cried in terror, even as his face went slack. "*End* thi—"

And she did, decisively, the brilliant flash blotting out even her vision. Wincing, she lowered her hand, shaking out energy as the metal octopus slowly disintegrated, tentacles coming apart, trailing disturbing pieces of blackened grease as they flopped to the ground ... until, at last, the puzzle that had been Erskine mercifully fell apart.

Grimly, she inspected the oh-so-real looking probe that had once been one of Erskine's most entertaining parts, but a quick scan revealed that he had not planted its gearwork seed. The tiny monstrosity could have lain dormant in her for years, waiting for that one vulnerable moment ... in which it could have seized the Burning Scarab's power.

Jeremiah knelt, brushing the hair of her cadet self. Between the bruise on her brain and time lost in hospital recovering, it was a wonder she'd ever graduated—but no wonder that she'd thwarted a Foreign Incursion in Academy. She hadn't. Just meddling, by her future self.

Jeremiah reached to collect Erskine's lantern, and drew a breath: it was an anti-Scarab weapon. If she'd intervened, as she'd planned to before Anderson's counsel, she would have died. Then her eyes turned towards her own Lorentzian lance, and she gasped: it was genius.

She had been an engineer. Easy to forget, with a brighter career as an Expeditionary Ranger behind her—and now a billion years of Scarab knowledge rattling around in her head—but Cadet Specialist Engineer Jeremiah Willstone had been a *good* engineer.

Jeremiah glanced at Erskine's remains: yes, even *despite* her meddling, it was really the cadet's cobbled-together weapon that had done the parasite in. The aetheric energy delivered by the lance was still cascading through the thing's gearwork, frying circuit after circuit.

Anderson spoke true: she shouldn't second guess herself. Even without Scarab eyes, the cadet had seen Erskine was infected, and had crafted the means to deal with him. Even though her elder self came back for mop-up, wasn't it honest to credit her younger self the victory?

And, technically, wasn't it still her in Academy, in either case?

"Congratulations, Cadet," Jeremiah said quietly, great brass wings spreading in pride as she regarded her younger self. "You've thwarted another Foreign Incursion in Academy, and I can tell you with authority you'll have a bright future."

# SOLARPUNK GAUGUIN

## Part II

### *By Janice Thompson*

What caused the seas to freeze, that swelling cold
Was finally discovered, but was manifold.
In brief it was a global stark magnetic shift
That set those in the threatened north and south adrift
In every cart or craft or way that could be found.
To hope of safety every single soul was bound.
So Mette, her children, and all of her other kin
Moved over sea and land and melted sea again
On to Tahiti's vibrant coast, now safe and warm.
Upon the shore Paul stood with waiting open arms,
And as she spied him, Mette spontaneously raced
To share such ardent kisses, such intense embrace,
There rose a hearty cheer from all who saw them there
With huge congratulations to the blissful pair.

Then to their home Paul led his grateful family,
Which he had crafted knowing all that they would need.
Transitioning was difficult at first for those
Who to their former situations were disposed,
Who started their new life confused and overwhelmed,
But slowly each adapted to this gentler realm.
There was no going back, no use in fighting fate,
Which to this paradise they must somehow relate,
So used their second chances to adapt anew
Whatever trade or talent they already knew.
Between the natives and those from the north displaced
There grew a true conjoined respect, and quiet grace.
A blending of their finer aspects came to be
The base upon which every person could agree
Not only on this island but for all confined
Within that life sustaining and most temperate clime.
And with the artists Paul had known, plus many more,
There formed a colony of mutual support,
While scientists opted to harness solar rays,
And cloth was spun of bamboo in amazing ways,
Where sunlight played upon thin sheets of colored glass,
Which on the floor and walls a vibrant image cast,
As Paul applied his skill to this, his current art.
Mette so adored her husband's work with all her heart.
Their children grew and prospered as do all who live
Where plenty fosters freedom and all souls forgive.

# HOME

## A Boston Metaphysical Society Story

### By Madeleine Holly-Rosing

The demon had fulfilled his promise and Duncan lived long enough to die in his mother's arms. As his spirit lingered, he watched Mae change her mind and decide to go and live in Philadelphia. He overheard later that she married another escaped slave by the name of Emmet Rochester. Though he tried to reach out to his Aunt Dara to learn more, his death frightened her and she refused to communicate with him in his spirit state. It made him sad, but Duncan understood.

His family left Boston not long after Aunt Dara and his mother died. He had hoped that one of the tenants over the years would be able to sense his spirit, but no one had. It wasn't until long after the House Wars that a young Irishman with bright red hair and a dash of freckles across his face marched into his family's old tenement that Duncan knew something had changed. This one was different.

A stout woman with dark red hair and not much older than the man, followed him in and watched as he strutted around the room.

"This will do just fine." He gestured to the surrounding rooms. "Better than Dublin. Aye, Mrs. O'Sullivan?" he asked in a thick Irish brogue and gave her a wink.

Not impressed with the apartment, she sighed, picked up a bag and placed it on the table with a clatter. "Aye, Andrew. It'll do."

Andrew's eyes flickered around the room as if looking for something hidden.

Duncan sensed the unease in the man as he saw his back tense up and his jaw clench.

"Why don't ye go and introduce yourself to the neighbors?" Andrew forced a smile. "I'll take care of the unpacking."

Erin looked worried for a moment, but then her eyes lit up. "I'd like that."

"Then off with ye!"

Andrew held his grin until his wife shut the door behind her. He whirled around, his eyes darting about as if to catch sight of a fly.

"Better ye come out before I get angry," Andrew ordered.

Duncan's spirit coalesced into an opaque vision of the man he once was.

"Ye died young." Andrew sighed.

The word "Aye" wrote itself in the dust on the floor.

"No need to tell me the details now. I know the missus can't see you, but there'll be no wailing or caterwauling in the middle of the night. Understood?" Andrew ordered the ghost which hovered in front of him.

Duncan pointed to the floor.

The words "Talk?" formed in the dust.

Andrew's face softened. "Aye. I imagine it be a wee bit lonely here. What's your name, laddie?"

The dust shifted again. "Duncan."

# PLAYING CHICKEN

*By Dover Whitecliff*

UNCONVENTIONAL:

Sometimes allies can be found
Where you least expect.

*Kyree's Profound Aphorisms*
as dutifully transcribed by Kenna Wolfesdaughter

"So what happened?" Blue asked as we hiked up the ridge.

"I won. Fa got the whatever-it-was. And that was my first visit to 'Raro." All of a sudden, it dawned on me that I had gone a full fortnight without having to have the spotlight on me. A real holiday for a change. Granted, it was so Blue could help me figure out how to use my new clockwork eye, and involved training the likes of which I'd never thought to undergo. And that's without mentioning sprinting through an obstacle course of Blue's own devising with his sister's polka-dot bloomers wrapped round my head to block sight in my good eye. Trust me. Better if you don't ask.

"'I won'? That's all I get?"

"Technically, we could still go up against each other in the arena. You think I'm giving away all my secrets? Why are we looking for a clockwork yak again?"

"As long as I'm house sitting, I take my brother's liege duties. And that means helping the tenants." I knew my partner's hair had enough undyed blue in it to put him higher up on the Kinship food chain, but I still had trouble equating Blue, hot exo-suit Middleweight, with Pascal Azure Lovelace, third son of the royal Duke of Lovelace. "The bay is right over here."

"Well, if raiders are using the bay as a base to steal from the farms on the estate, I'd rather see them before they see us. Best go low."

He crouched and made his way forward, then eased down on his belly. After a moment, he motioned me forward. "Wolfy, is that who I think it is?"

I shimmied up beside Blue and looked over the edge of the sea cliff toward the coral outcropping in the middle of the bay. No raiders in sight. Coiled around the tenant farmer's missing clockwork yak was—

"Yup. Dragon," I confirmed. Well, technically it was a *moʻo*, a sea serpent. There hadn't been a sighting of a true dragon since the Sundering. It was about then I realized that Blue had said *who*, not what, and sight clicked with memory. The violent clash of serpentine colors with the crystal blue waters of the bay was all too familiar. "Wait. No. It can't be. Not *him*."

"Sure looks like him."

*"Dimpledarling?"* Maroon back, *check*. Mustard belly and dorsal spines, *check*. Wiggling chartreuse ear fins, *check*. Steaming nostrils, *check*. Toothy grin, gaping Void on a stick times 436 teeth for both jaws, *check*. And this one was the real thing, not some submersible amusement ride in Su Chan So Lake.

"I guess they had to get the design from somewhere. I wouldn't have thought to see that color combination again, ever, let alone see it in nature." Blue shuddered. "Time to put that eyeball of yours to work. Sight it in and tell me how far the outcropping is from the top of the cliff."

I pulled the eyepatch from my right eye and blinked twice until a tapestry of numbers came up. Distances, I'd come to realize after smacking into trees enough times. It took a few mind wrenching seconds to overlay what I was seeing with my good eye with the numbers from the clockwork, but I finally got them lined up without wanting to heave.

"Maybe 1,500 feet, give or take." I sized up the competition. The bay itself had almost no cover and, even though there was a boat-sized stream flowing into it, I was certain sure that, being a sea serpent, Dimpledarling could swim faster than I could and catch any raft with a yak on it. "LUPA's claws could take it out, if I could get to the belly, but I haven't gotten her back yet. How about I run interference and you slice and dice." It wasn't much of a plan, but without my exo-suit, I was more an *amuse-bouche* than a threat.

"The bay is the treasure of Duoros, and a protected habitat. No can do."

"Right then. I'll lure it out of the bay into open water, *then* you slice and dice."

"Um. No. It doesn't work like that."

"We can't kill it?"

"We can't even paint it a less revolting color." Blue thought a second, then smacked me on the shoulder as he pushed to his feet. "Up you get. We've got a yak to rescue."

"Forget the gods of 'Raro. I've obviously cheesed off the whole bloody pantheon." I rolled over on my back and demanded of the unforgiving sky. "What part of '*I'm on bloody holiday*' are you not understanding?" Blue laughed and held out a hand to pull me up.

"Come on, Wolfy. Got an idea. You're gonna love it. Just need a few things from the workshop."

A few things turned out to be a wagon full of random scraps that made no sense to me, but I had no doubt that Blue, being Boffin Supreme, would snap his fingers and they'd somehow transform into a miraculous contraption that would not only take care of Dimpledarling, but whip up a perfect bowl of fried noodles and short ribs with a nice strong cuppa once we were through. We pulled into a clearing a way down the cliff from the bay, and Blue put me to work unloading. We worked in relative silence, save the occasional *"put that there,"* or *"pass me the spanner would you,"* until—

*BWAAAK!*

I jumped and spun toward the sound, spanner in hand and ready to throw. "What in the Void was that?!"

"Take a look." Blue snickered. "Scary monster. Much worse than a sea serpent."

Nothing in sight save us, though the underbrush shivered and shook. Something was out there. I turned slowly and listened. Clucking and scratching? To be fair, I'd had a rough five months between taking the Solstice games, having a bomb blow up in my face, losing an eye and getting a clockwork replacement that I was only just figuring out with Blue's help, breaking into and out of prison and keeping Dimpledarling's mechanical cousin from diving down the spillway of the Dai Sun Dam to bust it open and flood the Great Exposition of Duoros, but it was still bloody embarrassing. I put on the *I didn't just jump out of my skin for a chicken* look. Which fooled exactly nobody.

"Feral chickens?"

"Something like that." He lay under the wagon unhitching the dozen poles of scrap iron that hadn't fit anywhere else.

*BWAAAK!*

It, no *he*—it was definitely a rooster—burst through the brush and into the clearing in a flurry of glossy black and gold feathers. Wicked sharp beak. Talons the size of daggers. Beady little eyes that glared *you are so dead* with an eloquence rarely seen outside Kyree's face. The top of his crimson comb easily came up to my hip.

"That's not a chicken, that's a bloody *kaiju!*"

"That's not a chicken. It's a Qubalayo. Think of it as giant chicken with attitude. We call that one Boris."

"Boris."

"Boris," Blue confirmed.

"I have no words."

"Good, because this isn't going to build itself. Come on, Wolfy, help me wrestle these into place." I kept one eye on Boris and the same one on my work, being as I had put the patch back on, and held various poles at odd angles while Blue bolted them together. Boris strutted and bobbed around the clearing, poking his head into everything, sidling up to supervise and then pecking at me, pushing with his bum to chivvy me around as if he were the director of operations and not Blue.

"Bugger off." I shoved Boris away with my knee.

*BWAAAK!*

"And this lot does what exactly?" I ventured to ask once all the bits and bobs seemed to be in final position. The whatever-it-was had two uprights braced and bolted for stability and attached to a rectangular frame on wheels. What looked like a paddle wheel for a steamer was mounted to one side with a crank and gears to turn and lock it, and then one long pole stuck up from the top cross bar with a rope and a sling hanging down.

"You played Siege of Inarion with your mates, right?"

"Is that a game?"

"I take it that's a no."

"Got no memory that far back. If I did, I haven't a clue."

"Ah. Forgot about the memory thing."

"You've been saving that pun for weeks. Haven't you."

"Guilty as charged." Blue grinned. I forgave him since he had taken off his shirt to work. A pleasant view always improves my mood.

"So. Siege thing."

"You know what a catapult is? Old style weapon?"

"Seen the paintings. This doesn't look like that."

"Catapults work because you pull down on the throwing arm and hold it under tension. When you let the arm loose and it hits the cross bar, whatever's in the bucket takes all that tension and uses it to fly. With me so far?"

"It makes rocks fly."

"In Wolfy-speak, yes. It makes rocks fly." Damn if he didn't do a spot-on impression of me. "But Dimpledarling is in the middle of the bay. Made with the scraps we have here, a catapult would fling a rock that would either fall short, hit him, or hit the yak, none of which is helpful. Still with me?"

"And we can't just take it closer because Dimpledarling will tear us apart and eat us."

"Exactly." Blue pointed at the sling. "But, by moving the throwing arm to the top crossbar, taking the bucket off the end and replacing it with the rope and the sling, and switching the spool of rope with the paddle wheel and gears, we can make the rock fly farther and hit behind Dimpledarling. The splash should lure him off the yak and out to the mouth of the bay. We just need to test the distance first."

I helped Blue haul the arm down and heave a fair-sized rock onto the flattened sling. Blue walked around adjusting this or that. Meanwhile, Boris and I were locked in a contest of wills. He would wait until he thought I wasn't looking and rush me, and I would dodge. I would surreptitiously kick at him, and he would dodge. It was a coming down to a fowl sort of standoff.

"Yo, Wolfy! Anybody home?"

"Sorry. What do you need?"

"See that stick over there by the paddle wheel? Pull that, would you?"

I turned to look in the direction Blue was pointing. "What? This?" Boris took advantage of the distraction and sidled up to peck at my knee when I looked up at Blue for confirmation. "Oy!" I shuffled him out of the way, herding him back with my boot. "Shoo! Damn bird. Whole bloody island and you have to muck about right here." I groused and stomped over to the stick Blue had jerked his thumb at. Yanked hard. THUNK! The net shucked up and around the rock, and the line went taut, pulling back, up, and over. WHOOOTHUNK! The log swung forward. *Now hang on. Something's missing. Where'd the bloody bird go?*

The net furled and disgorged its cargo. *BWAAAK! BWWAAAAAaaaaaaaakkk!*

"What in the Void was that?"

"You don't want to know."

Blue shaded his eyes to follow the rock through the sky. It wasn't alone. "You didn't."

"All on him. Shouldn't have wandered over the business end of your contraption. Damn, Blue, that's badass."

"Not bad for an hour or two, some scraps, and some elbow grease."

"What are you going to call it?"

"No idea. Just something in my head. What do you think? Over Thrower?"

"Boring."

"Rock Chucker?"

"Nah."

"Fowl Flinger?"

"Fowl Flinger. Works for me." I peered over the edge in time to see the Qubalayo unfurl his huge black wings to glide the last few bits to the beach below. I saw a flash of gold from his chest as he turned tail and sprinted toward the cliff. "You've got to be kidding me. He's coming for us."

"Seriously?"

"We'd better be off the cliff before he gets back to the top."

"Right then, let's move the Fowl Flinger into position. I'll get Cyril's airboat and bring it down to the mouth of the stream. When I give the signal, pull the lever. Probably not enough time for a second shot."

"Forget time to reload, it takes both of us at full strength to pull the arm down."

"Point taken. If Dimpledarling decides he wants lunch, I don't suppose you could distract him and then run like the wind?"

"I don't think Kyree's *Eyes on Me* training extends to dragons, but I'll give it my best shot."

"That's the spirit! Let's do this."

The hardest part was the waiting. I kept watch up top, but Dimpledarling seemed to have a thing for the clockwork yak. Fa's bedtime stories always mentioned dragons liking shinies. He coiled and uncoiled around it, rubbing against it, occasionally slapping his tail in the water. I was beginning to wonder if a rock would be enough to dislodge him from his prize.

It seemed an age before I heard the hum of the airboat, but finally the nose nudged toward the mouth of the stream. Blue crouched in front of the fan. I hoped like the Void that Dimpledarling kept his attention on the yak for at least a few more minutes. Finally, I saw Blue's hand go up and drop. I turned back toward the Fowl Flinger. Did a double take. Boris. Sitting on the rock.

"We're not playing, Chicken." I hissed and shooed, but Boris stood his ground, cocked his head at me, and bobbed toward the lever. I walked over to it and put my hand on it. He bobbed toward it again, glaring. "That's a bloody great dragon down there, you idiot." I realized I was trying to reason with … a chicken. When did it come to this?

*BWAAAK!*

I took that as the order to pull. Boris took off with the rock. WHOOOTHUNK! The rock splooshed in the bay behind the sea serpent. Dimpledarling turned and slithered partway into the water. Blue gunned the engine, trying for speed. Dimpledarling heard the airboat, turned back. Saw Blue. Damn. Damn. DAMN!

"Oy! Dimpledarling! Up here!" I jumped and down, waved my hands, bellowed and whistled. But Boris was quicker.

*BWAAAK!* He angled his wings and glided just out of reach over Dimpledarling's head. The sea serpent thrashed and uncoiled, leaving his perch and diving after Boris, now heading for a sandspit at the mouth of the bay. *Not bad for a giant chicken.* I kept watch while Blue wound the yak, walked it into the boat, and took off faster than an Angora stampede.

Eyes turned when we rolled back into civilization at sunset. Me riding the monobike along the dock and pulling the Fowl Flinger, with Boris proudly sitting on the top crossbar, and Blue in the airboat with the clockwork yak at the prow.

We dropped off the yak with the farmer's family to much rejoicing. They insisted we eat and celebrate with them, so, of course, we had to demonstrate the Fowl Flinger as after-supper entertainment. Boris loved that. Kept strutting over to sit on the sling, insisting on another ride. Wonderful. We'd created a giant chicken with addiction issues. Blue, as his brother's ducal proxy, knighted Boris for service to the Lovelace Family, creating The Most Royal Order of Dragon Distraction.

We left Boris and the Fowl Flinger with the farmer and his family, and continued on by moonlight. By mutual agreement, we stopped for a cold one in Kusini-town before heading back to the manor house. The pub was crowded and I got jostled on the way to the bar, but the bloke apologized. "Nice ink." He said as he left. No pity. No revulsion.

"It really is." Blue handed me a pint and ran his hand down my arm. "Give me a She-Wolf over a giant chicken any day or night."

# INTO THE ORDER OF GLAUCOS

*By BJ Sikes*

*The next morning*

Theo woke, head throbbing, and with a mouth that tasted like something died in it. He smacked his parched lips together, rubbing his tongue against fuzzy teeth.

*What happened last night?*

The last thing he remembered was the cool breeze across the back of his neck as he lay facedown on the bed.

The sun now blazed in through his open curtains. Memory returned. Last night, he had shuffled away from the window after the monsters had disappeared, trying to move quietly, slowly, in case they were still out there in the dark watching him.

He shuddered at the remembered images, shadows still lurking at the edges of his vision. What had he seen out there? Had it all been a hallucinatory nightmare or were there really monsters lurking in the nighttime streets of Nassau?

Theo struggled to his feet, wincing down at yesterday's wrinkled suit. He noted splotches of something sticky and brown on his trouser legs. Juice, he suspected, from the rotten fruit that urchin had thrown at him.

The clothes peeled from him like the skin of a ripe peach and he dropped them to the floor for the servants to deal with. He rang the bell for water, arrogant in his nudity as he tapped his foot, waiting. With brusque words, he ordered a bath, oblivious to the grumbles and dirty looks thrown his way by the beleaguered maid. He stank. It was time to get clean.

Grumbling servants carried in buckets of steaming hot water and dumped it in the tub, splashing water on the floor as they worked, but Theo was past caring. As the last of them departed, with nary a word in his direction, he sank into the water with a sigh. His body felt heavy and hard to move. He soaked and let the warm water soothe away the last of his nightmares. Stomach grumbling, he thought that some food would perk him up. He dragged himself out of the bath sooner than he would have liked, dripping more water onto the floor, and scanned the room for his belongings.

*Shocking level of service in this supposedly fine establishment. They haven't even unpacked my clothes.*

Speckling the floor with droplets of still-warm bath water, Theo unearthed clothing from his steamer trunk and threw it on.

ᘓ৪৹

Theo invaded the hotel dining room in his creased beige linen suit and unshaven face. British expatriates enjoying their Christmas dinner filled the grand room with its large French doors open to the gardens. He caught glares and moues of disgust at his appearance.

The head waiter, a man of Caribbean ancestry, approached him, looking him up and down.

"Sir? Have you a reservation?" His tone anticipated Theo's lack of planning.

"What?" Theo rubbed a hand across his unshaven chin. His eyes were still bleary from the night. "I'm a guest here. Why would I have need of a reservation? What a preposterous notion."

The head waiter's face changed, grew more obsequious, but still doubtful.

"Of course not, sir, right this way." He gestured towards a secluded corner of the dining room, sheltered behind potted plants. Theo sighed.

*Ah good. Secluded away from all of those happy families.*

He glanced around the room as he followed the head waiter between tables and guests at dinner. He caught a glimpse of something long and thin under a tablecloth—a tentacle? He jerked his gaze away from it. Could he still be suffering the effects of the *Psilocybe?* The sunlight caught on a crystal wineglass, scattering a rainbow across the table. He squinted and looked away, catching the eye of a man grimacing down at his meat before taking a large bite with sharp, sharp teeth.

*Those teeth don't look right. Too many, too pointed.*

Theo's breath grew ragged. The walk to the table in the corner of the room seemed endless on his shaky legs. He slumped into the outstretched chair and wordlessly took the menu from the waiter.

"Mutton chop, eggs, tea, toast," he told the man. Something simple and homey would settle his nerves. He realized that he hadn't eaten anything at all since yesterday's luncheon. That would account for his jittery nerves, of course. He averted his eyes from a palm frond waving in the breeze from the open windows. It reminded him too much of giant tentacles waving in the torchlight.

The food arrived, looking reassuringly normal. No weird appendages or sharp teeth. Just good, solid English food. He sawed off a piece of the mutton and chewed. The tough meat reminded him of the meat from those giant Oriental bovines, yaks or something. He grew calmer as he worked through his meal, but then voices from behind the palm trees broke into his solitude.

"How could you possibly sleep through that racket yesterday evening, Harold?" A woman's voice, shrill and petulant.

"Well, my dear, I had had a whiskey or two and I was quite fatigued from the lawn tennis game."

"Impossible man. Mabel, did you see those outlandish costumes? And the noise was simply beastly."

"Yes, I did. Were those supposed to be monsters? Ridiculous! It is a barbaric festival and it ought to be abolished. Why, if Britain still ran these islands, there'd be none of this Junkanoo nonsense."

"I completely agree. I think it makes the native people too wild. Did you see them dancing … if one can call that *dancing*."

Theo sat still, taking it in, holding his breath. So he hadn't imagined the monsters of last night, but neither had he seen a nightmare of savagery after all. He motioned to the waiter. Theo could feel judgment pouring off the man despite his impassive face.

"Last night … this Junkanoo thing. What was that all about?"

"It is a Christmas festival, Sir. The people of the Bahamas enjoy singing and dancing. We create our own costumes from paper and such for the Junkanoo *thing*."

"That was people out in the streets last night … dressed up in paper?"

The man's face didn't change.

"People? Yes, sir. Of course. Will there be anything else?"

Theo waved a hand in dismissal. So the terrifying fiends had been made of paper. How ridiculous. He'd been petrified while under the influence of the fungus. He laughed a little at himself and finished his breakfast.

Standing to leave, he caught sight of a party of British officials in full dress uniforms accompanied by women in white lace and lawn gowns. Small children in party dresses sat at a nearby table. The Ambassador Sir William Grey-Wilson, his staff, and their families, presumably. Theo sauntered over to their gathering, forgetting the state of his clothing, and hailed Lieutenant McLachlan as he approached.

"And a Happy Christmas to you, Mr. Cooke," replied the soldier. He stood to shake Theo's hand and introduced him to the ambassador and the rest of his party. Sir William seemed cool in his demeanor, unsmiling as he greeted Theo.

*Oh dear. Have I already offended him?*

At that thought, he remembered the state of his clothing and apologized for it, explaining that the maid hadn't unpacked his luggage. A tight smile flickered across Sir William's face.

"Ah yes, I couldn't imagine why else you would be in the dining room in that state, especially on Christmas Day. Will you be joining us for services later, Mister Cooke? We'll be at Christ Church Cathedral at one o'clock."

Theo's heart sank. Church services? He'd hoped to avoid the obligatory rituals here. Thinking fast, he demurred.

"I'm afraid I won't be able to join you. I'm Catholic actually. I'll be attending services at St. Francis Xavier."

"Heh-heh, d'you know some of the Anglican Churches Over-the-Hill out-Rome Rome. You might feel at home if you were allowed to go over there," Lieutenant McLachlan interjected.

Looking displeased, Sir William dropped the subject and began a long discourse on the importance of Theo's agricultural mission in the Bahamas. Theo struggled to pay attention. His work seemed distant and unimportant. Despite knowing that he had seen people in costume last night rather than monsters, horrific appendages, sharp teeth in a flash of a smile, and other disturbing images continued to lurk at the edge of his vision.

The ambassador finally wound down and Theo made his excuses, bowing.

He wandered out of the dining room through the open French doors and into the hotel's luxuriant gardens. Green glossy leaves and brilliant flowers in pink and orange filled his vision. Theo gulped a breath of thick, wet air. His boots sank into deep grass and he moved into the mass of vegetation, intending to escape the people behind him. Drops of water fell on his face from the overhanging bushes as he pushed his way through.

A woman's voice, singing, chanting, calling out names in a strange language, reached him before he saw her standing ankle-deep in the surf. Theo stepped out from the dense foliage onto a sandy beach and there she was. Her arms, bare and bronzed, outstretched towards the ocean. His eyes lingered, caressing her uncorseted curves, visible through a clinging white cotton dress. Her red-gold hair tumbled in rough curls down her back.

As if she sensed his gaze, she looked back over her shoulder at him. Her eyes were tawny and reminded him of a lion he'd seen in the London Zoo, glittering and predatory. The woman's tanned face appeared older than he expected from her figure.

"A wave of strong emotion has your astral body in great agitation."

Theo gaped at her bizarre statement.

"What?"

She turned to face him, her own face grave and thoughtful.

"Your aura is full of pallid grey and dragon's blood. Something has frightened you badly, but your lust is rising."

The woman was obviously insane. Aura? Astral body? He ought to turn and leave but his curiosity urged him forward.

"You're new here. The Bahamas are full of hidden danger, hidden from all but those of us attuned to the spiritual world. The monsters walk the streets and none see them. They show themselves at the Junkanoo—"

Theo interrupted her, frowning.

"The Junkanoo? Why, they're nothing but men in paper costumes!"

The woman's face creased with a slow smile.

"That's what they want you to believe. Beings from the next higher plane of nature show themselves on the outer edge of the physical field during the Junkanoo. The monsters gambol through the streets of Nassau, feeding off the madness, the excitement, the energy of the real people out there. It recharges their corporeal forms for the entire year, so they can do battle with each other."

She sounded so sincere, like she believed every word of the nonsense she spouted. Perhaps the sun had addled her brain. Theo decided to play along a little longer.

"You're saying that the Bahamas are inhabited by monsters that feed off people's energy? And you are the only person who knows this?"

Her eyes flashed with anger and she raised her chin.

"You British are so prosaic. You can't see anything beyond the material world. Except you did see something last night, didn't you? And now you're terrified, afraid that you're losing your sanity."

Her words shook him. Were the apparitions last night more than drug-induced hallucinations? Nausea rose up his throat with breakfast heavy in his gut.

"I ... I saw something, something horrible." His breath caught in his throat. He gasped for air, feeling the trembling take over his body again as horrific images flashed through his mind.

"Yes, you saw them. The monsters with mouths full of sharp teeth, the monsters writhing with tentacles and claws. You saw the Old Ones." She sounded so matter-of-fact, so reasonable. He nodded his response. She reached out and grasped his shoulder. Theo flinched from her sudden proximity. How had she reached him so quickly? The heat from her hand seeped through the linen of his suit and a swell of calm moved through him.

"You don't have to be afraid of them. The monsters you saw are simply the avatars of powerful gods. They would share their power in return for your devotion. Think of it, Theo. Power over the weak and the meek. Power over those who oppress you, manage you."

*Theo? How did she know my name? Who IS this woman?*

His mind flashed to his wife, timid and bookish, so unlike the bold hussy scrutinizing him here on this beach. How far away Clara seemed. Seeming to sense his inattention to her, the woman spun away from him and strolled away along the beach.

"Wait! Come back? I don't even know your name!" He called to her retreating back. She glanced over her shoulder.

"Lydia. And you are a fool, Theo Cooke."

"But … wait! Tell me more!" He stumbled through the sand after her. She strode on, treading on the more solid beach next to the water.

"Are there more people who know about these god-monsters?"

He caught up to her, realizing the trick of walking near the water. Hang the damage to his shoes. She shot a sideways glance at him but didn't respond.

"You're American, I presume from your accent. Do you live in Nassau? How did you find out about these god-monsters?"

"You're full of curiosity, now? My knowledge was passed to me by savants in the Order. We live on Andros Island, preparing for the advent of the Old Ones. We knew you were coming, so I came to Nassau to meet you."

"How … how did you know about me?"

The woman halted and turned towards him.

"Theo, you are more than you realize. You must come with me back to Andros. The Order sent me to retrieve you. Your destiny lies with us. Your every wish will become a reality. No more will you suffer the indignities of those beneath you. You will be powerful."

Theo stared at her. Could this be something he'd been searching for? A break from his old life? Duty niggled at him and he couldn't shrug it off. He made another attempt to resist her.

"But, my job … I have an assignment here. I can't just leave with you."

Lydia smiled, her mouth twisted.

"I am well acquainted with the British ambassador. We'll get you reassigned to Andros."

Theo frowned, not sure if he wanted to let this Order take over his life. He gazed back towards the hotel but he and Lydia had walked far along the beach and he couldn't see any signs of civilization. She moved closer to him and turned his shoulders so he faced her.

"I think you'll like the Order. We don't have silly notions of morality."

He looked into her tawny eyes, level with his. Lydia leaned closer and kissed him on the mouth. Groaning, Theo grabbed her waist and pulled her close, returning the kiss. The Order might be just what he needed.

CʒꙄᴑ

"We'll send for you as soon as the ambassador approves your reassignment to Andros. I'm sure there'll be no problem."

Lydia's confident smile settled Theo's nerves. He hated the idea of her leaving so soon. They had had barely a week together before she announced that she needed to return to Andros Island. He nodded and took her hands, rubbing her skin with his thumbs. He leaned in to kiss her goodbye, oblivious to the bustle of the harbor.

"Be safe, my darling. I'm counting the seconds until I see you again."

She smiled in return and caressed his face, then turned and walked up the gangplank of the small boat waiting to take her to Andros. The crew cast off and the boat pulled away from the pier. Lydia leaned against the railing, calling out goodbyes and waving. Theo returned her wave, his face split in a grin, but tears choked him. He stood on the pier waving and watching until the small craft disappeared over the horizon.

# THE CONFECTIONER'S TALE

### *By AJ Sikes*

Yes, I am just twenty years old. I came back from the front lines and have healed. I've been looking for work for two months now.

–

Cannoneer, yes. I was—

–

Oh, my leg. They've given me this wooden one for now, but the doctor is working on a new prosthetic. He says it will look just like the real thing. Of course, the officers will get them first. They need them, you know.

–

Well, yes, you're right. I suppose I do need one, but … well you know how these things go. And anyway, I shouldn't think it would be too much trouble having me helping out around the kitchen, will it? I mean, with customers. They won't have to see me.

–

Indeed? Well, thank you. Sorry for troubling you.

–

Across the street? The shop there is also looking for help? I'll try it. And thank you. Good day.

#

Hello. Good afternoon, madame. I understand you have employment to offer. Is that correct?

—

Yes, the man across the street. He sent me here.

—

I had asked him for work, yes. But ... well, my leg, you see ....

—

I am perfectly capable of doing most kitchen work, yes. Perhaps a bit slower than I was before, but I can pull my own weight.

—

Yes, I can cook. Though I confess a preference for dessert work.

—

Indeed, that is a rarity in these times. The war is over, mostly. But who has the ingredients to make pastry except for the people in the Old Quarter, eh?

—

I did live there once, yes. I suppose it's not good trying to hide. You can see it in my face, can't you? I tried to be a man among the people. I thought the war would have leveled all those walls between us, but perhaps I was naïve. I'll be going, then. I'm sorry to disturb you. Thank—

—

Yes, my family does still live there, and I do know some of the merchants. One in particular is a friend of mine. He also left a bit of himself in the mud beyond the hills. His left arm.

—

Of course, yes. I spoke to him just the other day, in fact, and he was happy to provide me with ingredients.

—

My parents? They believe me dead. I had my merchant friend take them a letter while I was in hospital. He'd written it on a piece of officer's stationary we'd nicked back in the trenches. Made it look official, you know. My parents were never much for details except those involving coin and crown, and I'm afraid they were quite convinced of my demise in the war.

It's only my leg that got left in the mud, though.

–

After what I saw there, I could never go back to my old life. The people there … they have no idea what is happening around them. None at all. Not like the old fellow who worked the cannon with me. He knew what was happening. He'd seen it, and do you know who he was?

No, I shouldn't—I promised him I wouldn't trade on his death, just as he had promised me. I should go. I'm sorry for—

–

Yes, I do intend to work as a cook. A pastry cook if at all possible. If I'm to do anything with my hands in the future, it will be some form of art. A feast for the eyes and tongue.

I've brought a sample. I'd meant to share it right away. It may not be as fresh anymore, so I won't be surprised if you turn your nose up at it. It's here in a parcel. Could you—Yes, thank you, just open my satchel. It's right on top.

–

Yes. It is chocolate. The dessert is not of my own invention, I must admit. But I think you'll like it.

–

Of course, please. No, no, you have it. Ah, and this is your husband? Good day, sir. Yes, I was just asking your wife about employment. I've brought a sample of my pastry work, which I would like to make for your shop.

–

I am honored that you like it, madame. Won't you try some, sir?

—

No, I insist. None for me. Please, you finish it.

—

Thank you, sir. Madame, thank you, too. Thank you. It's a privilege to share it with you, really. I've been turned away by so many shops. All because of my leg. I know it's unsightly—

—

A fellow cannoneer gave me the recipe. It was on our last night together, before an enemy cannon found us and threw him into the sky and my leg along with him.

—

Tomorrow? Yes, I ... I could come back tomorrow. What time?

—

Too early? I shouldn't think so, no.

—

Haha! I see, you spoke in jest. You are right, sir. A military man does not know an hour that is too early. And is this fine for a uniform?

—

You'll have a set of whites for me? Again I am grateful to have found you.

—

A question for you? I admit I hadn't thought of any. But now that you ask ... will ... that is, do people from the Old Quarter ever buy from your shop? Will they eat the food I make?

—

It is an odd question, yes. But—

—

Not ever? They think this neighborhood "too low" to grace it with their presence? Preposterous.

—

Yes, well, as my friend from the trenches would say, "More for us then, eh?"

# FLOWERS OF PARIS

### By Sharon E. Cathcart

1889

Thaddeus Flowers awoke in a bed not his own, head pounding. He'd definitely taken too much absinthe at the Café des Artistes last night, and was not entirely sure where he was. The bistro was in Montmartre, but he might be anywhere from there to St. Michel.

Raking his fingers through his dark hair, Thad sat up slowly. The dull light filtering in through the curtains showed a respectable enough room; his clothes were draped across a chair … on top of what looked like a petticoat.

Oh, dear God. Not again.

This really was becoming a habit … and one that Thad needed to break.

Eventually.

The girl sat up and pushed her blonde hair out of her eyes.

"You can leave the money on the washstand as always, Thad."

Thank God, it was only Colette. Thad was a regular in her crib.

"Who is Arabella," Colette asked as Thad dumped a handful of coins next to the bowl and pitcher. At his surprised look, she explained. "You talk in your sleep."

Thad shrugged his shoulders, dressed himself, and stepped out into the harsh morning light. He squinted as he made his way to the shady side of the street and walked to his own garret room. The concierge, Madame Solange, would probably not be up yet—he hoped. He was in no mood for her lectures, and he needed to sober up for his meeting that afternoon in the Marais.

Arabella Abingdon. He could hardly wait to see her again. It had been what, seven years, since they'd met in London? He'd never forgotten her striking beauty, her intellect—who knew that a woman could understand science so clearly? And now, she had someone in Paris who could help him make his dream of airship transportation in cities come true.

Or so she said.

Back in his room, Thad re-read the letter for what seemed like the hundredth time.

"My dear Thaddeus:

You must meet me Thursday next, four o'clock in the afternoon, at the address below. A long-ago friend from my boarding school days has married an absolute genius. I showed him your plans, and he's made a model for your flying machine. Don't be late.

A.A."

The address was a townhouse in the Place des Vosges; Thaddeus had made a preliminary trip to take a look at the place. A fashionable address, to be sure; probably the home of an old man in his dotage who had taken a young wife. Still, curiosity compelled him to be there at the appointed time. Especially since he'd never managed to adequately recreate his flying machine concept; other drafts just felt wrong after Arabella's disappearance, and he'd eventually abandoned the entire project.

Now it was that Thursday. Thad laid out his clothes, brushed the dust from the fashionable frock coat, and made sure he had clean linen. He would wait to shave until closer to departure time; that way, he would present a better impression. A look in the glass suggested a trip to his barber might be in order, but the funds he'd paid Colette were the last he'd had in his pocket. That also meant a trip to the bank.

So much for the quiet day he'd planned to pass before the appointment.

Arabella Abingdon had been the stuff of dreams, for the most part. Their first dinner together had ended in her rooms off of Manchester Square. There, Thaddeus had yet another surprise; he had never imagined that a woman could match his ardor in bed—unless, of course, she was a prostitute, in which case, one never could be truly sure. As it had not occurred to him that a woman could be his intellectual equal, so it had never occurred to him that a woman might also have physical desires of her own.

The entire experience had been eye-opening for him. Then, as quickly as they'd met, she was gone—to Menlo Park, New Jersey … if the address on her first letter to him was anything to go by. Letters after that came from all over the world.

And now, both of them were in Paris.

Thaddeus presented his card to the majordomo who answered the door. He was a trifle disturbed to note that the servant was better dressed than himself. He wondered who his tailor might be, and then wondered whether it was an appropriate question to ask of the proverbial help. The man was tall and slim, with dark blond hair and a fashionable Van Dyke beard; he leaned heavily on a cane when he walked but still retained an air of dignity. Thad followed the fellow down a hallway that opened onto a parlor. There, he found Arabella sitting with a chestnut-haired beauty.

"Thank you, Gilbert," the latter said as she stood to greet their guest. "I'm Claire LeMaître. You must be Monsieur Flowers. Arabella has spoken highly of you." She extended her hand.

Thad took her hand and bowed over it, a trifle surprised to be greeted in English. "I am delighted to meet you, Madame LeMaître. Miss Abingdon tells me you were at school together."

"Yes, we were at the same boarding school in Switzerland. Before we go in to meet my husband, would you like some tea?"

Thad declined, so Claire asked Gilbert to let the maestro know that they would be joining him in the study shortly.

"I should warn you, Monsieur Flowers, that my husband suffers a physical deformity that embarrasses him greatly. He will be masked; do not let it frighten you."

Thaddeus nodded his understanding, trying to contain his excitement at seeing his design in action. He and Arabella followed Claire down the hall.

"Where did you get my drawings," he whispered. "I've wanted to ask you that for ages."

"You gave them to me, Thad."

"I did?"

"Yes, you did. I should have known you wouldn't recall; you'd had rather too much whiskey when you asked for my help. And there was no reason you couldn't have asked, other than your own embarrassment, given all of the letters we've exchanged."

Arabella seemed poised to say a great deal more on the matter, but their conversation was cut short by Claire opening the door to her husband's study and ushering them in.

Monsieur LeMaître was not, as Thaddeus had expected, an elderly man. In fact, he was not yet middle-aged, tall and well-built. The unmasked side of his face was that of the most elegant dandy; his black hair was perfectly cut and his green-gold eyes riveting. The hand he extended to Thaddeus was long and elegant, the handshake demonstrated a grip of steel.

The masked man then kissed his wife on the cheek, and held chairs so that she and Arabella could be seated.

"Monsieur Flowers, I have wanted to meet you ever since Mademoiselle Abingdon showed me your sketches. I will show you the model I made, which improves on your design."

"Please, call me Thaddeus or Thad. Monsieur Flowers make me think you want to talk to my father."

"Then you must call me Erik. Now, to the business at hand."

He led Thaddeus to a table near the window, where a copy of his sketch was held down by weights at each corner. In addition to equations written in Arabella's hand, there were additional sketches, more equations in a different hand that could only be Erik's, and the entire balloon segment lined through.

"You see, I looked at what you had originally planned with the balloon. It is impractical, either with your original three balloons or a larger single one as with the new idea you concocted with Mademoiselle Abingdon. You looked at her engine solely as a way to create steam to make the balloon lift ... but you failed to take into account the condensation that would inevitably develop inside the bag itself, rendering it useless. No, my young monsieur, you only thought it partway through."

"I beg to differ, sir. I spent years working on this concept."

"Then I am surprised that you failed to take into account the easiest way to make your airship work. Remember, there is no need to overcomplicate most things. You need not rig something complicated, for example, to make a backdrop fall to the stage; you have only to untie the ropes that hold it in place."

What a peculiar example, Thaddeus thought. What on earth would make a man create such an analogy?

"In any event, I did some more calculations, and then revisited the works of Leonardo da Vinci to confirm my thoughts.

Thus, I have created a scale model of your airship … using Mademoiselle Abingdon's engine and my improvements."

He opened a drawer and took out what looked like a small boat. It was Thaddeus' beautifully painted gondola in miniature, complete with ten little dolls as passengers, all fashionably attired. Their clothing was to scale, right down to the hats. Each had a lap rug over his or her knees. Unlike Thad's design, with the three balloons, there was only a series of blades at different places on the exterior, the same gold as the boat's trim. Another departure from Thad's design was the domed glass covering on the boat, which would render the gondola weatherproof. The metal framework holding the glass in place was a series of elegant curlicues that hid the joints.

"That's very pretty," Thaddeus said, a trifle disappointed.

"It's more than pretty," Erik replied drily. He flicked a switch on the back of what Thaddeus could only think of as a toy and a tiny motor could be heard warming up. Soon, the blades began to spin, faster and faster. The little gondola scooted across the table and into Erik's elegant hand. He held it aloft … and let it go.

Thaddeus was sure that it was going to crash to the ground … but it didn't. Instead, it flew straight until Erik retrieved it to stop it from hitting the wall.

"Of course, you'd have someone operating the tiller to steer," he said pointing to an elevated seat in the back with a uniformed doll before he switched off the motor. "My friend, your basic idea is pure genius. It will revolutionize travel in large cities. You just need to have competent boatbuilders, ironworkers, and glaziers to make it for you."

"Now, if you'll excuse me … I have an opera to compose."

The masked man bowed gravely and exited, closing the door behind himself.

"An opera? Really? I thought you said this man was an inventor."

"He's more than that, Thad," Arabella replied evenly. "If you ever want a full character of Erik LeMaître, you could ask around the Opèra Garnier. They will tell you stories that will make you think you're in the midst of a penny dreadful. But that's really not the point, is it?"

Thad thought that maybe, just maybe, he now understood the point of the backdrop story.

Turning to her friend, she said "Thank you again, Claire, for arranging this meeting. I have every confidence that Mister Flowers here will be in touch regarding the necessary schematics. I will call on you again tomorrow. Thad, let us be gone."

Gilbert, the majordomo, held outer door open after Thad and Arabella had donned hats and wraps.

"I think, my friend," she said as she tucked her gloved hand into Thad's elbow, "that you and I need to go celebrate."

Erik came to the door as they were leaving.

"Monsieur Flowers, if I could have one more word with you, please."

Thaddeus followed him down the hallway, Arabella and Gilbert waiting in puzzlement.

"I would suggest, if you intend to woo Mademoiselle Abingdon, that you spend a little less time in bistros and a little more at her side. Open your hand, sir."

Thaddeus did so, and Erik dropped two metal disks into his palm.

"Take her to see that godawful tower of Eiffel's that they've just opened, and then take her to the opera tonight. You can return the tokens later. Good day to you, sir."

Thaddeus thanked him, and put the tokens in his inside coat pocket, after noting where he and Arabella would be seated for that evening's performance at the Opèra Garnier.

Box Five.

# REACHING ATLANTIS

*By Michael Tierney*

Some time later, Captain MacNee awoke. The last thing he remembered was the airship being swept into an updraft preceding a storm front. *I guess we didn't reach Atlantis in time,* he mused. The gondola of the airpirate ship *Daedalus* was in shambles, some of the windows were smashed, and crewmen were lying dazed on the floor. MacNee shook his head to clear it. He stood up unsteadily and exhaled puffs of icy mist.

"Wake up, Sherman," he yelled to his first mate. "Jenkins, to the helm!" The crew gradually stirred and wearily came to.

"What's our status, you lazy louts? Altitude, heading. Get a move on."

The helmsman said, "Captain, the altimeter shows 20,000 feet! That can't be right. We've never flown that high." He paused. "Sir, 20,000 feet and falling rapidly!"

*Well, that explains the temperature,* MacNee thought, *and why we passed out—who knows how high we went inside that storm?* He gingerly picked his way to the rail through the broken glass and chunks of ice sliding across the deck. Brilliantly sun-lit storm clouds loomed behind them in a deep blue sky. Looking down he could see the outlines of fields far below. Outside the gondola, icicles hung from the guy wires. And now that his grogginess was fading, his air legs told him that they were indeed descending.

"Drop the emergency ballast. We have to reduce our weight."

While water was usually used as ballast in airships—readily available and easily dumped—*Daedalus'* emergency ballast was lead shot. The cost in buoyancy in carrying several hundred pounds of lead weight was worth the ability to lose weight rapidly.

The ballast flowed out from beneath the floor of the gondola. As it did, the captain waited for any indication that their altitude was leveling.

"Ballast away, Cap'n," said Sherman.

"It's not working, sir," said the helmsman, "12,000 feet and still descending."

"It's all this damned ice. It's weighing us down. Roll the ship from side to side—see if we can dislodge it."

The elevatorman turned the control wheels to move the port and starboard elevator flaps in opposite directions, to tilt the entire ship sideways in a roll. As the deck tilted, anything not secured slid around uncontrollably. After a few tries, a rumble from above was followed by the sight of sheets of ice, seemingly acres of it, careening past the broken windows of the gondola. Soon enough, the airship leveled off, and even rose a little.

"Adjusting buoyancy, sir. Our altitude is 5000 feet."

"Well done, men. I dare say that was enough excitement for one day. Navigator, any idea where we are?"

"I'm sorry, sir. Once we got swept up in those storm clouds, I lost our bearings. Did we go past Atlantis?"

"Sherman, what does the ship's chronometer read?"

The first mate removed the clock from its protective housing. "Smashed. Not operating, sir. It stopped a few minutes after we entered the storm. There's no telling how long we were unconscious. We may have flown past Atlantis altogether."

MacNee looked at his first mate with a questioning glance. The captain found his brass spyglass rolling around on the floor by the helm, and surveyed their surroundings. "I can see what look like farm fields, and a few small towns. There is a good road network, but I see no railways." He looked further to the horizon. "Wait, I see a city, or what might pass for one. There's rising smoke and steam, and a number of roads seem to head for it."

Sherman came over next to his captain, and spoke discreetly. "Play it up a little more, Captain. Remember, sir, the men are expecting Atlantis."

MacNee hissed, "My God, man, are you still going on about that? Look, we were almost killed being sucked into that storm. By the grace of God, we weren't. We should be pretty damned glad about still being alive and not perpetuating this charade about Atlantis."

"But, Cap'n, the men, they were so close to mutiny. I'm not sure they would be too glad to know you lied to them about Atlantis. Would they … sir?" he added greasily. "They might want a new captain at some point."

As MacNee listened to his first mate, his hands gripped the rail ever tighter, until his fingers were white with tension. He felt enraged, enraged that he had been too weak to stand up to Captain Redbeard exiling them from the rich North Atlantic trade plunder, and especially too weak to be an able captain of his crew. But at this moment, he was most angry about letting his first mate talk him into this asinine scheme.

"Two points to port, helm. Head toward the center of that city," he snapped at Jenkins at the helm. "But first let's land and see if we can get some idea of where we are before we drop down in an unknown city. Who knows, maybe we are at Atlantis."

As the ship descended, MacNee could discern more details on the ground. "There's considerable destruction below. Almost as if an army had passed through destroying everything in its path."

The first mate jumped in, "Plato's stories tell that Atlantis was a war-like civilization. Perhaps one of their enemies has attacked them."

"Yes, Mr. Sherman, that must be the explanation," said the captain looking at him while rolling his eyes. "Helm, two miles ahead is a crossroads, land next to it. We'll see if we can learn anything on the ground."

The helmsman deftly steered the airship down, turned it into the wind, and landed it in a field near the intersection of two country roads. While the crew moored the airship to the ground, MacNee and Sherman jumped down out of the door of the gondola. MacNee looked around at their surroundings. While the fields had obviously once been plowed, they were now left fallow. No crops grew on the bare soil, and even the weeds were failing to thrive. About a half-mile up the road stood a farmhouse and a barn covered in acres of ice, but no people could be seen. It was almost as if the population had fled.

"Cap'n, look at this," the first mate cried from the road junction." When MacNee reached him, he smiled and pointed at a road sign, fallen and partially broken off. On the remaining bit was written, "ATLANT".

"Oh, geez," said the captain. "Really?"

"Take it as a stroke of luck, Cap'n. The men are expecting Atlantis and here's just the evidence we need to keep them satisfied that we're on the right track."

"Don't you find it a bit odd that there's no one around? Look at the desolation?"

"No people mean easy plunder for us."

"Yes, unless someone else has already plundered it. You've really done it, Sherman. What now? Look around, the land is in ruins. There's no plunder here. It's even worse than the Mediterranean."

The first mate leaned in. "Listen, Cap'n, we got into this mess because you wouldn't stand up to Redbeard, and let him push us out of the North Atlantic plunder. Remember, one word from me, and the crew will know just what kind of tales you've been telling. And then I take over the ship and you get stranded in this godforsaken place—or worse."

MacNee knew that what his first mate was saying was true. His command depended on the men believing in him. He would just have to go along and play it out and hope that sometime, somewhere, the status quo would change, maybe with a little push.

A few of the crew had gathered around the fallen signpost. "Look, Captain. You were right, sir." One of the brighter crew members—the one who had had a primary school education and had sounded out the letters—pointed at the sign. "It must be Atlantis, sir. We've found it, and soon we'll all be rich as kings! Three cheers for the captain!"

The men's cheers sounded hollow in the desolation. MacNee smiled tiredly and said, "All right, men, back aboard. Let's head for that city we saw ahead," he paused. "Let's head for Atlantis."

As the airship reached the outskirts of the city, Sherman kept up his promotion of what they would soon find. "Just think, men. The legends of Atlantis tell of a land where gold is so bountiful that they pave the streets with it! Pick up a few gold cobblestones and you'll be set for life."

"Perhaps you shouldn't excite the men too much before we even reach the city, Sherman," said the captain loud enough that the crew could hear as well. "I seem to remember another part of Plato's story about how the people grew corrupt and greedy, and that to punish them the god Poseidon destroyed Atlantis. Why do you not mention this part of the legend, Sherman?"

"Is that true, Captain?" asked the helmsman. "Was Atlantis destroyed? Then what are we heading for."

Sherman jumped in. "That's just one interpretation of the story, you see. Many other people have believed that Atlantis wasn't totally destroyed and have searched for its treasures over the centuries."

"And has anyone found it yet, Mr. Sherman?" asked the captain.

Just as he was about to answer, a crewman cried that they had reached the city. MacNee looked over the bow and saw ruins below. The streets were laid out in neat blocks, but most of the buildings lining them were demolished. Here and there a spire rose up undamaged. MacNee wondered if the Atlanteans marked their churches with spires as they did in England, and if they somehow had been spared the destruction. The airship continued to descend, but even at this altitude, MacNee could finally make out people in the ruined city below, walking aimlessly along the streets. One building, a large brick structure with a two-story tower, sat behind an open square large enough for *Daedalus* to land in.

As the ship descended, the passersby could not help but notice it, which generated some excitement in the populace. By the time *Daedalus* was on the ground, a large crowd had gathered. The crowd parted as a thin man with a receding chin and stern demeanor strode out of the brick building toward them. MacNee and Sherman climbed down from the gondola and met him.

"Now, see here. What kind of nonsense is this contraption? Who are you?"

"Captain James MacNee of the airship *Daedalus*, sir," said the captain bowing his head slightly.

"What army are you with?"

"No army. We are, um, an independent outfit."

"From what country?"

"We come from across the ocean, from a land called England."

The thin man looked somewhat confused. "Yeah, England. I could tell that much from your accent."

MacNee seemed reassured that the Atlanteans had heard of England. "May I ask who you are, sir?"

"James Calhoun, mayor of the city of Atlan—"

"Ah, yes. In our language, we call your city Atlantis. And we also call a city's leader, 'Mayor'. Perhaps our two lands are not too different from each other."

"What in tarnation are you talking about? And why are you here?"

Jenkins called down from the window of the gondola, "We're looking for treasure."

"Treasure? Look around! The Federals already took all our treasure, and destroyed our buildings and railways and farms from here to the sea. There ain't no treasure left," the mayor said with a bitter laugh.

MacNee leaned in towards his first mate, "The Federals must be from the country that invaded them."

The first mate stepped forward. "If I may, Mayor Calhoun. We have come a long way to find your city. The stories of its magnificence have reached even our land."

"They must be carpetbaggers, Mayor," said a man from the crowd. "Northerners coming down here to loot and plunder.

"Loot and plunder, that's our motto!" cried Jenkins again.

"Jenkins, be quiet," hissed the captain.

"I assure you, Mayor Calhoun, that I am not from the North—I grew up in Kent," said the first mate. We have no desire to inflict any hardship upon your city. If you could give us just a small amount of the fabled treasures of Atlantis, we won't bother you anymore."

"Is that a threat?" asked the mayor. At the same time, the crowd pushed forward around the gondola.

"I think it is time for us to depart, Mr. Sherman," said the captain pulling his first mate's arm as he started climbing the ladder to the gondola.

"Wait. What did you say his name was?" Calhoun asked.

"Sherman, William Sherman," the first mate said, holding out his hand. "At your service," he added politely.

"He must be his son! Get him! Grab the carpetbagger before he escapes!" cried various persons in the crowd. Sherman's arm was snatched from MacNee's hand, and Sherman was pulled into the center of the roiling crowd. MacNee jumped up the ladder and issued the order to depart.

Within seconds the propellers were turning, the elevators adjusted, and the ship soaring into the sky. MacNee could see Sherman, down in the center of the crowd, still struggling against the strength of the ten men who held his arms and legs.

MacNee quickly sized up the situation. He considered an attempt to rescue Sherman, but concluded that the growing mob would render it a futile exercise. And once the option of rescuing his first mate was eliminated, he realized that Sherman's capture by the Atlanteans also solved his personnel issues with his first mate. Sherman's mutinous intents were no longer a problem, and to the crew, the loss of booty could be blamed squarely on Sherman.

"Odd that they should find Mr. Sherman so disagreeable," mused Jenkins at the helm.

"Mr. Sherman has that effect on some people at times. Most people at most times, actually," said the Captain.

"Heading, captain?"

MacNee thought. Since he had no idea where they were, and no clear desire to go anywhere in particular, a heading was of little consequence.

"We were heading westerly when we encountered the storm, I believe. Head due west, Mr. Jenkins. Let's see what we might find." MacNee strolled around the gondola, pacing slowly with a sly smile on his face.

"Have I ever told you gentlemen about the legend of El Dorado, the lost city of gold?

# THE LAST STAND OF JOHNNY CHIMES

*By Richard Lau*

"Could be a trap, sir."

The commander of the 7th Cavalry nodded at his officer's assessment, momentarily regretting his decision to divide his forces into three battalions.

Still, he had two hundred men behind him, and before him was … what?

A single figure stood about a hundred yards from where Lieutenant Colonel George Armstrong Custer, also known as Yellow Hair to some friends and foes, had brought his men to a halt.

It could have been a scarecrow, for all its lack of movement. A very shiny scarecrow, with sunlight shooting off of it in all directions.

"A warning of some sort?" asked Custer, as his horse uncharacteristically shifted nervously under him.

His scouts, many of them Crow, told him they had seen nothing like it in their encounters with the plains tribes. They had also said they had seen a village larger than any they had ever seen before. More ponies than they had ever seen, too.

Custer had his fair share of experience with renegade tribe members. And he didn't like the strangeness of the situation.

This military action should have been a typical *hammer and anvil* maneuver, with Major Reno attacking the village from the south and Custer pressing on to attack the village from the north.

But as Custer moved his troops forward, hidden from the village and Reno by rocky bluffs, he encountered the lone figure in their path.

He gave the order to approach slowly. Perhaps this was some new offering of peace and surrender?

Custer could feel the tension growing thick around him, from the pre-battle nervousness of his men to the restlessness of the horses who were moving much slower than they would have liked.

It was clear now that the figure was not human at all, or even stuffed cloth, but some sort of metal statue. Gold, perhaps?

And the statue was calling to them. In a flat monotone that was undeniably European in accent, it repeated its message, "Go back. Leave these people alone."

"Ah," thought Custer. So there it was. A challenge. To him. To his cavalry. To the authority of the government of the United States. So be it. He should hear the gunfire from Reno soon.

He drew up right to the statue, meaning to kick it over in disdain.

But then he heard the chimes.

From somewhere within the statue, barely audible over the annoying recorded voice, was the sound of a music box.

"How odd," Custer thought, trying to identify the tune.

The preoccupied cavalry leader didn't realize his hesitation made him a perfect target.

An impatient sharpshooter, Sees Over Mountain, grew tired of the inactivity of the rifle pressed into the skin of his russet cheek. One could only hold a coiled snake so long.

Yellow Hair had confronted Brass Man with no sign of turning away. So be it.

Sees Over Mountain pulled the trigger. Before he could fire another shot, a flag bearer and several others surrounded the falling figure, righting him on his horse. The entire mass of soldiers surged forward, their orderly formation breaking into confusion.

Guns erupted everywhere, including the two in the hands of Johnny Chimes.

Not far away, Major Reno was facing his own problems. The Native encampment was much larger than he had estimated from the scouting reports. He also did not expect mounted Cheyenne and Lakota warriors to ride out and meet him before he could even reach the southern end of the village.

Now his forces were struggling to maintain their skirmish line, and Reno glanced with envy at the isolation of the lone covered wagon on a slight, nearby hill.

The wagon was too far away to be threatened or pose a threat to anyone. Anyone close enough might still miss the figure huddled at the base of one of the wheels in the shadow of the wagon.

Gustaf Hoffman, the man who had created Johnny Chimes, pressed the upturned collar of his coat against his ears. The effort did little in keeping out the shouted commands, the war whoops, the thunder of metal raindrops, and the screams of pain from those they hit.

He thought of Europe, of the persecution his people had faced there. Europeans called this land "the New World". The Native tribes, for whom this land wasn't very new at all, called this place "home".

But the land was older than any of those peoples. Hoffman wished he could escape into it, sink into it, become part of it, for land that old must have seen so much violence and bloodshed over the years that the current slaughter would fade into insignificance. At least that was what he hoped.

With irony, he realized that, for many of the battle's participants, his wish of returning to the earth was being fulfilled. It was as if he felt the individual death of each red-, white-, or blue-coated soul.

Hoffman mentally escaped into the world of gears and steam technology, as he often did during times of stress. He thought about the modifications he had made to Johnny Chimes, the mechanical man that was like a son to him.

He had installed narrow cartridge-feeding tubes in Johnny's arms, refilling his guns automatically straight from the palms into the handles, increasing the pistols' capacity. Additional chambers affixed to Johnny's back held even more ammunition. The weapons in Johnny's hands were literally miniature Gatling guns.

The new and improved Johnny Chimes was so weighted down that a horse running into him would effectively be running into a thick, deep-rooted tree. The horse would lose. Its rider would lose more.

Hoffman didn't have to leave the shelter of the wagon to know the devastation Johnny was laying down. He knew his designs, the weapons, and their effect all too well. He didn't have to witness the carnage. His guilty imagination was horrible enough.

Modifications in threat detection strained the capacity of Johnny's physical frame, but this was balanced by the elimination of subject recognition, for unlike bounty hunting, war did not require identifying a specific person.

Hoffman had cautioned the tribal leaders to warn their warriors to stay out of Johnny's way.

To his surprise and pleasure, there was still room for the little music box. Like a real human being, there was always room for some good in a person's heart, including Johnny's.

He had heard about redemption for Man. Would there be redemption for Johnny, especially after today?

While Hoffman tried to mentally escape the battle, the battle physically came to him. Like a stray ant, a blue-coated figure slipped around the rear of the wagon, intending to use it for protection.

The soldier was startled to encounter a civilian, but then his expression turned to anger.

"Goddamn injun gunrunner!" spat the soldier and raised his rifle in final judgment.

A pointed island of rock abruptly surfaced through the front of the soldier's ocean-blue coat, surprising both men.

The cavalry man clutched at the wound, but there was too little to grab with the arrow's wooden shaft still inside his body. He twisted one last time and fell over.

Hoffman crawled over to the body. The soldier's eyes were open but seeing what Hoffman hoped was a better world.

A shadow fell over them. "Not again!" thought Hoffman, spinning in his crouch, almost falling over.

It was the old Sioux chief, the one who had approached the inventor and his metal bounty hunter in the town of Snakebite, where Hoffman had sympathized with the chief's tale about his people's plight and persecution. The tale cut close to his heart and provoked memories of his family who had faced similar circumstances across the sea. It had outraged his sense of justice and torched his desire for revenge. He had taken the situation personally and made the cause his own.

The chief had told him, "Sitting Bull has already had a vision at a Sun Dance gathering. We will resist being herded onto a reservation. An army like your metal friend may give my people a better future. Will you help us?"

Hoffman had admitted that he was just a man, not a factory, but he still agreed to change Johnny Chimes from an instrument of the law into a renegade killing machine.

Johnny, of course, had no opinion and just did as he was programmed. With circular reasoning, Hoffman wished he could program Johnny to develop an opinion of his own and provide advice and counter-argument. Maybe one day …

Hoffman suddenly became aware that much of the gunfire had stopped. He pressed his hands into his thighs and slowly rose on stiff, cramped legs.

Standing, he was only a little taller than when he was sitting. He resembled a small ball balanced on a much larger ball that was perched on two stovepipes. Johnny was, ironically, more ideally proportioned, but his shape was made from molds, not genes.

A stray shot here and there made Hoffman flinch, but, for the most part, the only things that reached his ears were the wails of women discovering fallen loved ones or the final death whimpers of those seeking a merciful, quick end.

Johnny was supposed to return to the wagon as soon as the metal man no longer detected a threat. Something must have gone wrong. As much as he disliked it, Hoffman would have to go onto the battlefield.

Putting on his bowler, which added a good four inches to his height, Hoffman realized that in his formal black attire, he looked like a doctor or an undertaker. To the wounded and dying soldiers, his manner of dress would give them false hope or, even worse, false relief.

He had no fear of the Indians, as they were called by the soldiers and others who had sought to restrict their freedom. A great presentation had been made of him and Johnny to the village in the prior week. There was a big discussion of whether or not the non-Native and his machine could be trusted, much less put into action. By now, he was as well-known as some of the chiefs.

The edge of the battlefield was horrible and grew worse with each step.

When he had reached the peak of the ridge where Sees Over Mountain had fired his first shot, Hoffman stared at the spot where he had positioned Johnny to confront the soldiers.

His metal creation could not be seen.

In the area around where Johnny had stood, the bodies of men and horses were piled high, stuck in unnatural, agonized poses, as if sculpted by an untalented artist or a far too-talented one with a vision of Hell.

Horses and men, of all colors, all bleeding red.

But where was the one of brass? The one who bled black oil and white steam? Where was Johnny Chimes?

Out of respect for the fallen, Hoffman removed his bowler. His round baby cheeks were wet, though running with sweat or tears, he could not tell. This was his doing. Not Johnny's. For Hoffman was the one with the heart, the conscience, and now the overwhelming grief.

He stooped to pick up an abandoned pistol lying nearby, intending to join the dead that surrounded him.

A flash like the shimmer of a distant star caught Hoffman's attention and stopped him.

Johnny! Hoffman squinted. But his invention was moving away!

Hoffman dropped the pistol and moved toward the steep downward slope.

"No."

The single, calmly spoken word struck like a physical blow.

Hoffman immediately recognized the old chief's voice, dry as the wind, heavy as the mountains. The old man appeared by Hoffman's side as if suddenly solidifying out of the lingering gun smoke. In one hand he still carried his bow. In the other hand dripped the freshly retrieved arrow from the soldier that had tried to kill Hoffman.

"Do you know where Johnny's headed?" he asked the chief.

"Your friend is heading toward the reservation. Many of the Sioux are headed that way, too."

Hoffman was surprised. "Back to the reservation? I thought this fight was to stay off the reservation!"

The reply came as flat as the plains and as soft as the whispering of the wavering grass that grew there. "This fight was about having a choice, not a fate forced upon us."

"But why is Johnny going there?"

"I only said he is headed in that direction. He may stop before, change direction, or pass on through. He follows his own path now."

Though the chief's words were not technical, his description of Johnny "following his own path" alarmed the inventor.

"He was supposed to return to the wagon! He must be damaged in some way!" Hoffman panicked, his head filling with images of stuck gears, bent rods, and burnt wiring. "Still, whether he goes to the reservation or not, I can't have Johnny be the cause of any more death!"

Hoffman had started moving forward again when the old chief gripped the inventor's arm, his thin fingers the branches of an iron tree. Hoffman grimaced, noting that it was the same hand that had held the now-dropped arrow.

"Johnny is of no danger to anyone," the chief said.

Hoffman looked at the chief, who was gazing into the distance. "My braves said Johnny had stopped shooting long before he moved off."

"But there still must be something wrong!" insisted Hoffman. "Johnny needs me."

"No, he doesn't." The chief's answer was as firm as his grip.

But what could the old Indian know about Johnny's workings? He may be a wise leader, experienced in plains living and tribal politics, but he was probably one of the least mechanically minded people Hoffman had ever met.

The chief went on, as if reciting an ancient song, and perhaps he was. "A bow string eventually breaks. A knife grows dull. The best arrow will lose itself. A favored spear bends with age. All weapons tire of killing."

Now the chief's sad, almond eyes turned to the inventor. "And like the greatest warriors, your friend Johnny is a weapon. And he is tired."

The two men stood together but worlds apart. For one man, Johnny's fate had already been decided and accepted. For the other man, it was a struggle between what was desired and what was right.

For history, The Battle of Little Bighorn was where Custer's hammer snapped like a toy drumstick, where Reno's anvil collapsed as rotted wood, but for Hoffman, it was where Johnny Chimes made his last stand.

# ABOUT THE AUTHORS

## Sharon E. Cathcart

Books by award-winning, internationally published author Sharon E. Cathcart provide discerning readers of essays, fiction, and non-fiction with a powerful, truthful literary experience. A former journalist and newspaper editor, Sharon has been writing for as long as she can remember and always has at least one work in progress. Her primary focus is creating fiction featuring atypical characters. Sharon lives in the Silicon Valley, California, with her husband and an assortment of pets. Her website is *www.sharonecathcart.wordpress.com.*

## Lillian Csernica

Lillian has published *Ship of Dreams*, a pirate romance, under her romance pen name Elaine LeClaire through Dorchester Publishing's Leisure Imprint. Her short fiction has appeared in *Weird Tales, Fantastic Stories*, and the newly released anthology *After the Happily Ever After*. Lillian's historical short fiction has appeared in *These Vampires Don't Sparkle* and *Alterna-TEAs*. Two paired stories are included in the Clockwork Alchemy 2015 anthology *Twelve Hours Later*. Another pair of stories set in the same series appear in the 2016 anthology *Thirty Days Later*. Born in San Diego and a veteran of historical reenactment, Ms. Csernica is a genuine California native. She currently resides in the Santa Cruz mountains with her husband, two sons, and three cats. Visit her at *www.lillian888.wordpress.com.*

## David L. Drake and Katherine L. Morse

David L. Drake and Katherine L. Morse are the award-winning, San Diego-based authors of *The Adventures of Drake and McTrowell: Perils in a Postulated Past,* a serialized steampunk tale detailing the adventures of Chief Inspector Erasmus Drake and Dr. "Sparky" McTrowell. The duo's many adventures are provided in weekly penny dreadful-style episodes at *www. DrakeAndMcTrowell.com.* They have produced four novellas since 2010: *London, Where it All Began; The Bavarian Airship Regatta; Her Majesty's Eyes and Ears;* and *The Hawaiian Triple Cross.* Drake and Morse won a Starburner Award for the radio show based on their first story, which has run multiple times on Krypton Radio. When not cosplaying their alter egos at conventions all over the West, they are both research computer scientists specializing in distributed modeling and simulation. Mr. Drake is a nationally ranked foil fencer. Dr. Morse is an internationally respected expert on standards, but prefers to be recognized for her cookie baking skills. They throw awesome parties, if they do say so themselves.

## Anthony Francis

By day, Anthony Francis programs intelligent computers and emotional robots; by night, he writes science fiction and draws comic books. His short stories in the anthologies *Twelve Hours Later, Thirty Days Later,* and *Some Time Later* are prequels to his steampunk novel *Jeremiah Willstone and The Clockwork Time Machine.* Anthony is also the author of the award-winning urban fantasy novel *Frost Moon* and its sequels *Blood Rock* and *Liquid Fire,* all starring magical tattoo artist Dakota Frost. Anthony lives in San Jose with his wife and cats, but his heart will always belong in Atlanta. You can follow Jeremiah Willstone at *www.jeremiahwillstone.com* or *www.facebook.com/jeremiahwillstone*, Dakota Frost at *www.dakotafrost.com* or *www.facebook.com/dakotafrost*, or Anthony himself on his blog *www.dresan.com*.

## Madeleine Holly-Rosing

A TV, feature film, and comic book writer, Madeleine is the winner of the Sloan Fellowship for screenwriting, and the Gold Aurora and Bronze Telly for a PSA produced by Women In Film. She also won numerous awards while completing the UCLA MFA Program in Screenwriting. Her steampunk comic, *Boston Metaphysical Society*, was nominated for Best Comic/Graphic Novel at the 2014 Geekie Awards. Her novella, *Steampunk Rat*, was also nominated for a 2013 Steampunk Chronicle Reader's Choice Award and is part of the anthology based in the same universe called *Boston Metaphysical Society: Prelude.* The first Boston Metaphysical novel will be released in 2017. The comic and her blog can be found at *www.bostonmetaphysicalsociety.com*.

## Richard Lau

Richard Lau is an award-winning writer who has been published in newspapers, magazines, and the high-technology industry. He has won first, second, and third place in a single local flash fiction contest and had five of his plays selected for a ten-play show. This is his first publication in an anthology. He thanks Barbara, his first reader, for her support and his parents for all those trips to the library.

## T.E. MacArthur

T. E. MacArthur is an author, artist, and historian living in the San Francisco Bay Area with the loving ghost of her one-time companion, Mac the cat, and her new bouncy kitten, Calypso.

Writing is her obsession, driving her to brave a trek all the way to Iceland for research. She has written for several local and specialized publications, and even had an accidental stint as a sports reporter for Reuters News.

*The Doomsday Relic* is the latest in The Volcano Lady series, following the adventures of Victorian lady scientist Lettie Gantry, through the worlds of Jules Verne and altered history. The Gray's Shilling serials, gazettes, and books continue thrilling adventures, following the time honored cliffhangers of dime novels, penny dreadfuls, and weekly serials. To put it mildly, T.E. has a love for all things Victorian (history and clothing from 1870–1890 in particular) and is having a lifelong affair with the writings of Jules Verne.

## AJ Sikes

AJ Sikes writes noir urban fantasy and has published multiple short story stories and the alternate history novels, *Gods of Chicago* and *Gods of New Orleans*. He offers professional editing services to writers of speculative fiction, non-fiction, and academic material. He served in the US Army, holds an MA in Teaching English to Speakers of Other Languages, and taught university level ESL writing and composition courses. He's a woodworker and toy builder in his spare time. AJ keeps a blog called Dovetails (*www.writingjoinery.wordpress.com*) where he talks about the similarities between woodworking and writing. Find out more about his editing services at *www.ajsikes.com*.

## BJ Sikes

BJ Sikes is a 5'6" ape descendant who is inordinately fond of a good strong cup of tea, Doc Marten boots, and fancy dress. She lives with two large cats, two small children, and one editor-author. Her stories in this anthology are prequels to her upcoming novel *Sand and Bones*. News and other info can be found on her blog at *www.bjsikesblog.wordpress.com*.

## Janice Thompson

Janice Thompson has been writing poetry for more than fifty years. She composes tightly woven, unforced verses that allow for as many levels of interpretation as are possible. Much of her poetry hearkens back to the English Lake District poets. JaniceT has been an avid fan of the Steampunk genre since the early eighties, and its influence on her is apparent in some of her "steamier" poems, such as "Twist" and "Train of Thought". Samples of her work have been posted on her blog at janice-t.weebly. com. Her published works include the Echoes, Neo-Victorian Poetry series, as well as *A Compilation of Echoes*. Samples of her work are posted on her blog at *www.janice-t.weebly.com*.

## Michael Tierney

Michael Tierney writes steampunk-laced alternative historical fiction stories from his Victorian home in Silicon Valley. After writing technical and scientific publications for many years, he turned his sights to more imaginative genres. Trained as a chemist, he brings an appreciation of both science and history to his stories. His debut novel *To Rule the Skies* was published in 2014. Visit his blog at *www.airshipflamel.com*.

## Harry Turtledove

Escaped Byzantine historian Harry Turtledove made his first sale in 1977, and has been telling lies for a living full-time since 1991. He writes alternate history, other SF, historically based fantasy, and, when he can get away with it, historical fiction. He is perhaps best known for *The Guns of the South*; recent books include *Joe Steele*, *The Hot War: Bombs Away*, and *The House of Daniel*. He and his wife, writer Laura Frankos, have three daughters (one also a published author), one granddaughter, and two cats, Boris and Natasha. Watch out for Natasha. She beeps.

## Kirsten Weiss

Kirsten Weiss worked overseas for nearly fourteen years, in the fringes of the former USSR and in Southeast Asia. Her experiences abroad sparked an interest in the effects of mysticism and mythology, and how both are woven into our daily lives. Now based in San Mateo, California, she writes steampunk suspense and paranormal mysteries, blending her experiences and imagination to create a vivid world of magic and mayhem. Kirsten has never met a dessert she didn't like, and her guilty pleasures are watching *Ghost Whisperer* and drinking good wine. Get updates on her latest work at: *www.kirstenweiss.com.*

## Dover Whitecliff

Dover Whitecliff was born in the shadow of Fujiyama, raised in the shadow of Olomana, and lives where she can see the shadow of Mt. Shasta if she squints and it's a really clear day. She is an analyst, an editor, and a jack-of-all-trades, but mostly a writer who has been telling stories since forever, and who won her first ten-speed as a fifth grader with a first-place entry into *Honolulu Advertiser*'s "Why Hawaii Isn't Big Enough for Litter" contest. Her short stories in the anthologies *Twelve Hours Later, Thirty Days Later*, and *Some Time Later* are companion pieces to her first solo novel *The Superspy with the Clockwork Eye*. She lives in Sacramento, California with her very patient husband and several hundred bears. Visit her at *www.doverwhitecliff.wordpress.com.*

# ABOUT THINKING INK PRESS

Thinking Ink Press was founded in 2014 by five Bay Area authors with a love for the printed word. Following a preview release of the *24 Hour Comic Day Survival Guide*, our first official release was *The Parents' Guide to Perthes*, a guide for parents of children with Legg-Calvé-Perthes disease.

Since then we have published fiction in a wide range of sizes: the flash fiction postcards *White Mice* and *Finnegan's Firewall*; pocket-sized, origami-inspired Instant Books including *Jagged Fragments*, *Small Surprises*, *Wild Hair*, and *Bees*; chapbooks such as *Sibling Rivalry* and *Beyond the Fence*; illustrated children's books such as *Hip, Hop, Hooray for Brooklyn Bunny!*; full-length fiction anthologies such as *Twelve Hours Later*, *Thirty Days Later*, and the forthcoming *Some Time Later*; and full-length novels, including *Debris Dreams* and the forthcoming *Shattered Sky* and *Luna's Lament*.

Our goal is to find awesome things and to get them into your hands. Our ambition is to find new ways to do that. And our commitment is to produce high quality books that show through and through our love of the printed word. You can find us online at *www.thinkinginkpress.com* or contact us at *contact@thinkinginkpress.com*.